chaos

(Agents of Evil, Book Two)

By

Megan Duncan

Weinmeier

All rights reserved.

Copyright © 2012 by Megan Duncan

First Edition: June 2012

This is a work of fiction. Any resemblance of characters to actual persons, living or dead, is purely coincidental. The author holds exclusive rights to this work. Unauthorized duplication is prohibited.

For information:

http://meganduncan.blogspot.com/

A very special thanks to my amazing family, and my spectacular fans. I couldn't have finished it without you.

1

There was nothing quite like the sound of shells being cocked in a shotgun. Once, I found the click and swish of the metal sliding against itself frightening, but now I couldn't think of anything more comforting.

I've been known to clean my shotgun, disassembling and assembling the parts for no other purpose than my own sense of relief, and the assurance that when the next attack came, and I knew it would, I would be ready.

Tonight, I was ready.

My fingers gripped the cold metal with a familiar tension of fierce determination. The gun cocked easily in my right hand and I rested the weight of it on my shoulder, ignoring the instantaneous, but fleeting pain it caused when it struck my scar.

The wound had healed, in a way, but I knew somewhere deep inside me that it would never stop hurting. A constant reminder of the pain I endured on the journey to what we thought would be our salvation. We were wrong. As I pushed the memories away, burying them into the deep abyss of anguish in my soul, I ran forward to the front lines.

"Ready?" I asked only slightly winded when I reached the perimeter of our make-shift compound within the military base.

"Yup," Max replied gruffly.

I eyed the other survivors that lined the perimeter and nodded. All of them were prepared. We had done this many times before and there was no reason to think we wouldn't prevail again. In fact, these attacks were becoming more of a nuisance than anything else.

Just a few short weeks after Max turned the emergency message back on people started to slowly trickle in. We were amazed, at first, by the number of survivors. A few dozen might not seem like a lot, but in times like these we considered ourselves a small army.

At first, we rejoiced, considering so many survivors a victory in our favor, but that slowly began to change. Where there were people; there were demons. Not long after the first survivors crawled onto our base, so did a new menace - the spider demons.

After the first attack, we barely survived and the creatures have continued to assail us ever since. We rose from the ashes of that night, shuddering at the corpses of those we could not save. When I looked into Max's eyes, I immediately recognized an emotion in him that was unhinging itself inside me as well.

No longer were we focused on just survival, or simply protecting ourselves. My eyes hardened as something broke inside me and all I could think of was revenge. Since the instant demons first stepped foot into our world, everything had turned to chaos. It was time we brought chaos to them.

"They're coming!" a man shouted from my left. A nearby tower pointed a light in the direction he indicated and we saw them.

Our shifting bodies rustled the air around me as we all prepared for the attack. My eyes surveyed our line, everyone was in their position, everyone was armed. Their faces were hard and determined; with every attack, they became less fearful. With every victory, we became more powerful.

The swarm of spider demons writhed along, tarnishing the deep blue horizon as it migrated toward us. The sound of thousands of spider legs skittering across pavement and earth made the hair on my arms stand on end.

My attention locked onto Max as he gripped the submachine gun in his hands and charged the swarm. A violent war cry spilled from his lungs as he sprinted. We all followed after him bellowing our own threats.

I lengthened my stride to match Max's, and caught up with him just moments before the first spider demon came within range. Our eyes linked for the briefest of seconds, the horrifying images still lingering within them, and we turned to face our enemy.

Gunfire crackled and sparked in the night as the first wave of spiders crashed into us. Their giant, leggy bodies gave them ample height. Standing at nearly seven feet tall or more, these monsters loomed above us, attacking mercilessly.

We ran between their legs, spraying our bullets upward into their abdomens. Spider demons weren't difficult opponents, as long as you didn't get within reach of the pincers near their faces.

"Stay away from their faces if you want to stay alive!" I screamed into the night.

After endless hours of studying their behavior, Carter discovered the spiders' weakness. Without him we might not have been able to handle their attacks. The problem wasn't so much the deadliness of the spider attacks, but their sheer numbers. They could easily consume us all if we didn't know how to bring them down. They almost did.

I bobbed, weaved and ducked between their monstrous, pole-like legs, the earth pounding and rumbling beneath my feet as the spider demons savagely tried to kill us.

Max and I always ran further into the fray than the others, who preferred to stay on the edges, waiting for the demons to come to them. No, we couldn't fight like that anymore. I knew we were being risky; cheating death with every step we took, but in a world like this, after what we'd seen, you could say we'd been doing that for a long time already.

The ring of Max's blade being pulled from its sheath pealed through the night, interrupting the drone of arachnids that deafened my ears and flooded my brain. I knew that sound. It was time to take these damn spiders down and send them back from whence they came.

Slinging my shotgun's strap across my back, I pulled the two long, hunting knives from their casings on my thighs. It was time for some dirty fighting.

I knew Max was somewhere nearby, even though I couldn't see him. With my jaw clenched, and spider demon hair follicles rubbing the flesh of my arms red and raw, I gripped my blades tightly. We were in so deep the monsters wouldn't know what hit them. They never did.

Max and I were getting awfully good at this. With the spiders' attention focused solely on the base, and the line of men and women defending it, we easily wove our way beneath them, deep into the heart of the horde.

My chest heaved a steady breath as I pulled my arms into a wide, winged arc. My muscles twitched in preparation; I needed to be fast. I needed to be *really* fast. I expelled another breath, hearing the shrieks of nearby spider demons, which caused the others to slow their pursuit toward the base. Immediately, their pea-brained attention moved toward the noise. Max had already started his attack, and by the sounds of it, was taking out quite a few. If I didn't get going I would be in trouble.

I sprang into action, running at full speed as I whacked the spindly legs of the spider demons with my blades. Their heavy bodies thudded to the ground behind me with every limb-breaking slice.

I snapped my arms like a rubber band with every blow. Each hit had to count. Each hit had to take out a leg of a spider demon. It didn't take much force, but there were a lot of spider legs between the base and where I was.

Taking off their legs not only kept them from moving closer to the base, but it also disrupted their senses, somehow disorienting them. Carter tried to explain it to me once, but I didn't need to know the how or why, all I cared about was that it worked. I vaguely remembered something about his theory that they have kind of bee colony mentality.

****

"Like some sort of demon network?" I asked him.

"That's one way to put it. They are still individual demons, but I think they have similarities much like a beehive, or a colony of ants would. You can tell that just by how they attack the base." He began drawing a schematic on some scratch paper.

"I get it," I said the annoyance rising in my voice as I ripped the paper out from under his pencil.

"If that were true," Carter grinned defiantly at me, yanking the paper back from my grasp, "then you wouldn't need me to tell you how to kill those creepy crawlers, would ya?"

"He's got a point," Max chimed in. He planted a boot onto a chair, leaning on his knee as he eyed Carter and me.

"Just tell us how to kill them, Carter."

****

The spotlights of the base grew closer, their bright beams cutting through the mass of web-spinners that loomed above me. I was almost to the end of the line. The thought of getting so close to being done renewed my energy, temporarily helping me forget the burning sensation in my arms. I had to ignore my muscles' painful protests caused by the demands I was subjecting them to. All this pain would be worth it in the end.

I sliced through the last set of spider limbs and dove forward before the massive body could fall on top of me. If I got trapped underneath one I'd be a goner. They didn't need their legs to eat you, a fact one of our survivors learned all too personally.

Stretching my arms, I lunged forward like a baseball player trying to take home base. The not so pleasant, but familiar, sensation of bristly hair rubbing against my legs sent my arms clawing frantically at the ground. I growled and grunted in frustration; I couldn't allow myself to scream, even though I wanted to. I could see the outline of our small army not far off. They would hear my call, but so would the spider demons. Then I would have to deal with more than just one clawing at my legs.

I allowed myself a few mere seconds of panic then swallowed hard and flipped my body over. My legs resisted the twisting sensation as the spider demon gripped tighter. My bones were threatening to snap, and tears of infuriated rage fused with pain began to burn my eyes.

I couldn't let this one demon take me down. No, I wouldn't allow it.

It held onto my leg feverishly; its own fallen limbs twitching sporadically on the ground. It was trying to pull me into the swarm, no doubt to feast on my flesh, but luckily for me, this spider demon had no meal coming tonight.

Of its eight legs, five had been severed; two on one side, and three on the other. The spider kept toppling over every time it rested its colossal weight on the other three legs. Stupid demon.

My knives skidded across the dirt when I jumped out from under the demons. I had to get to one of them. I reached back, twisting and over-extending my back muscles further than my body was willing to allow. I was certain I could feel them tearing, ripping under my flesh, but I couldn't think about that. I had to focus on reaching the blade and slicing off the demon's claw-like leg that was clamped around my foot.

With a roar of pain, I clasped the knife in my hand; and in one swift, but painful movement, I hacked off the spider's appendage, narrowly missing my own foot.

I scooted myself backward frantically. The spider demon couldn't crawl anymore, but I didn't want to be anywhere near it. Hands caught hold of me, lifting me upward, and in my panicked state I raised my knife ready to strike. I whirled to see whatever was behind me, and prepared to plunge my knife into it.

"Whoa! It's just me, Abs. You're okay." Max raised his hands in surrender. Relief washed over me and I fell into his open arms, silent tears streaking down my dirty face.

I might have been tough. I might have been on a war path to kill demons, but for some reason when one got hold of me I almost always panicked. I was constantly trying to be tougher than I really was, whether to convince myself or everyone else, I wasn't sure. But Max was always there for me, lifting me up when I fell and renewing my resolve that someday I could be as tough as I wanted. As tough as he was.

He held me close for a brief moment, long enough for my ragged breath to return to normal. There was still fighting to be done.

When Max released me, I felt something hit my foot. I looked down to see the spider demon dragging itself toward me.

Wow, this one was not going to give up.

This time, however, I kept my cool and didn't panic. Max made a move to dispatch the demon for me, but I lifted my hand to stop him.

"I've got this one," I said with deadly resolve. Lifting my shotgun off my shoulder, I loaded the last shell that hung from the strap across my chest, cocked it, and blew the spider demon's brains into a slimy puddle of goop. With a kick of my boot, I flung off a splatter of gore that landed there.

We ran up to the line of people guarding the exterior fence of our makeshift compound, and joined their fight against the last remaining demons. Swiftly, we dispatched them. With only a few dozen headed toward us, it was easy to take them as they struggled to climb over their fallen comrades, their bodies still twitching and jerking.

It was a sight to turn even the strongest stomach, but the more I saw, the more normal it became. It was the sign of another victory for us, and something we *deserved* to see.

"That'll do it," Max exclaimed to the crowd as the last demon was killed. It dragged its body along with only half a limb working. Still, it came for us. They always came for us.

"The clean-up crew will be here soon enough," I added following everyone back into the safety of our perimeter and its ten-foot fence topped with barbed wire.

I waited as Max and another man I couldn't remember his name, maybe Henry, secured the gate. Our part of the job was done for the night and we didn't want to be anywhere nearby when the "clean-up crew" arrived.

"You did good tonight," Max smiled at me slinging his arm over my shoulder and pulling me close. His expression had lost some of its steeliness. I knew mine had too. We always felt better after a victory. There was nothing quite like the feeling of knowing we had accomplished something. We would all be alive for another day and that felt good.

"Thanks. How many do you think we got tonight?"

"Oh man, I would say at least a fifty. That swarm seemed to be one of the bigger ones we've encountered." We were walking through the halls of the housing units and people gasped at Max's words as we passed them. Most of the newcomers were still uneasy about staying here. I couldn't blame them. Before, occupying one place for too long felt wrong, but that was starting to change now. We had a defensible location. If we had a chance of surviving anywhere, it would be here.

"Hmm... I guess that'll keep the clean-up crew busy enough tomorrow. Should buy us time to scout the city. What do you think?"

All the weeks we had been here, we hadn't found time to do much scouting. I was becoming almost as eager as Carter to see what we could find. Just for different reasons. He was certain we might find more clues as to what really happened at the base, and the military that used to be here. He had some hair-brained idea that the military left to fight against something within the city. It was a little farfetched, but as with most of his ideas I just rolled my eyes.

I, on the other hand, wanted to gather supplies, and if we were lucky, maybe even find some survivors. Maybe they would know what really happened to the base. So far no one who had entered our compound was originally from here, so they had no clue as to what went down.

"Yeah, I think with a swarm that big, it'll give us a good chance. The longer we keep waiting, the more likely our window of opportunity will fizzle out."

"What window of opportunity?" Carter, my brother, asked as we entered our room. Carter, Taya, Max and I all shared a room. Not for lack of space. We tried separate rooms at first, but it didn't feel right to be apart. We just felt safer this way.

"Heading into town," I answered Carter's curious look as I dropped my shotgun onto my cot and began the annoying job of taking off my gear. The hardest part were the combat boots. I always had Max tie them for me. He had the muscle to make them extremely tight, which was always a good thing when fighting demons, but it didn't take long for my feet and ankles to begin screaming in agony.

I looked at Max for him to explain when I saw the look of excitement on Carter's face, his journey book clutched tightly in his hand. My brother was starving for new details, still clinging to the hope that he could put all his information to good use and save mankind. Max and I both agreed that we didn't want Carter to go. Since our fight with the madman, John, Carter's vision just hadn't been the same. His face received some serious damage and didn't heal right. He hated being kept from doing anything because of it, but it was just too dangerous for him now. He couldn't fight like he used to. Even his aim with a crossbow was leagues from what it once was.

"Great! When are we going?" Carter twisted around on his cot to face us.

"*We*," I said pointing to Max and me, "are going at first light." I glanced to Max for confirmation, and he nodded as he changed his shirt. I felt my cheeks flush with heat and quickly turned away. I couldn't let him distract me when I was trying to yell at my brother.

"Don't start that argument again, Abby!" Carter's irritation began to rise. I turned my back to him as I dropped my boots on the ground.

"*Carter*," I sighed in my whiniest breath. "Please don't start. I'm tired and I don't want to hear it right now, okay?"

"No, not okay! You're my little sister and I'm not letting you scout the city alone. You think just because you can go out and fight spider demons, you can take on whatever is out there waiting for us?"

"You know I won't be going alone. Max is going with me and we are assembling a team."

"So, why can't I be part of that team?"

I could see the pain lingering in his expression as he asked the question. His eye twitched awkwardly. He knew the answer, and I didn't need to tell him. He was a liability now. *I* had to be the one to look after him and he hated it. I couldn't blame him though. He was my big brother, but he could no longer do the things that he felt the title embodied.

"Dude," Max said as he plopped down next to Carter on his cot. "You know why." He placed a comforting hand on Carter's shoulder, which he shrugged off.

"Abby's not healing right either, but you're still letting her go." His face looked angry, but not his tone. That was just his expression now and we were all starting to get used to it. His injured eye kind of drooped sleepily, making it seem like he had a permanent scowl, which was very uncharacteristic for my brother. Well, at least before everything happened, it would have been.

As much as I wanted to crawl into bed, I couldn't. After an attack, the four of us always did a walkthrough of our camp to check on everyone. We were much like shepherds, herding our flock, making sure the "big bad wolf" hadn't done more damage than we knew about.

Except in our case, our flock was comprised of people and the big bad wolf was made of savage demons.

Having given up the fight, for now, Carter followed Max and me out of our room. I slung my shotgun over my shoulder, unwilling to let it leave my side, even when I knew we were relatively safe, for now. I think all of us had learned the hard way that there really wasn't such a thing as "safe" anymore. Taya's words echoed in my head at the thought.

"There is no such thing as safe. There is alive and there is dead. Everything in between is just dumb luck."

"You've got that look on your face," Max commented as we rounded a corner and headed to the cafeteria. It had become our pro tem assembly room after attacks and everyone was making their way toward it.

The discussions and reports were relatively the same every time, but we didn't want to leave anyone in the dark as to what was going on. Carter and Max both agreed that ignorance meant death. I concurred.

"What look is that?" I feigned ignorance even though I knew exactly what he meant.

"You look like one of those kitten posters. All helplessly clinging to a tiny branch, with the phrase, *Hang in there!* on the bottom."

"You look freaked out," Carter added for good measure.

"So?" I snapped.

I was getting really sick of them trying to read my facial expressions. They didn't understand women before the apocalypse; and for the life of me, I didn't understand what made them think they could now.

"*So*, you're going to make people worry. We won tonight. It was a good night."

I rolled my eyes at Max and groaned. "They *should* worry," I raised my voice a little too loud, and several people looked my way. I gave them weak smiles and they continued on.

"See!" Carter piped in again. "Just because the world has gone to shit around us doesn't mean these people don't deserve some sense of peace. We might not have much here, but at least we have some semblance of safety; some tiny bit of security in a world of chaos."

I avoided their gazes and stared intently forward. The doors to the cafeteria lay ahead, and as each person entered I got a peek into the room and the small assembly of people gathering there. I knew Carter and Max were right, but I had a really hard time concealing my feelings. Especially on nights when a spider demon got a little too close for comfort. It just rattled my nerves.

I adjusted my shotgun and gave them as confident a smile as I could. Ushering the last few people into the cafeteria, we walked in and joined Taya up at the podium. She had taken it upon herself to start these gatherings, and even at her young age, people revered her with rapt attention.

Most of the survivors who managed to get to our base were just people who had been holed up in their houses, hiding and waiting for help to arrive. Very few of them saw or encountered the things that we did. Lucky for them.

With each group that arrived, Carter and Taya would convey our tale. Most sat quietly with horrified looks on their faces. Then Carter would go through his demon book, and instruct everyone on what we had learned. We wanted everyone to be able to defend themselves and know what they were up against, if our worst-case scenario were to ever happen - if demons ever crossed into our compound.

Few ever spoke up when Carter asked if they had any facts about demons to add that he hadn't already mentioned. Either they were scared, or just didn't want to relive their experiences by saying the words aloud. Occasionally, some would approach Carter later on, telling him what they saw. He would add it to the book and tell them how brave they were and how every bit of information would help us in our battle. I knew he was trying to instill them with the same hope he had - that someday we *would* defeat the enemy, and the world would finally be ours, once again.

Max walked up to the microphone and cleared his throat as the crowd hushed. Carter, Taya and I lined up behind him. "As you are all probably well aware, we won tonight!" The crowd cheered his announcement.

I surveyed the room, spotting the men and women that fought beside us lining the walls, still in defensive stances, even though the current threat had been defeated. A feeling of intense pride swelled inside me for these people. I remembered each of their faces as they entered our compound on their first day. They looked utterly broken and afraid, but standing here tonight they appeared more like warriors. Men, women, young, and old.

We weren't in this alone, and I knew that each one of them would do whatever it took to maintain the peace and safety we had established. Finally, the last remaining threads of fear dissipated inside me.

Max's speech was uplifting, raising even my spirits. He was becoming quite the leader and I imagined that in some small way, he was living his dream of joining the military. Even though this version was much more twisted than he ever previously hoped for; he was still defending the innocent, protecting the helpless and saving mankind. A smile pulled up the corner of my lips. I was so proud of the man he was becoming.

Everyone applauded after Max ended his report, and Taya stepped forward to give her standard cautionary warning. "Tomorrow there will be limited access until the cleaning crew disposes of the spider remains. So, if you *have* to go outside, please use caution and inform the nearest guard where you're going. Does everyone understand?"

All nodded their heads as they turned to exit the room. I had to hide the smirk that appeared on my face.

Sometimes, it seemed Taya must have aged ten years since arriving at the base. She sounded so much like a strict teacher; it was both funny and comforting. She wasn't much younger than I, but I still felt guilty that she had to grow up so fast. Then again, everyone had to. I guess that's why no one had a problem with us leading the group. Age wasn't an issue anymore. It was just human versus demon. No shades of gray, just black and white.

Taya turned to look at us as the crowd moved away behind her, releasing a tired sigh. "I hope they don't show up early in the morning. I can't ever sleep with all the noise. It's too friggin' creepy."

I nodded my head in agreement. I didn't think anyone could sleep through the noise. Our "cleaning crew," as we fondly called it, were merely vulture-like demons. They were huge, scavenging birds that ate whatever was left behind of the spider demons. After the first brutal attack on the base, we somehow fell into an uneasy alliance with them.

We killed the spider demons and they disposed of the carcasses. I almost lost the entire contents of my stomach the first time I saw them picking at the mutilated remains; and knowing that they ate their own kind was horrifying. Sure, it worked out for us, because they didn't attack live prey, but it was still disgusting.

The demon birds, our cleaning crew, would completely vanish until there was another attack; and the following morning at dawn, they would reappear. Their skin-prickling shrieks reverberated through the predawn air, waking everyone up as they fed off the carnage. I couldn't help feeling like we were feeding them. It was better than the alternative though. Demon remains were much more preferable than human remains when it came to feeding demons.

"They *always* come at dawn," Max replied smiling and handing her two foam ear plugs. "Here, use these. It helps a little."

"What will you use?"

"I'll be fine." He waved her off, and she smiled.

"Are we still on for tomorrow?" she asked me.

"Yeah. As soon as we get back."

Taya beamed before heading out of the cafeteria. She had been begging me to help teach her how to shoot and though at first I had tried to pawn her off on Max, she had still wanted me to do it. I finally relented and agreed. There was still an unspoken tension between us, but things had improved. I knew she would always harbor some anger toward me for what happened to Judy, Norah and Savannah. Their deaths were difficult on all of us.

I didn't take it personally anymore. It wasn't me she was truly mad at anyway, she just needed something tangible to target her anger on, and that just happened to be me.

"I suppose you're going to start letting her go on scouts now, too?" Carter asked hopping down from the stage.

"Carter, don't be stupid." His pouting sessions usually didn't last this long and I was starting to get annoyed.

He stormed off with no response other than dramatically trying to slam the cafeteria door, which he failed at miserably. It's hard to slam a door that self-closes.

"Abs," Max said my nickname admonishingly.

"What?" I shrugged my shoulders before jumping down to the floor. We held hands and walked back to our room.

"He beats himself up enough; you don't need to as well."

Since Carter's injury, Max had become overly protective and somehow hyper-aware of his best friend's feelings, which made me feel slightly guilty. Carter was *my* big brother and that's how I should have been treating him.

"I know, but..." I sighed pushing through the cafeteria door. The hallways were mostly empty as people rushed to get as much sleep as they could before the demon birds came and woke everyone up.

"Imagine how you would feel if I wouldn't let you fight with that shoulder of yours."

I rubbed the mentioned shoulder that still remained sore. "First of all, you can't tell me what I can or cannot do," I said bumping him with my hip. "And second of all, I would feel like crap," I admitted.

"Ya know, sometimes it seems like you're the big sister and he's your little brother."

"Mhm. The tables have turned and Carter doesn't like it one bit." I lost the giggle that started to build in my chest and continued. "He knows he can't fight anymore, and I hate having to keep telling him 'no' every time he asks. I just wish there were other things he could do to occupy himself."

"Maybe we should find him something to do?" Max suggested. "So, he feels like he *is* contributing."

I nodded in agreement and let Max pull me under his arm as we rounded another corner on our way down the hallway where our room was located. I wasn't sure we could find anything that would keep Carter busy. I knew when it came down to it nothing would suffice except fighting beside us. He wasn't willing to sit around while we risked our lives to defend this place. I couldn't blame him one bit for that. I would be doing the same thing. Busted shoulder or not, I'd fight until my last breath.

Our room was already dark by the time we got there. Taya was squirming under her covers, trying to get comfortable and Carter was motionless with his back toward the door. I knew he was still upset and only feigning at being asleep, so I walked quietly to his bed and sat down. Placing my hand on his shoulder, I bit my lip trying to think of what to say.

"I'm sorry." That was all I could come up with and I felt like a horrible sister.

When he didn't respond or even flinch under my touch, I tried harder to think of something. Sorry wasn't enough for how I'd been treating him. He only wanted to help defend everyone and I just kept snapping at him. I *had* to remember how Carter got hurt in the first place. It wasn't because he was being careless; it was because he was trying to defend Norah. He had been brave and I needed to remember that.

"I'm a jerk, okay?" He stirred a little, so I continued. "Alright, I'm a giant jerk!" I let out a small laugh. "Does that make you feel better?"

Carter rolled over and looked at me, a small smirk breaking on his face. "Not much, but it's a start." I slapped his arm.

"Seriously though, Abby, I can still fight; you just gotta let me prove it." He pulled himself up into a sitting position. "Just because I can't shoot doesn't mean I can't do anything."

"I know." I looked up to see Max smiling at us. I knew he was happy we were making up.

"And just because you say I can't, doesn't mean I won't go anyway. If I want to go on that scout tomorrow, I'm going to go," he said sternly. I opened my mouth to protest. "Shut it! I won't go *tomorrow*, but I *will* go on the next scout. Got it?"

"Yeah I got it," I said giving in. He was right. If he really wanted to go there wasn't anything I could do to stop him.

"Now stop worrying about me so much, that's my job. I'm supposed to look after you, not the other way around. I promised Dad I'd protect you, and damn it that's what I'm going to do." His tone was lighter, and somewhat playful; but at the mention of our dad the mood died.

"Alright, big brother. So, do you not hate me anymore?"

"I never hated you, you're just a brat." He squeezed my sides and I jumped out of bed with a squeal.

"Some of us are trying to get their beauty sleep, ya know?" Taya grumbled from under her covers which only made us all giggle.

It was nice not to be at odds with my brother anymore, and even nicer to hear him laugh again. It was a long time since any of us laughed.

I crawled into the cot next to Max's and snuggled in for the night. We weren't actually sharing a bed, but it was still nice to be close to him. Someday, the four of us would have to feel secure enough to sleep in our own rooms, but for now this would do. I turned to face Max, and squeezed his offered hand. It was as much intimacy as I allowed in our current living situation, even though I was almost certain I was ready for more. Max's patience about it made *me* feel more like the guy in the relationship. The fact he never mentioned it, made me think even more about it. My last remaining thoughts were of Max and me going out on our first real date. There was some serious lip action happening, and I was almost certain I went to sleep with a smile on my face.

2

As expected, the bone-chilling screeches of the demon birds tore me violently from my sleep. Even though it wasn't the first time, it was no less unsettling. I wanted to stay in the dream world I had created, where Max and I could be together, living like normal teenagers. But apparently, the demons had other plans in store for me.

I knew burying my head under the covers, and trying to get more sleep was an option, but a futile one. But, there was no way I could fall back to sleep and definitely no way I'd be able to return to my dream.

Wiping the sleep from my eyes, I yawned and looked over to see Max's cot was empty. I wasn't surprised. He had always been more of a morning person than I ever could be. I dug under the bed where I pushed my boots, and pulled out the watch I dropped inside one of them. Six thirty. Damn, it was early.

I found the room completely empty after I convinced myself to crawl out of bed. It was nice to have the privacy, but I felt the immediate need to be near people. Taya, Carter or Max, it didn't matter. Being alone sparked the tiniest flicker of panic to twist in my chest.

I knew exactly where I could find Taya. Whenever "clean-up crew day" came around, she would lock herself up in the storeroom and claim to be cataloging our inventory. But what she was really doing was avoiding the noise. Being in the center of the building without windows was excellent for smothering the demonic screams outside. She was never a big fan of our "arrangement" with the demon birds, and their piercing cries bothered her more than anyone I had seen. No doubt immediately after the first deafening shriek, she promptly got dressed and busied herself with her task.

I figured that she already knew exactly how much of everything we had in there by now, but if that's what got her through the day I wouldn't question it.

I decided on a sink bath to conserve water, so I stripped down and immersed a washcloth until it was dripping wet. Doing a quick, but thorough scrub-down, I rinsed off and threw on some clean clothes. Today was our first off-base scout, and I was both nervous and excited. A change of scenery might do me a little good. Maybe all my stress and nerves were just from being cooped up in the compound for so long?

I yanked on my last clean pair of cargo pants and a faded Star Wars t-shirt. I definitely had to do laundry when we got back. Knowing Max and Carter, they were probably much worse off than I. They were wearing clothes that had already worn more than twice, or even three times. Of course, I could have looked through Taya's clothes, but she absolutely wouldn't have had anything scout-worthy. I couldn't fight demons and walk miles on end in frayed jean shorts, or a pair of flip-flops. The thought of being able to wear flip-flops was appealing though, despite it not being an option.

Stomping my foot firmly into a boot I sighed. It wouldn't take long before it became a torture device attached to my foot. If I found some sneakers, I definitely intended to trade these suckers in. No doubt about that.

Pulling open the door, I was assaulted by the noise of the busy hallway. With the demons outside having their "breakfast," everyone tried to keep themselves busy with inside chores. I dodged several bulging sacks of laundry as I made my way through. At least someone would have clean clothes around here, but sadly, it wouldn't be me - for now.

I nodded my head and gave polite smiles to all the passers-by knowing that if I offered more I'd be slammed with an endless barrage of questions about today's plans. I had been cornered one too many times by some of the residents here, and had to learn my lesson the hard way. Trying to be polite, I once answered so many questions that I ended up not going on an on-base scout. Sure, there hadn't been much action on that scout... Okay, truthfully, there hadn't been *any* action at all, and they didn't find anything, but it was an excuse to get out and do something useful.

"Speak of the devil," Max announced as I entered the weapons room. I stuck my tongue out and walked purposefully toward him.

He was seated at a large, round table with an expansive map sprawled out in front of him. I recognized two of our best fighters, Grant and

Drew, at the table with him. They looked up and nodded in greeting, their grim expressions never leaving their faces.

They were an unusual pair and didn't say much, but their skills spoke volumes. The two had shown up at the base just a handful of days after we did staggering in, looking much the same as we. They were decent guys, and I liked them, even though I hadn't been able to get more than a couple words out of them. The fact that Max took immediately to them was enough for me. They were at least five or more years older than Max, but it was apparent to me they looked up to him with respect.

Grant was a shaggy, dirty blonde-haired guy, with a tan that wore heavily on his skin, aging him well beyond his years. If I had to guess, I would say he was from California. He probably spent all his life surfing, or checking out girls on the beach.

Drew, however, was the complete opposite. He had strawberry blonde hair, that was cut short, and flawless skin. In fact, when I met him I recalled instantly feeling jealous that my skin wasn't as luminous and clear as his. For a guy surviving an apocalypse, he always looked incredibly refreshed. My theories on what he did before coming here varied from day to day. Some days I thought he was a math geek, and would have been best friends with Carter; while others I thought he was a probably an architect. I surmised that theory the day he drew up plans to build the perimeter fence around our compound. I have to admit it did save our butts, and on more than just one occasion.

Of course, those were all just guesses because they never spoke of their pasts and I never asked. Come to think of it, no one did anymore. There wasn't any point. Nothing would ever be like it once was. Even if we did win the war, and drove all the demons from the earth, things could never be the same.

"So, what's the plan boys?" I asked as I grabbed a chair, scooting close to the table to rest my elbow on the map.

"Well," Max exhaled leaning back in his chair as he stretched. "We are trying to decide whether or not we should hit a housing development here," he pointed to an area on the map, and I looked, "or try and hit up this Walmart over here."

"How do you know there is a Walmart right there?" I asked.

Grant tossed a crinkled piece of paper toward me, and I grabbed it. I pressed it firmly against the table, trying to flatten it out with my palm before reading. It was a receipt from Walmart with the address printed on the bottom.

"That answers that then." I tossed the paper back to Grant. "Honestly, I don't think there will be much left there, and we'd be better off salvaging whatever we can find in the houses. That store would have been the first place people would have looted. Don't you think?"

"I would disagree." The sound of a door shutting soundly, but not violently, followed the voice. "It is the wisest course of action to target the area with the most potential in return, rather than to waste hours searching houses, and risk coming back with nothing."

I turned toward whoever had just entered the room and interrupted our meeting to yell at them. I was surprised by whom I saw. It was one of our most recent arrivals, Rembrandt, or Remie, as he said he preferred to be called.

Remie and a small band of survivors had arrived just five days ago. A more accurate description would be that they had just barely made it. More than half their group nearly starved to death, or died of thirst, and the other half were brutally wounded.

We didn't have any doctors, just a woman who was a retired school nurse. But in this world of chaos, that was as good as it got.

It was touch and go for a while, but seeing Remie out of bed for the first time gave me hope for the rest of them.

"Lookin' good." Max rose from his seat locking arms with Remie. "You sure you're up to this?"

"Never felt better," Remie said with grim determination.

Unlike Grant and Drew, I knew exactly who Remie was before the demons, and not just because of the uniform he wore. He was a soldier through and through. Demon apocalypse or not, he had training that nothing, and no one could erase. To him, this was a war like any other. We had a clear enemy and he planned to fight to the death to destroy it. I definitely didn't have anything to say against that.

I sat in silence, observing Remie and Max together. I had the feeling that someday, Remie would take leadership of our band of survivors. And somehow, I knew Max wouldn't mind that at all. Remie was everything Max wanted to be before the world turned to shit. I could see it in his eyes now. To Max, Remie was a hero, a leader. Even though I'd never seen him in a fight, I was starting to share the same conclusion. The few times I visited our medical room, I saw how Remie's fellow survivors acted toward him. They looked up to him, and were more often concerned with his state of health than their own. That had to be a good sign.

"The Walmart is closer than the housing development. We'll hit that first, and if it turns out to be a dead end, we should still have enough time to scout some houses for supplies," Remie said and everyone nodded in tacit agreement.

Max looked up at me to see if I would protest, but I just shrugged and stood up to get ready. I still didn't think it was a good idea, but we needed supplies and arguing would just waste more precious time. These days, time was as valuable as food and water.

Everyone got busy loading gear and weapons. Max and I attached our hunting knives, strapping them to our thighs in their usual positions.

"It's a good plan," Max said watching me toss my shotgun strap over my chest.

"There's no such thing as a good plan anymore. You know that," I whispered back to him. I didn't want anyone else in the room to hear me. It wouldn't be good for morale. "But we've got to do what needs to be done. We need supplies, and if you guys think this is our best option then that's what we are doing," I said with as much solid determination as I could. In truth, I'd follow Max into the gates of hell if I had to. If he believed it would end this war, I'd do it.

Max smirked slightly at me. We'd had this conversation before. He knew I'd never let him fight alone, no matter how bad the plan; and I'd never turn down an opportunity to kill another demon. Every one of their deaths was one step closer to the end of our hell on earth.

I leaned up against the lockers that lined the wall behind me, watching Remie across the room. He jumped onto one of the benches that was angled toward the lockers on his side, and looked out the small window above them. No doubt, he was just watching the demon birds devouring the spider demons' bodies. I watched the first time, but I couldn't stomach it anymore. By the look on Remie's face when he averted his eyes, he couldn't either. It was just physically disturbing on an entirely new, gut-wrenching level.

"Let's head out," Max ordered as he opened the door. The one he chose led straight to the outside, instead of back through the hallways of the compound. That way we could skirt the exterior of the building avoiding detection by the demon birds who were enjoying their feast. It was pretty rare for them to attack while they were eating; their attention locked solely on the decomposing bodies; but the prospect of a human meal might be too hard to resist. We preferred not to give them any options in that regard, which is why we avoided going outside as much as possible.

By distracting the demon birds with a free meal, we had the best chance to head into the city for a quick scout. At least this way, we were sure one demon species stayed busy enough not to notice any of us.

We jogged on in silence, and only the sounds of our labored breathing and boots thudding against the hard earth were audible. Max took the lead as he always did with me right behind him. I always had his back. Behind me was Remie, and I hoped he was as ready to fight as he said he was. One minor mistake and it could cost me my life. Picking up the rear were Grant and Drew, which relieved me. I knew they wouldn't let anything sneak up behind us.

It was a decent thirty-minute jog to the back corner of the base. We'd camouflaged our own hidden exit through a pile of burned-up cars. As expected, Carter was already there waiting for us. I could tell immediately by his lack of gear that he wasn't coming with us after all, and for the first time I kind of regretted my decision.

"Hey," I said as I came to a slow stop in front of Carter. I shouldn't have been so tired, but my gear was heavy and the day had already started getting hot.

Carter grabbed hold of my shoulder and grinned at me through thin, closed lips. "Stay safe, okay?"

I nodded at him, trying to resist getting too emotional. I couldn't allow my feelings to bubble to the surface. Not now, and maybe not ever again. Being emotional could get me or someone else killed, so I buried away the sadness I felt at seeing my brother and gave him a quick, but fiercely strong one-armed hug.

"Always. We'll be back in a few hours."

Our exit was one of Drew's building projects. It concealed a really big break in the exterior fencing of the base. He arranged a large pile of cars to be precariously stacked on top of each other. If a demon tried to crawl up it from the outside, the cars would crush the monster by collapsing.

In order to get in and out, only we knew where there was a narrow crawl space at the bottom of the pile. Not the most comforting place to enter, crawling under tons of rusted metal, but it was working well so far at keeping the demons at bay. I either had to crawl through there or take my chances with the barbed wire fence. I quickly decided against the latter.

I pulled my shotgun from my back and dropped to the ground. Pushing the gun in front of me, I crawled through the narrow space trying not to inhale too much of the fine dirt that puffed into my face. Over the hard earth and loose gravel stinging against the skin of my arms, I army-crawled my way under the ominous wreckage. The nearly twenty-foot distance seemed much longer than it really was, but Max was on the other side waiting for me, and that propelled me forward.

I grabbed his outstretched hand and allowed him to pull me all the way out. "I've got ya," Max said as he helped stand me up. The tiniest little squeeze from his hand sent ripples of desire to flood my body.

I knew Remie was right behind me and these were the last few moments of privacy that Max and I would have for a while. It was just a dozen cars between everyone else and us, so we took our last moments and enjoyed them as best we could.

Our faces, beaded with sweat from the burning sun, found each other like magnets. My lips locked onto his as if his kiss were sustaining my life. I kissed him passionately as he pulled me closer to him because it was never close enough. Our bodies tingled madly with desire as his hands gripped my hair, and I dug my fingers into his back. Maybe it was because we knew we might die on this scout, or that we'd been holding back our desires for so long they were ready to explode. Either way, Max and I needed each other as much as we needed air.

The sound of Remie shoving his gun out of the crawlspace severed our connection, and I gasped when Max broke away from my lips. "I love you Abs." He brushed his thumb against my cheek and planted a firm, but very passionate kiss on my forehead.

"I love you more," I whispered at his back as he walked away to help pull Remie out from under the cars.

I watched mutely as one-by-one, our scout team emerged from under the meticulously placed wreckage of burned-up cars. I knew there was no way this was going to be an easy scout. Unknown dangers awaited us, and we had no choice but to confront them and hope to come back alive. We needed supplies to survive and the only way to get them was to risk life and limb doing it. To most, it would look like a lose-lose situation, but the five of us knew better. Any shot at living was worth dying for.

It was a very long, hot jog. But, looking at the upside, the Walmart was also a straight shot from our compound; one of the perks for choosing a small town as our base of operations. We only had to take the main highway all the way down, just nine short miles. No sneaking through dark, dodgy alleys where any number of demons could be hiding. It was just open, and mostly empty, highway. If anything were going to attack us we would definitely be able to see it coming, or so I hoped. I already knew first-hand how one second everything seemed fine and secure, and the next, tiny, gremlin-like demons were squeezing through the windows, like maniacally possessed rats.

We could have taken a government car, but we had decided against it. At least not until we found new supplies. Driving down there with a noisy military vehicle would have been just plain stupid. No, we had to take our chances on foot for now. If we didn't find anything, we could jog back; hopefully without any demon noticing us at all. In and out. That was the plan, and hopefully, it was a good one.

I swiveled my shotgun and let it rest against my chest; trying to keep it from bouncing against my back as I ran. It was too distracting and I needed to focus on my breathing. We weren't going fast, but we weren't going slow either. Max led us at a steady trot. The heat of the day made it hard to keep our pace going for very long. I didn't know how he managed to maintain it. I still hadn't acclimated to the excessive heat here. I disliked every aspect of the desert, and missed the smell of the clean air back home more often than not. The endless green pine trees and the sweet coolness of the breeze... All I could see here in the desert was dirt, and more dirt.

"What I wouldn't give for a nice cool breeze from home right now," I said mostly to myself.

"Shoulda chose a base in California," Grant said. "We could be jogging along the beach right now." He looked at me with a weak smile, sweat sliding down his temples.

"Yeah, jogging down a beach with thousands of demons right behind us," Drew countered sarcastically.

"So? Maybe they can't swim?" I jested enjoying the lightness of their moods which was a rarity to see.

"Stay focused," Remie wheezed the order as he jogged past us.

Drew, Grant and I exchanged looks, and I knew they were coming to the same conclusion as I. Remie wasn't lookin' too good. I knew he would refuse a break if I suggested it. That's just the kind of man he was. From the stories I heard, he would push his body way beyond its limits. I was almost envious of his drive and stamina, but not quite. Sure, it was a useful tool to push your body to the max, like a well-oiled machine, but your brain is also part of that machine. I liked to think that the few moments of relaxed normalcy that I allowed myself might help keep me sane. I knew I could drive my body into the ground. While getting to the base, I had almost done just that; and somewhere along the way, I almost lost my purpose and who I was. I didn't want that to happen again. Remie would just have to learn for himself... or not. You can't kill demons when you're dead.

I sucked down a small gulp of water from the camel pack strapped to my back. After moistening my mouth, I increased my speed to catch up to Max. My hair was drenched in sweat and sticking annoyingly to my neck and face. Even with my hair up in a ponytail, I didn't feel any cooler. I watched him for a moment before I spoke. He was definitely as tired as any of us, but I knew he would never be the one to ask for a break. It would have to be me, but I really didn't care. I didn't think it made me look any weaker. In fact, I thought it made me look a bit smarter.

"Think we can take a five-minute breather?"

Max looked at me almost surprised. Not by my question, but because he hadn't noticed me jogging beside him. "Yeah. Just five minutes though."

He raised his hand in the air to signal the rest of the team and headed down the embankment of the highway. I rolled my eyes, but followed after him. Men. Apparently it took more than an apocalypse to teach them that they didn't need to act macho *all* the time. I could see in all their eyes that they were grateful for the break, but if anyone were to ask them, they would all say they didn't really need it.

We found an abandoned truck that provided some shade from the late morning sun and sat down in the dirt. "We've got to be more than halfway now, right?" Max nodded at me while he drank from his camel pack. "Good. So, what's the plan when we get there?"

"Split up, grab what we can, and get out," Remie answered for Max.

"Whoa. Wait a second." I looked at Grant and Drew's faces to see if they were as surprised as I was. Max's, however, was grim. "We don't split up." I waved my hands to include, Max, Grant, Drew and me. "That may be how *you've* done things, but we don't work like that."

"Well, that's how you're going to do things from now on," Remie countered. He adjusted his weight so he was squatting. The sun blinded him, making one of his eyes squint sternly at me.

"Max? What the hell?" I turned to him. I didn't recognize Remie as the leader. As far as I was concerned, Max was in charge and always had been.

"Yeah, man!" Grant and Drew agreed. "We didn't sign on for a suicide mission."

"Every mission is a suicide mission," Remie said in a low growl.

"Maybe when you're in charge!" Grant retorted. "Sure explains why your team came back only half alive!"

Grants words struck a nerve in Remie and I clearly saw our team spirit unraveling.

"Guys, calm down. Remie has a point. If we split up, we can get in and out of there quicker. We can also search more of the store in one pass than if we go in one large group." Max pleaded his case, but we weren't convinced.

"And who put him in charge?" Grant asked clearly not happy about the change of command. Neither was I. This was stuff they should have discussed while on base, not during a scout. It was never a good idea to do or say anything that might rattle your team while on a scout. That was just common sense. Wasn't it? You needed to stick to the plan as much as possible. Any deviation could get someone killed, or seriously injured

"Nobody is in charge! Just stop thinking about saving your ass for a second and look at the big picture. We're out here to get as many supplies as we can, as quickly as we can. Other than spider demon attacks, we haven't seen any other demonic activity in almost two weeks. We all know that we won't see any spiders for a while. This is our best chance to stock up and you all know it."

He had a point. Sort of. But we still didn't like it. "We aren't just worried about saving our *asses*," Grant argued his tone menacing. That made it even more frightening, considering his usual laid-back demeanor. "If *we* die, then there won't be anyone to bring any of the supplies back. Did you two masterminds even consider that?"

"Listen," Remie said as he stood up obviously tired of his battle trying to avoid the ray of sun that dappled his face. "If you ain't willing to take some risks for the people of this compound, then why don't you just head back? Do some laundry or something?"

Grant bolted from his seat his fists clenched and ready to slam into Remie's face. "Screw you, man!" Spittle dripped from Grant's lower lip as Drew restrained his friend. I put myself between the two when I saw Drew's eyes more or less threatening to let him go. As much as I would have liked to see Remie punched, we couldn't afford it. Not right now.

"Calm down!" I ordered Grant. He softened when I locked my eyes with his, but his expression remained wild.

"This P.O.S. is going to get someone killed!"

Max pulled Remie away, speaking in hushed tones as they went. I knew he could alleviate some of the aggression. Remie was obviously used to being the leader, and I didn't doubt that he knew what he was doing, or he wouldn't have made it this far. However, he had to realize the same thing about us. We might all be young, but every one of us had killed more demons than we could count. That had to mean something. Besides, he and his team were the reason we had to go on this mission in the first place. Our supplies were nearly wiped out shortly after they showed up.

"I know," I agreed with Grant.

We were all willing to risk our lives to get supplies. That wasn't our argument. We just didn't want to do it stupidly, and Remie's idea was stupid. No matter what the situation, splitting up was bad. That's how Carter got hurt. Instead of coming back and getting Max, Taya and me; he attacked John's men and nearly got himself, as well as Max killed. I shook off the memory preferring not to relive the horrors of that night.

Grant, Drew and I reloaded our packs and waited while Max calmed Remie down. After a few minutes, they walked back to the truck and grabbed their bags. Remie looked calmer, but he also avoided the angry glares from Grant and Drew.

"We'll go in groups of two," Max commanded. "Abby, you're with me. Grant and Drew; you two are obviously together, and Remie will go in alone. Everyone cool with that?"

Grant and Drew nodded somberly. They had never much liked Remie since he arrived at our base, and this was just fuel for the fire. Something about him rubbed them the wrong way. Maybe because he was an authority figure, maybe their personalities just clashed, or maybe they didn't want anyone encroaching on Max's role.

No one spoke the rest of the way. I caught Grant and Drew exchanging odd glances when Remie jogged past Max and them, putting himself in the lead. I couldn't help rolling my eyes. This issue with Remie would have to be dealt with as soon as we got back to the base. He couldn't just barge in and start barking orders at us, and we couldn't just attack him for it. We were supposed to be fighting demons together, not each other.

If Remie wanted to take the lead, he needed to do it the right way. But I sure as hell wasn't going to help him until I talked to Max. In the end, it would be his opinion that determined our move; even though I already knew what he would say.

The parking lot for the Walmart was just as I expected it - a disaster. Abandoned cars were randomly scattered everywhere; and trash piles sat in loose heaps however and wherever the breeze placed them. Many of the vehicles had their windshields smashed in and their doors left ajar. It didn't take much to guess what happened here. So many people in one place... It would have been like a demon buffet! Thinking about it caused bile to climb up my throat and I swallowed hard to keep it down.

We jogged halfway into the parking lot before Max and Remie ducked down behind a minivan. I followed their lead and squatted beside a nearby sedan. It was a tiny, two-door beater, with rusting paint and a makeshift window, made of clear plastic and duct-tape. I rested my weight heavily against it, and as I plopped myself down, the car slightly jostled. By the looks of it, this car would have probably fallen apart if anyone tried to drive it. Its owner wouldn't have made it far, if they had ever made it out of the Walmart alive, that is.

Grant and Drew knelt down beside me. Max gestured with his hand for us to come forward. We needed to make a plan. The last time we entered a store like this, it didn't go very well for us. We definitely weren't willing to make that same mistake again.

"Okay, Grant and Drew, you two head toward the food," Max said without emotion. His game face was on now, and I saw that the same went for the rest of the guys. At least, they knew when to drop their bull-crap and get to work.

"We got it," Grant said catching the empty duffel bag that Max tossed to him.

"Abby and I are going to look for whatever medical supplies we can find." I nodded my head in understanding allowing my game face to ensure him that I was up to the task. Our eyes locked for the briefest of moments, and the same bubbling chaos beneath my exterior was visibly evident in him as well. Neither of us would ever say it aloud, but we were both secretly hoping to find some demons inside. We both eagerly wanted to take them out and eradicate some more demons from our town.

"What about him?" Drew asked. He was pointing toward Remie, who jogged ahead to duck behind another car, closer to the entrance.

"He's going to, hopefully, stock us up with some weapons. They won't be anything fancy, but this town must have some sort of hunting section in their Walmart."

The fact that Remie would be getting us weapons seemed to oddly please the guys. They nodded their heads and watched silently as Remie stalked quietly to the entrance vanishing inside. Grant and Drew locked fists with us before following suit. I watched them more vigilantly than I did Remie; scanning the surrounding cars to be sure nothing was there watching, waiting for a chance to ambush them. I even sniffed the air to satisfy myself that there weren't any demon hounds around even though we hadn't seen any since our arrival at the base.

"Everything is gonna be fine," Max said. He was obviously watching me with a concerned look on his face.

"I know that," I replied in my usual, stubborn tone.

Max took a deep breath, shuffling the trash at his feet as he scooted next to me. "You ready?"

I smirked at him with a crooked grin, and pulled my shotgun free. "Let's go."

3

Max followed as I took the lead, shotgun at the ready to blow away any demons that tried to block me. I quieted my steps, as much as I could, weaving our way between the mess of cars and abandoned carts. At the entrance, I took a deep breath before the building swallowed me up, fortifying myself for whatever awaited us inside.

It took a moment for my eyes to adjust to the darkness of the store. Luckily, this Walmart was built with skylights, so some of the sun's rays dimly lit the eerie building around us. Max stuck close to me as I headed toward what I assumed was the pharmacy. If I remembered correctly, it was usually found around the shampoo and makeup aisles.

I kept my ears finely tuned to any noises around me, and other than Max's and my breathing, there wasn't another sound to be heard. Sure, that was a relief, but kind of creepy too. Silence always seemed to unnerve me more than anything else.

A flash of movement on my right caught my attention and I instinctively swung my shotgun in that direction. Max froze and aimed his weapon in the same direction. "What do you see?"

"Not sure."

I squinted as if it would improve my vision. My eyes began to sting slightly when I realized I wasn't even blinking, so I allowed them one solid squeeze shut before opening them again. I walked sideways to get a better vantage point, never lowering my gun away from the section of the store where I saw movement. Max took a few long, silent strides across the open aisle to peer around the corner. It was more than just trying to get a better shot at whatever demon might be stalking around. He was putting himself between the demon and me.

I allowed one tiny smile to crack my hard exterior before focusing back on what had to be done. I tightened my grip, lowering myself to one knee. I needed as steady a shot as possible in this situation. I didn't want a stray pellet to hit anything that wasn't a demon. Max looked back at me to ensure I was ready, tensing his jaw muscles before bounding further into the aisle his gun raised.

We froze as we stared down the aisle and saw nothing. My heart was pounding in my chest and thumping in my ears. Adrenaline was preparing my body for the attack we both expected, but there was nothing but silent emptiness.

"You sure you saw something?" Max asked without ever taking his eyes away from the dimly lit aisle.

"I'm pretty sure." The intensity of the silence around us started to make me doubt myself. Even the particles of dust that glinted in the few rays of light seemed to float softly in the air, as if they had never been disturbed. Maybe it really was all in my head?

I looked at Max shrugging my shoulders apologetically when another flash of movement caught my eye. This time, Max saw it too. Our bodies instantly tightened and we instinctively raised our weapons as we found our target in the cross-hairs. The sound of our weapons being cocked echoed throughout the store, causing the dark figure to stop moving. The haze of dust and shadows blurred my vision. No one even flinched. Max and I kept our weapons aimed and steady, and the shadowy creature stood still in the distance, like a deer caught in car headlights.

"What is it?" I whispered under my breath to Max.

"I don't know. I've never seen a demon freeze like that."

"Me neither."

My instincts were screaming for me to shoot, but my eyes said otherwise. Something wasn't right and Max felt it too. He must have, or he would have shot instantly and asked questions later. Nerves prickled my skin as the figure took a step backward, slowly bathing itself in the light that sliced through the darkness from one of the store's skylights.

It was Grant.

Fear distorted his face as he took another step to further illuminate himself. A bulging sack teetered on his back. I sighed heavily; releasing the air I had trapped in my lungs, and lowered my weapon. The bag on his back made Grant's dark figure look like a hulking mass, much larger and more oddly shaped than any human.

I saw Grant expel a breath and look visibly relieved when Max too, finally lowered his weapon. Grant had come *very* close to getting shot, and he knew it. Max waved his hand as he let out a short, bird-like whistle to Grant, who replied before dashing into a dark aisle behind him.

"That was close," Max said turning to me.

"Too close," I concurred.

We dashed past two more aisles before we found what we were looking for. As expected, the medical supplies were pretty much nonexistent. Max took the far end of the aisle while I searched whatever was closest to me. I swept my eyes across the shelves, fiddling with boxes as I went. There were tons of boxes of simple Band-Aids. I knew they wouldn't be of much use, but I opened them anyway; dumping their contents inside my bag. Band-Aids couldn't heal a demon wound, but it was better than returning to the base empty-handed.

Max jogged to my side with a handful of vitamin jars and dropped them in my bag. He pulled out a box he had stashed under his arm and wagged it in my face.

"What's that?" I asked.

"Ibuprofen."

"Awesome."

I snatched the dust-covered box from him and stowed it away. That was definitely a good find. Max winked at me making my cheeks blush wildly before jogging toward the pharmacy counter. He slid across it to get to the shelves that stood behind. There were plenty of boxes in there, but there was another problem - we didn't know what a lot of those drugs were. It could be pretty risky taking anything not knowing what it was, but then again, it might be better than leaving them here.

Unraveled ace bandages littered the ground at my feet and I bent down; picking up the ones that weren't covered in blood. I shoved them into the bag with everything else. I walked toward the pharmacy counter, leaning my body against it. It was just the right height to press awkwardly against my hip bones, so I stepped back and tossed my bag onto it. Little to no light filtered into this small, closet-like area, and I wouldn't have known Max was even in there, if it weren't for the beam of his flashlight that danced around in the darkness as he moved.

"Find anything?" Even my whisper seemed too loud in the complete silence of the store. Max mumbled back a reply that I couldn't understand. I guessed he probably had his tiny flashlight braced between his teeth while he searched the shelves. I wanted to go back there with him and quicken the process, but someone needed to stand guard in case any demons showed up.

With my shotgun in hand, I hopped onto the counter, my back facing Max while he searched for prescription drugs. I scanned the surrounding aisles slowly. This place was just a little *too* quiet. In fact, I wasn't sure I'd ever been anywhere that didn't have at least a few demons around. But if they weren't here that meant they were somewhere else, which was really good for us, and really bad for someone else.

The sound of Max dumping a shirt full of pill bottles onto the empty counter startled me, and I jumped off the counter with incredible speed; ready to fire at whatever needed shooting.

"What the heck, Max?" I hissed at him. "You scared the crap outta me."

"Sorry." He smiled at me, obviously amused by my reaction.

I smiled back at him, but stuck my tongue out too. I didn't realize I was so on edge. Something was obviously affecting me, but I just couldn't put my finger on it. Maybe it was my enduring pessimistic nature always kicking me in the butt, and never allowing me to feel like things would really turn out okay. I thought I was over that, but maybe not. When things were bad, I hoped and prayed they would get better, but once they did, I would count the days 'til something else went wrong. That's probably what it was. My internal clock was counting the days, and I thought time was about to run out. Something bad was going to happen, and I just didn't know what it was.

I shook out the sudden tension in my body and looked through what Max collected. "Anything good?" I asked looking at his face as he examined a tube.

"Anti-itch cream," he answered as he handed it to me.

"I said anything *good*, you dork."

"What? It could be useful after a spider demon attack." He winked at me.

He had a point. Their bristly legs always made my skin itch. I tossed the tube into the bag and grabbed a blue box off the counter. "Lots of allergy meds. They won't do much good, but might as well take them."

"I guess we're good?" I asked Max as he slid across the counter and shoved his arms through the straps of the bag.

"Do you think we should look through some more aisles? We haven't been here that long. I thought I saw some stuff on the shelves over here." Max pointed with his flashlight to an aisle off to the side of the pharmacy.

"How did you see way over there?"

"There was a small window on the pharmacy door in there that looked out into this aisle. Let's take a look."

"Okay."

I speed-walked the short distance to the aisle Max pointed out, and smiled proudly, stifling a gasp. It was a clearance section, but that's not what made me smile. There were countless bars of soap and bottles of hydrogen peroxide. Not being in the pharmacy section, people must have overlooked this area.

"Jackpot!" I beamed up at Max planting a quick kiss on his surprised face. I pulled away from him to start loading our treasure, but he snatched my hand, pulling me back.

"I guess I'll have to start finding soap more often," he smiled wryly.

"I guess you will."

We kissed passionately again. Something about finding anything we knew would be helpful in our survival ignited a blaze between us. I wrapped my arms around his neck, my toes barely touching the ground as we kissed. Our lips broke away, allowing the warmth of our mouths to mingle together.

I pulled away before my emotions got the best of me, showering his face with a series of quick pecks before dashing to our treasure. It was Christmas morning, dropping the bars of soap into our bag as we went. When we emptied almost two shelves, we stuffed the remaining space of the bag with the peroxide, nearly clearing off an entire shelf.

"Not a bad haul," Max proclaimed as he hefted our now bulging sack onto his back.

"Not bad at all," I agreed. "We should head out. They're probably waiting for us."

Max and I made it to the end of the aisle before a thought popped into my head, stopping me dead in my tracks. "Max, wait." I pulled onto his hand to stop him.

"What?"

"I've got an idea."

I ran back to the remainder of our supplies and quickly starting snatching the bottles and boxes, moving them to the bottom shelf where they would be less visible. We didn't know for sure whether there were other survivors in the city, but I didn't want them stealing any of our find. It was selfish, I knew, but we had a lot of people depending on us too and they also needed these things. We would have to come back again soon to get more.

I ran back to Max's side and patted him on the shoulder. "Let's go."

"What did you do?" Max asked, as we walked hastily back to the entrance.

"Made sure no one else could find it," I said coolly.

"Hey," I waved to Grant and Drew as we exited the store. The sun was beating down hard so I shielded my eyes from it.

Max dumped our bag next to theirs and took a long swig of water. The shade inside the store was nice and cool, and the heat from the desert sun outside was hastily breaking through that coolness.

"Get anything yummy?" I asked Grant nudging their bag with the tip of my boot. They had the job of scouring the food shelves. I hoped they had found something better than what had sadly become our standard diet at the compound. Canned tuna mixed with some kind of canned vegetable, and a random assortment of mismatched kinds of noodles.

"If you think dried beans are yummy, then yes, we did."

"That's all you got?" I asked disappointed. I took a seat atop my bag and sucked some water from my pack.

"Nah, we got a couple other things," Drew tried to reassure me. "Some questionable canned meat, old, dehydrated soups, condiments, spices and pickles!"

"Pickles?" I looked up at Drew like he had just spoken in another language. The excited expression on his face was completely alien. I'd never seen him so happy.

"Ya know, those sour green things?" he mocked me.

"I know what they are! I've just never seen you so excited before."

Grant slapped Drew across the back of his head and mumbled something under his breath.

"What the hell? Why did you hit me?"

Grant simply rolled his eyes, but I quickly caught onto the issue. Apparently, the pickles were supposed to remain a secret. I locked eyes with Grant for the first time since inside the store and smiled at him with a wink. "I won't tell anyone if you won't. Your pickle secret is safe with me." I drew an "X" across my chest to validate my promise. I figured I owed him one for almost killing him inside a Walmart.

"Do I even want to know?" Max asked as he joined our conversation obviously only hearing the tail end.

"Probably not," I said stifling a fit of giggles.

"Where's Rembrandt?" Max asked bringing the levity back down to our normal intensity.

"I dunno. Haven't seen him since he went in," Grant answered.

"If he's going to keep us waiting for long, it better be because he found something really good," Drew added.

Max waved them off with a groan. He was never one for holding grudges against people, or allowing people to be bad-mouthed even when they deserved it.

"If he's not out here in ten minutes, I'm going in to look for him. Abby, Grant; you two should start looking for a decent car for us to head back in," Max ordered. Normally, I would have started arguing his decision, but his tone and the flexing of the muscle in his jaw told me he wouldn't have it any other way. He was getting worried. Being separated always put us on edge. Just another painful reminder of the past that would forever haunt us.

The ten minutes waiting for Remie to exit the store went by ever so slowly. Max fidgeted restlessly, his eyes never leaving the entrance for more than a second. I knew what he was doing; running through every noise and movement he heard while we were in there in his mind, like a movie. Probably every smell too. I'd done the same thing, I'm sure we all did. There weren't any demons in there, so Remie wasn't in any immediate danger. Unless, of course, he managed to get himself hurt some other way. *Or* maybe it had been so long since our last scout, we were all starting to lose our survival instincts. Maybe the prickling of the skin and eerie vibe that seemed to permeate the air whenever a demon was around didn't work as enough of a warning anymore.

Nah, I couldn't believe that was possible. There was no way I could ever forget the terrible way my body reacted while sensing a demon was nearby. Everything just felt wrong; and there was no way to ignore it. Max was just being paranoid.

My muscles screamed at me as I got up and walked the short distance to where Max knelt beside a giant bus tire. I sat down hard on the first step of the bus entrance and squeezed his shoulder. I opened my mouth to reassure him, but wasn't sure what to say. I could say everything would be okay, and it probably would, but we never knew for certain.

"He knows what he's doing, Max. Remie wouldn't have survived this long if he didn't." I figured I'd give it to him straight. Giving him the "every thing's going to be fine" speech would only make him more paranoid.

"I know. I just..." He stretched his upper arms backwards, causing his joints to pop with the motion. He was tense and stressed and I wished I could rub his shoulders to make him feel better, but now wasn't the time.

We didn't speak for a long moment. I rested my elbows on my knees and propped my head up as I gazed at Max's fingers. He was fidgeting with the strap of the hunting knife on his thigh. I felt completely mindless as I watched without blinking until a saddening thought sizzled into my mind. Ever since we arrived at the base, Max had shouldered all the guilt caused by the deaths of Judy, Norah and Savannah. Even though Taya blamed me for what happened to them, it was Max who suffered their passing with the most intensity. He confessed to me one night, after Taya and I had gotten into one of our usual fights that it was truly his fault they died. I just thought he was just trying to make me feel better, but he was being honest. He really did blame himself.

Remie might have been a jerk sometimes, but Max considered him a part of the team; and if anything happened to him I knew Max would take it hard. Any loss, even someone that everyone didn't always get along with, would be difficult to swallow.

"It's going to be okay," I said my cheesy comfort line not sounding so bad after all. Not only did I not want Max to endure such guilt, but it was also a dangerous distraction; and he had to focus on our survival. And that included Remie's, so I vowed I would do whatever was necessary also. He would like to know that we could make a getaway if we needed to. I had to support him in that regard, and I knew exactly how to do it.

"Grant, Drew!" I said their names with sharpened clarity, as I rose in one smooth movement from my seat on the bus step. They jerked their heads in my direction, noticing the tone in my voice was one I hadn't used in quite a while. It was time I took charge and barked some orders around here. "See that Ford Explorer over there?"

They both nodded their heads noiselessly.

"Good. Get it started," I ordered flatly.

The two of them looked at me with complete shock for only a moment until I crossed my arms and stared them down, hard. I was going to be very pissed off if they didn't do what I said, and they could definitely see that one my face.

"Yes, ma'am," they said in unison, jogging over to the old, red Explorer I had pointed to.

"Max!" I said his name harsher than I intended still carrying the air of authority I was mustering to take control of the situation. He looked at me, slightly startled, unaware that I sent the guys off to get the car. "Get in there! And get Remie. Then get out. You understand me?" I pointed to the Walmart with my finger and flung my thumb backward toward the Ford.

He sighed heavily and hid his small smile, but not enough that I didn't notice it. I knew him too well to let him hide anything from me anymore. Knowing Max, I sensed he needed me to be who he knew I could be. A survivor, and a fighter, but most importantly, a leader. We both knew that there was no one else in this world we'd trust to lead our group. Sure, Max looked up to Remie, but I wasn't sure he trusted him entirely, yet. So, I stepped up to the plate and took the lead while the man I loved fought the demons inside him. The demons of guilt and doubt.

Max stood up and rolled his shoulders looking at me. It wasn't a loving gaze, but something else. His eyes held the deepest respect and gratitude. My body began to melt slightly at his expression, and I knew I would quickly turn to Jell-O. I couldn't let it.

"Go," I ordered again. Without a word, Max took off for the entrance of the store and disappeared.

I stared at the darkness that swallowed him for only a moment before pushing away the knot that was building in my gut. Max would come back out of that store and we would all leave this town in one piece. I *had* to believe that.

I gathered up our bags into one pile while Grant and Drew still struggled to get the Explorer started. I wasn't even sure if they knew how to jumpstart a car, but I expected they'd eventually figure it out. Hopefully, they'd watched enough movies and crime shows to get the general idea.

Five minutes later, the roar of the engine answered my doubts. The cheers from Grant and Drew inside the Explorer meant they must have doubted the very same thing. The engine struggled at first, but as it warmed up, it grew strong and steady. We had our ride out; now all we were waiting for was Max and Remie's return.

Grant backed up the Ford nearby, while Drew and I loaded our packs into the back.

"That everything?" Drew asked attempting to push the back door silently shut.

"Everything except the most important thing," I replied quietly looking back toward the store.

"He'll be out soon. Max doesn't know how to fail." Drew patted my shoulder then headed to the front of the Ford to talk with Grant. A single tear escaped my eye, but I didn't even notice it until its chilly wetness slid down my face, dripping onto my collarbone. Sure, it hurt when Drew patted me on the shoulder, but not too much. My emotions were getting the best of me and I needed to keep them in check.

Growling, I wiped my face off with my arm and leaned back against the Ford. The last thing I needed was for the guys to see me crying. With my shotgun resting on my knees, I steadied my breathing and regained the resolve I knew I had inside me. Max had to come back out. He and I were already too invested for him not to. We were going to save the world together. We were going to kill every last demon together and nothing could stop that. Period.

My pep talk worked. The chaotic resolve was back and burning beneath the surface.

I stood up from the Explorer, ready to charge into the Walmart, when Max and Remie came strolling out like they had just been out shopping on a normal Sunday afternoon. They each pushed a cart loaded with supplies, and my heart thumped in my chest with excitement. I looked back at Grant and Drew. Both their faces matched how I felt. Remie hit the jackpot.

As I jogged toward them, I saw that Remie's cart was full of weapons, but I couldn't tell what Max had. Whatever it was, his cart was full too. With a huge cache of weapons, Remie was sure to gain favor in our group now. I guess I never should have doubted him.

Max increased his speed when he saw me jogging toward him, and ditched the cart when we got close. He gave me a quick embrace and held my head firmly between his strong hands. "Everything okay?"

"Yeah. We got an SUV, and we're good to go. What did you guys get?" I peered from around Max's shoulder to eye the treasure. My attention flew directly to Remie's cart as he approached. "Holy crap!"

I flung myself onto his cart like a kid on an ice cream cone and pulled out one of the rifles.

"What's this?" The weight of the weapon didn't feel right.

"Hellz yeah!" Grant cheered jogging up to the carts with Drew hot on his tail.

"What kind of fire power we got?" Drew questioned as he brushed past Grant grabbing the gun from my hand. I was still staring at it in shock. The moment he took the weapon fully into his grasp, a look of surprise broke feverishly across his reddened face. "What the hell is this?" Drew held the weapon out like it was a severed demon limb.

"What's going on?" Grant snatched the weapon from Drew and they both inspected it.

I looked at Max, then at Remie, and neither of them looked happy. "These aren't real weapons, are they?" My question silenced everyone.

"No," Max answered, his voice dry and raspy.

For the first time, I *really* looked at Max's cart and saw what was inside. Dozens of containers of pellets. I picked up one of the jugs and sighed sadly. These stupid containers of bright colored BB's and plastic guns had just ruined everything.

"You spent all that time getting friggin' BB guns?" Grant said furiously. He threw the air gun into Remie's cart and shoved it at him. Craning his neck around to look at Max, he stretched so far it looked uncomfortable. "Why did you even waste the time bringing them out here, man?"

"They might not be useful against demons, but they can be used for target practice instead of wasting ammo. A trained army is always better in a fight," Remie explained shoving the cart back toward Grant.

"This isn't an army!" Grant shouted.

"That's enough," Max spat shoving Grant away from Remie. I lowered my eyes still completely disappointed in what weaponry Remie had managed to salvage from the store. Sure, fire practice was a good idea, but the switch from thinking we had some real fire power to realizing they were nothing but toys was a crushing blow, and a hard lump to swallow.

"There wasn't a single weapon left in the place." Max placed his hand on my shoulder and pulled me back from between Grant and him. If there was going to be a fight, he didn't want me to be in the middle of it.

"If there wasn't anything left, then why bring out these damn toys? What are we supposed to do with these? Pester the demons to death?"

"No," Max replied getting annoyed, "we are going to train everyone on how to defend themselves. It was better to bring out something than to come out with nothing."

Grant ran his fingers through his hair and huffed angrily. I understood his frustration. It was tough defending our base and even harder when every day our supplies dwindled further.

"We'll find weapons. We just need to look somewhere else."

"And where's that?" Drew asked as Grant skulked away kicking the trash at his feet.

"Here." Remie pulled out a crumpled piece of paper, handing it to Drew.

I squeezed next to Drew to get a glance at the paper and met Max's eyes with confusion. "You're not serious?"

"It's a good idea, Abs."

"We don't even know where to find this place or how much deeper into the city it is," I argued.

"It's a better chance than any other place to find what we need. No one would think of heading to a museum for supplies," Remie said matter-of-factly.

"So you think there will be weapons there?" Drew asked wagging the paper in front of Max.

"Yeah, we do. Or at least stuff that hasn't been picked clean to the bone already."

"It's a damned space museum! What weapons could it possibly have?" I couldn't believe they were serious about this. They were grasping at straws. I was all about getting the supplies we needed for the base, but it wouldn't do anyone any good if we died trying to get them. I could just imagine the look on Carter's face if we never came back. He and Taya would definitely come looking for us.

"Abby," Max spoke calmly as he tried to ease my anger. "This museum is one of the least likely places to get ransacked. It might not have *everything* we need, but there's a good chance that it hasn't already been picked clean."

"Museums have visitor centers, which means there might possibly be food and other useful items that are probably *all* still there," Remie added.

"We're more likely to find more useful supplies on base than going out there. Besides, we have a good enough haul for now," I said as I pointed back toward the Ford Explorer.

"You know we can't do that," Max sighed.

There were certain areas of the base that were fenced off when we got here, supposedly with good reason, but we didn't know for sure. Fences blocked off entire sections of the base; their doors and windows were boarded shut and entire entrances barricaded, but that wasn't what worried us the most. It was the makeshift signs that kept us at bay.

Smokers!
Danger!
Do Not Enter!

They hung everywhere, painted in bright, red paint on any flat object that could be found. They hung off the fences, smeared on trash can lids, and scraps of metal. It didn't take a genius to know what they meant. There was some kind of demon trapped on the base; behind those warning signs. So, we didn't go past them, and nothing ever came out. I wasn't one to ignore such obvious signs of caution. I wasn't stupid. I knew full well there were demons there, but it seemed much less threatening to venture out into our own base, than to search out a museum in the outskirts of a town we didn't know. If something were to go wrong, we'd be too far away to get help in time.

"Shouldn't we look for a police station or something instead? What weapons could that museum possibly have?" I snatched the paper from Remie's grip, almost tearing it. The paper was crumpled and covered in dust, with foot prints stamped onto it. Apparently, there was supposed to be an event held there several months ago - a chili cook-off. That cook-off never happened. Demons had invaded the world not long before this quiet little town could celebrate.

There were a few pictures on the flier of exhibits at the museum, but nothing looked useful to me. What could we do with a giant chunk of meteorite or old satellites?

"I'm with Abby on this. I just don't get it. There isn't going to be anything useful at this museum. You really want to travel out there to raid the gift shop? That's beyond stupid," Drew's tone was more disgusted than angry.

"What's the *real* reason you want to go there?" Grant asked rejoining the conversation.

Max avoided his gaze and I instantly knew he and Remie were hiding something. It wasn't like Max to keep things from me, or anyone else for that matter. Warning bells were blaring in my head. I stared at Remie defiantly, crossing my arms over my chest. It was Grant, Drew and I versus the two of them. They had to know that we wouldn't cooperate until they told us the truth.

"You've got to promise that what I tell you won't leave this group," Max instructed with hesitation in his voice.

"This isn't going to be good news is it?" I knew that when Max used this tone, things weren't good.

"Who are we going to tell?" Grant asked.

Max pinched the bridge of his noise as sweat beaded his brow. "Our generators are going out."

My knees began to buckle and I would have fallen to the hot pavement if there hadn't been a car behind me to catch me. That was the worst possible thing he could have said. I mean, I would have much preferred that he tell us we were out of food. But out of power was one problem that would be hard to fix.

The irritation that was grinding at our group since the scout began instantly dissipated. "Are you sure?" Drew asked his voice laced with concern.

"Yeah."

"Shit. This isn't good." Drew began pacing back and forth running his hands through his red hair. "I know it has been glitching out on us, but I thought we had a bit more time."

"Why didn't you say anything?" I asked Max.

"We didn't want to start a panic," Remie answered. I tried to hide my annoyance. He talked to Remie about it, but not me?

"Carter knows and so does Taya. They're going to try and keep it under wraps to avoid mass alarm," Max said.

"If the power goes out completely, people are going to notice. Then what are we going to do?" Drew asked.

Realization hit me as bile rose up in my throat. I stepped forward to answer Drew's question. I knew just what was going to happen. I knew what Max and Remie were trying to do, and as soon as I opened my mouth, the world began to spin. The bright, cloudless sky loomed into my vision, and just before my body should have slammed into the hard, black pavement Max's face came into view.

"Whoa, Abs, you okay?"

I blinked hard and focused on him, allowing my vision to cease its swirling. "Yeah, yeah. It's just this heat," I lied.

"Get her into the Explorer. The A/C seems to be working," Grant said.

I allowed Max to guide me into the Explorer while the guys loaded up Remie's scavenged supplies. Normally, we would have been eager to exit the store parking lot, but all eyes were on me. We were exposed in the heat for too long and I knew they were as grateful as I for the cool air.

"You were going to say something," Grant said encouragingly.

"Yeah." I hesitated for a moment. Despite already receiving bad news, it was hard to announce any more, but we all needed to be on the same page. Especially if we were going on a suicide mission to a museum, deep inside the unscouted city.

I looked at Remie, who was resting his elbows on his knees and rubbing his temples vigorously. "I know why you got the BB guns. It was a good idea." Grant and Drew looked at me like I was insane, and I had to raise my hand at them so I could continue. I didn't need them spouting off and starting another argument. I was finally starting to see in Remie what Max saw, and they needed to see it too. We *all* needed to get along and be on the same team if we were going to make it through this.

"Remie is trying to prepare us for when the generator goes out. There are lots of people in our compound that need to learn how to defend themselves and if these guns will teach even a tiny percentage of them to do that, then we're going to give them that chance."

They both opened their mouths to respond, but shut them again as the logic finally seeped into their thick heads.

"So, it's not just weapons you're looking for then? We need parts for a generator?" Grant asked.

Max nodded.

"And you think we can find these parts at the museum because you don't believe anyone would ransack the place?" Max nodded looking slightly relieved now that we knew the truth.

"Alright then," Drew said as he turned to face forward in the passenger seat. "Ya know, you two should have told us the truth from the beginning."

"It's a hard enough burden to bear. Max didn't want everyone else to have to carry that weight as well," Remie added sounding much softer than he ever had before. "Thinking that everything you've fought to guard and protect could fall apart just because of some rusted, old generators is pretty hard to deal with."

"Burdens are the hardest to carry when you carry them alone." I raised an eyebrow at Max, giving him the *"we're going to talk about this later"* look.

He might have been trying to save me from a whole truckload of worrying, but we also promised never to keep anything from each other no matter what. What we built at the compound was my responsibility too. He was always being the hero, the protector; but he needed to learn that sometimes he should step down and let someone else do the job. I didn't want him getting burnt out. Every so often the weight of emotional stress far outweighed anything else. I was starting to wonder if we had swapped personalities when we got to the base. I used to be the one who bore the weight of the world on my shoulders, but now it looked like Max shared it too. Or, to be totally honest with myself, I have to admit I still carried that weight, and my shoulders were getting awfully weary.

"So, what's the plan?" I looked at Max and then the rest of the guys. It was a very dangerous decision we agreed upon, but I knew every one of them felt the same way I did. If we had to get generator parts, then we weren't heading back to base until we had some.

"Get the parts. And don't get killed," Drew said flatly while Grant nodded in agreement.

"Sounds like a good plan to me," I added.

4

The small town made it easier to find the museum than I thought it would. There wasn't a single demon sighting along the way, which was a good thing, yet I still couldn't seem to relax.

We took Indian Wells Road until we reached Scenic Drive, and there it was, standing on the hillside to our right, reflecting the afternoon sun like a beacon.

The building looked unlike any museum I had ever seen. A giant, glass cube housed between two square concrete pillars. Darkened windows mirrored the outside world revealing nothing of what was inside. Actually, it was sort of pretty in a weird way. It looked more like a work of art than a museum for rockets.

The museum stood atop a hill on the outer edges of the town. It gave us a vast view of the entire city below which sprawled out further than I expected.

"Wow," I whispered quietly pressing my face against the glass.

Remie pulled into one of the many open spaces and we all piled out leaving the doors of the Explorer open. It made it easier to get back in, should we need to make a quick getaway.

I walked steadily away from the guys taking slow steps toward the edge of the parking lot. My feet kicked up the loose gravel as I dragged them along. Something about the view of the city drew me in.

"Looks almost normal, doesn't it?" Remie asked startling me, and making me swallow a pang of fear. "From up here, it almost seems like it could have all been just a bad dream."

He sounded almost sad as he spoke, and when I looked up at him he was gazing down at the city. The brim of his hat cast a shadow across his face, but I could still see the expression he tried to hide. He had lost someone. Everyone had, and even someone as tough and as cold as he couldn't hide that kind of pain.

"Would be nice to think we could just wake up and everything would be how it used to be," I agreed turning to look back at the city. Everything *did* look normal. There were no billowing towers of black smoke, no screams of dying people, and no shrieks or howls of demons. If only I could make myself forget how the world *really* was I might have been able to pretend it was just a normal Sunday afternoon.

I sighed.

"I had a daughter like you once," Remie said never letting his gaze waiver from the city. "She was very brave and smart." He gulped loudly.

"What was her name?" I asked curiously. It was rare for anyone to talk about their life before the demons and I was surprised that Remie chose to open up to me, but it was nice too.

"Zahara."

"That's a pretty name. How old was she?"

"She was ten," he said as he fiddled with something on his wrist. I looked down to see it was a pink and purple knotted bracelet. It must have been his daughter's. "She wanted to be an astronaut."

I heard the grief in his words. It must have been difficult for him to be here at a museum which painfully reminded him of what he lost. I wanted to comfort him, but I didn't know how. I also knew I wasn't very good at it. I never could find the right words. That was Taya's department. She had a much cheerier disposition than I could ever hope to have even during an apocalypse. I tried to think of what she would say in this situation and rested my hand atop his, searching for the words. I couldn't think of any so I simply squeezed his hand as he grasped tightly to the bracelet on his wrist.

"She would have loved this place," he sadly flatly as the emotion vanished, and he buried it somewhere deep inside him.

Remie finally tore his gaze from the city and looked at the exhibits that were housed outside the museum. Old missiles of various sizes, giant engines from a space shuttle, and several other things I couldn't identify. Carter would have loved this place too, but I kept that thought to myself. Unlike Remie's daughter, Carter *could* visit this place if he wanted to.

We should have made our way directly into the museum, but there was just something about this place that drew us to it. It was so unusual. This plain, uninteresting and simple town had a building that looked like a giant diamond sitting atop a mountain. What wouldn't draw a person's attention?

I looked back at the Explorer and saw that Max, Grant and Drew were busy unloading our bags so we could fill them with whatever we found inside the museum. Hopefully, we would find something. I scanned the surrounding hillside behind them for any movement, and didn't spot any demons. We hadn't seen any all day and I should have found comfort in that, but I couldn't. I was too pessimistic. Assured for the moment that we were safe, I turned back toward the front of the museum.

Remie was already walking among the antique space parts that were scattered artfully outside. He was adjusting his gun strap on his shoulder and although he looked relaxed, almost like he didn't have a care in the world, I recognized something quite different. I saw the tension in his jaw as the muscles flexed, and the whiteness of his knuckles as he gripped the gun that hugged his hip. Even his eyes were only half-observing the pieces he stood before as they panned around scanning the perimeter. Was he trying to act casual so he could bait any possible nearby demon? Was he trying to let it think it might catch him by surprise? Or was he always constantly on alert?

I stared down at my own hand that I kept atop my shotgun. I always gripped it like it would run away from me even though it was strapped across my chest. I guess I was just like him. I always had my hand ready to shoot at whatever might come at us. That's probably why I almost shot Grant inside the Walmart. I made a mental note to apologize to him later.

Rembrandt and I actually had a lot in common. Although we tried to relax, and embrace every moment of normalcy and peace that we could, somewhere deep down inside, we both knew down to our very souls that it was a lie. We instinctively gripped our weapons without even thinking, our nerves constantly tuned to the world around us without us even noticing. We were fighters through and through. If we were born this way, or because the world and the evil in it had made us like this, there was definitely no changing it.

"Hey, you two! Let's go. We're burning daylight," Max shouted from the parking lot. He was pulling his duffel bag onto his shoulder.

I looked at the horizon and he was right. It was late afternoon and would be dark in a few hours. Definitely, not the time of day I wanted to be out and about searching around for supplies. We needed to get in, get out, and get back to the base all before the sun went down.

"You ready?" Max asked as I jogged up to him.

"Yeah." My reply sounded breathy as I lifted the strap off my shoulder and held the shotgun firmly at my side.

"Let's go," Grant and Drew said in unison leading the way.

I followed after them with Max at my side, and Remie pulled up the rear. I glanced back watching him, and saw he was walking backwards keeping a wary eye on anything that might attack us from behind. He seemed awfully alert to me. Almost like he *sensed* something watching us. I gave him a quizzical look that he responded to with a stern face and then a wink. It *didn't* reassure me. In fact, I was starting to get the feeling that maybe something *was* watching us. But from where?

As we entered through the heavy glass doors and into the main entrance of the museum there was a sign that read, *New Mexico Museum of Space History,* perched above a greeting desk. The desk wasn't covered in trash or dust. It looked relatively normal and untouched, which was downright weird. Maybe Remie was correct, no one would have thought to raid a museum when the demons first attacked. Maybe we *would* find everything we were looking for. It sure would be nice to catch a break for once.

Out of the corner of my eye, I glimpsed the gift shop to my left. I signaled to Max that I was going in, and he nodded his head before instructing Grant and Drew to follow me. Remie stayed at the front entrance still glancing out occasionally like he expected a demon to come bursting in at any moment. I tried not to let the tension emanating from him distract me. We had a mission and I needed to stay focused. *If* demons attacked, we could handle it. We had all fought them before and would fight them again. Remie was tough, and anything that came through that door would have to go through him first. I smiled at that thought. Remie might not even leave any demons for the rest of us to kill.

"Damn!" Grant protested as we entered the gift shop.

Anything useful was gone.

"I don't get it," I said as I walked further in. It didn't look like anyone had ransacked the place, yet all the food supplies were gone. I ran my fingers across the empty hooks that were labeled, and used to hold chips and cookies.

"I guess someone got the idea before us," Drew said flatly with clear disappointment. He flicked magnets off a nearby stand, sending them scattering to the floor.

"There's still stuff here we can use," Max said not allowing us to get disheartened by this setback. "Abby, grab all those shirts and put them in the bag. Grant, you pack some of those mugs. We can always use more cups."

I saw Grant start to protest the order but Max's expression forced him to shut his mouth. In this new world, everything was useful, even something as simple as a cup.

Max didn't give Drew any orders, but he didn't need to. Drew was already gone and salvaging whatever was even slightly useful. I grabbed as many shirts as I could and stuffed them greedily into the duffel bag. I knew quite a few people who would be happy to have new, clean shirts.

On a nearby shelf, there were some toy space shuttles and key chains. I thought about it for a moment and shoved those in the bag too. We had some kids on base and I knew they had little or nothing to play with. It would please them greatly to have these, and a smile on a child's face would do us all good.

Max had gone behind the counter and was rummaging through the drawers, dropping things into a pile on the counter that he thought might be worthwhile. As I made my way toward him, I heard Grant mumbling under his breath. He and Drew were stowing small bags of nuts into the bag with the mugs. The clicking of the porcelain mugs moving against each other as they jostled the sack echoed throughout the room.

"Ooh, a lighter." I spied it on the counter with Max's discoveries and dropped it into the pocket on the side of the duffel bag. I dragged my arm across the counter spilling the rest of the items into the side pocket with it. There were a few more lighters, a pair of scissors, and some heavy duty tape, along with other miscellaneous items.

I tossed the bag onto the counter relieved to be free of the weight. "Think we'll find what we really came here for?" I asked Max in a whisper. I didn't want Grant and Drew getting anymore irritated than they already were.

"Honestly?"

I nodded.

"I don't know, but we've got to at least try." He looked over at Grant and Drew sighing. "Even if we don't find anything, we have to at least look everywhere for anything useful. Can you really go back to the base knowing you didn't do everything you possibly could to get what you needed to keep all those people safe?"

"Max," I rested my hand on his cheek and looked into his eyes. They were full of angst. "I have never had any doubt that you always do absolutely everything you can do to protect us. To protect me." His eyes flicked over to Grant and Drew, but I grasped his chin and forced him to look at me. "They aren't mad at you. They are mad at the situation. They don't want to fail any more than you do."

"You're right."

"Of course I am." I smiled at him glad that I could ease his tension, if only slightly. He had changed so much in the last few weeks. It was becoming glaringly obvious he carried the weight of the world on his shoulders; but in a way, we all did. Any humans who were still alive had the difficult job to protect our existence, as well as our world from the demons who wanted to rip it apart.

Drew cleared his throat causing Max and I to stop staring into each other's eyes. "We're going to throw this stuff in the Explorer. You two..." he gave Max and I a little smirk as we pulled our duffel bag off the counter and tossed it to Grant. "Don't have too much fun while we're gone."

"Oh, geez," I sighed at their backs as they walked out of the gift shop. They only made me blush a little, but I wasn't going to let that stop me from having a quiet moment with Max. We had both been on edge lately, and anything we could do to calm our nerves would be a good thing.

A tiny whistle tickled the air beside me and I turned to see Max leaning back against the wall, looking me up and down. I knew that look, but I feigned ignorance.

"What?" I smiled at him raising an eyebrow.

"Nothin'" he shrugged casually which only heightened our playful game.

"Get over here," I ordered leaning against the counter. I lifted my finger and beckoned him to me with a curl.

With one swift movement his lips were locked onto mine with fierce passion. His mouth was earnest and warm, filling me all the way down to my toes. As his fingers laced through my hair our lips parted allowing our tongues to dance together. The world of demons around us disappeared and for a single, blissful moment we were in heaven.

Like nearly all of our kisses; it ended as quickly as it began. I felt like I could kiss him forever, but as breathless as I was every time; I knew I would probably faint if I tried to.

"You're not the boss of me, ya know." His breath tickled my neck as he buried soft kisses against my sensitive skin.

"Yes, I am." I held back a sigh when the sensation of his touch extended down my spine. I would never get tired of that feeling. I'd known Max nearly all my life, yet every time he touched me it felt like the first time.

"What were you and Remie talking about?" he asked changing the subject after planting a final, but firm kiss on my forehead.

"Huh?" I was still lost in the excitement of our kiss.

"You, and Remie. You were talking just after we got here."

"Oh," I said surprised. I couldn't believe I'd forgotten. "He was telling me about his life before."

"Really?" Max seemed more intrigued than surprised.

I wasn't sure if I should tell him more than that. I didn't like keeping anything from Max, but I felt that Remie had told me those things in confidence, and I didn't want to betray that. But would it really be a betrayal? Knowing more about Remie had helped me to understand him better and relate to him. Maybe it would do that for Max too. Maybe it would bring Max toward fully trusting Remie in our inner circle. Perhaps then Max could be relieved of some of the burden he carried.

"What about his life?" Max inquired further when I got lost in thought. He walked around the counter and leaned against it beside me.

"He told me I reminded him of his daughter."

Max was quiet for a moment. "I didn't know he had a daughter."

"Yeah," I said the word and it hung in the air. "There's a lot we don't know about all of us."

"I know a lot about you," he replied smartly.

"Well yeah, we've known each other for years. What I mean is... I know he seems like..."

"Like the Terminator?"

I giggled at Max's analogy. "I couldn't think of the right word, but now that you say it, yeah, he kinda does."

"I guess in the end, the machine does sorta learn human emotion though, huh?"

I punched him in the arm and he laughed. I didn't realize how much I missed the sound of his laugh. "He's not a machine, dork. He's just hardened. Kinda like me," I admitted.

"You aren't hard," Max looked at me confused. "Why do you think that?"

"I am Max. You just can't see it. I try to be tough and strong. I try to hide my true terror, but all I really am is a scared girl who wishes things could go back to the way they were."

I wasn't planning to spill my guts to him, or to fight the tears that threatened to fall, but that's what I did. I never wanted to appear weak to anyone, and hated letting my guard down, but loving Max as much as I did, it was hard not to. My heart demanded that I breach the barrier and let him in.

"Abs," he spoke my nickname softly taking my face in his strong hands. I felt so small beside him, my cheeks filling his hands. "You *are* strong and tough. You never would have made it this far if you weren't; and neither would I. If I remember correctly, you saved my ass more times than I can count."

I sighed as a tiny laugh escaped with a single tear. "You've got a point."

Max nodded enjoying the small victory of having me admit he was right. For once. He pulled me into his arms, wrapping me securely as a sense of relief and security embrace me.

"None of us would have been here if it weren't for you, Abs. Not me, not Carter, and not Taya. You are tougher than you think, and the moment you let yourself believe that you'll be unstoppable. I almost feel sorry for the demons the day that happens."

I pulled my head from his chest and looked up at him. He was right. I knew deep down inside, I could be as strong as he said I could. I *had* been in the past. Life, the way it was now, was just so hard to endure making me strain to remember who I was and who I could be. With Max by my side, I knew I could do anything.

"I think I might feel sorry for them too."

He looked at me with a smile that lit up his face.

"Nah," we both said in unison as we laughed. He wrapped me tightly in his arms again and swayed me from side to side, rocking away the last shred of doubt that lingered inside me.

"Let's go see what's taking them so long," Max said giving me another quick kiss before grabbing my hand and leading me out the door. I spied a small necklace hanging on a jewelry rack beside the door. A silver chain with a pendant of a shooting star sparkled up at me. Something inside me made me pull Max to a stop and stare at it.

"What's wrong?"

"Nothing," I said simply clutching the necklace in my fist. I wanted to keep it. I wanted to remember this moment with Max. The moment he eradicated all the doubt inside me and allowed the true fighter I knew I was to emerge.

I locked the chain around my neck and gazed one last time at the sparkling pendant before tucking it under my shirt and heading out of the gift shop.

Max pulled apart the electronic, automatic sliding glass doors to the outside. He instinctively took the lead, and stepped out. We weren't even three steps out the door before I felt it. I knew Max sensed it too, because we both froze our bodies prickling at the sensation. The strange change in the air, the electricity of it, warning that a demon was nearby. I sniffed, inhaling only the hot dust of the nearby desert. No rotting corpse smell. So, we weren't dealing with a demon hound. That was good news, at least.

"I don't smell anything," I announced quietly to Max.

"Yeah, me neither. But that doesn't mean there isn't something out there. We need to find the guys."

We walked a good ten feet further from the entrance before we could see the Explorer and the situation we were in. I hadn't heard any gunshots, or any other kind of struggle for that matter. They had to be okay. I wasn't willing to lose anyone. Not again.

I grabbed the barrel of my shotgun, lifting it up in front of me. I didn't want to cock it just yet; the sound might draw unwanted attention. But I wanted to be ready.

Max looked at me and I nodded that I was ready. We both unbuttoned the sheaths for the knives on our thighs and I followed after Max on steady legs as he walked further away from the entrance.

The weight of my shotgun, my father's shotgun, rested comfortably against my shoulder. I found strength in that comfort believing somehow, and someway my father's spirit was still connected to it, and he fought beside me whenever I used it.

Max signaled for us to stop as we made it to the edge of the building. He peered around the corner to get a better view of the Explorer. I saw him wave his hand in the air making gestures I didn't recognize, but I could tell it was a good sign. His motions meant there was someone alive out there.

He whirled around and rested his back against the wall. His face was already shimmering with a sheen of sweat just from the few minutes we were outside.

"What's going on?" I asked. I wanted to take a peek around the corner and assess the situation for myself.

Max put a hand on my chest to stop me. "They're okay, but something is out there."

I swallowed hard and tightened my grip on my gun. Shaking off the tingling of my nerves, a deadly resolve burned through my body.

"What is it?" I questioned my voice suddenly sounding unfamiliar. It was so full of anger, but that was a good thing wasn't it? I needed to be angry.

"Not sure," Max admitted. "They're still hiding behind the Explorer, but they pointed toward the mountain. I think something is watching us."

"Shit," I cursed under my breath.

"What?"

"I thought I sensed that earlier. I think Remie did too."

"Why didn't you say anything?"

"Cause I knew Remie was on guard and he'd keep a lookout. Plus, we were going to make this fast. Get in and get out, right? I was just hoping we would go unnoticed."

"Well, we can scratch that hope," Max sounded a little miffed, but I ignored it. Now wasn't the best time to get annoyed with each other.

I pushed off Max's protective arm and peered around the corner for myself. I clearly saw Grant, Drew and Remie all squatting beside the Explorer their weapons at the ready. Grant saw me and waved for me to go back, but I shook my head. If there was going to be a fight, I wouldn't leave them alone.

"Why aren't they attacking?" I asked Max scanning the mountainside.

"No clue, but I don't like it."

"Me neither. We need to get them inside. If something is going to attack we are much better off not being out in the open, and calling more attention to ourselves. One pack of demons is enough; we don't need every one in the whole damn city coming down on us."

I rolled away as Max passed me; peering back around the corner toward the Explorer. I watched him as he gave directions on our plan. He pointed toward his eyes and then toward the mountainside. Then he lifted two fingers, waggling them to imitate running, before pointing to himself. Max and I were going to cover them as they took turns running toward us. I just hoped they understood the plan.

"They got it," Max said confirming my hopes.

"Good."

"You stay here, and I'm going to take cover over there." He pointed to a pillar directly across from me. "You know what to do."

I nodded. "Kill anything that isn't human."

Max smiled, but it didn't brighten his face. "Yeah. And Abs," he looked back at me drawing his brow low. "If anything happens you get back inside and lock yourself in. You hear me?"

"Nothing is going to happen." I wouldn't allow that thought to enter my mind. There was no possibility of failure. If I even toyed with the idea, if I even admitted that there was the tiniest, most miniscule chance that the demons might win this fight, I knew we *would* lose.

Max pressed his lips into a thin line and nodded. He knew I was right. I looked into his eyes and saw something shift. That same burning resolve that was inside me was bubbling inside him. No matter how afraid we were, no matter how much doubt battered our souls; we would fight these demons with as much fierce anger as possible. We weren't just fighting for our lives; we were fighting for our friends, for everyone that still lived in this world; wherever they may be. If we... *when* we killed all the demons that threatened us; we would be saving more than just the lives that stood on the line here today. Each dead demon meant another human could live. At least that's what it meant in our minds.

5

I embraced the anger inside me, and kneeled on the ground as Max signaled the first of our team to run toward us.

Drew steeled his resolve before stepping out from behind the Explorer. I saw him pivot to take one last look behind him toward the mountainside, and I swore under my breath. He just needed to run; Max and I would watch his back. It seemed like Drew stared at the barren mountain for ages, but it was only seconds.

My eyes traveled upward, and although I didn't see anything I felt the electricity building in the air that said otherwise. There was definitely something out there, but what was it? How could anything hide out there? This was a desert landscape; there weren't exactly trees, or large bushes to hide behind. No, just overgrown tumbleweeds and other sparse desert plants.

Drew took off at a run toward Max and me. My body started to watch Drew; to make sure he made it safely, but I knew I had to keep my eyes on the mountain behind him. I scanned every shadow inspecting every inch, but I didn't see anything. I was so focused, I didn't even notice Drew run past me until he planted himself beside me breathing heavily.

"Do you seem them?" he asked into my ear his breath hot against my neck.

"No, but I can feel them. What are they?"

"I don't know, but Remie thinks they are just being territorial, which is why they haven't attacked."

"Huh? What do you mean?" I'd never heard anyone describe demon activity like that. Remie was starting to sound a lot like Carter.

"He thinks they live in that cave up there." Drew leaned around me and pointed.

"I didn't even see that before," I sighed. I was a little disappointed in myself for not realizing it was there, but now that Drew pointed it out it was startlingly obvious. A small cave sheltered in the shadow of the mountain. I never thought about what demons preferred to live in. It was a disturbing revelation.

Max snapped at me to get my attention as he pointed back toward the Explorer. I nodded and got back to work. Now was not the time to talk. When I was back in my stance, peeking around the corner with my gun pointed securely at the cave, Max waved for Grant to come over.

Grant didn't stop to look and just ran over to us. There was no fear in his eyes, no hesitation, and no emotion. His fingers gripped his handgun tightly as he ran, and I knew he was fully prepared for anything that might come after him.

Movement caught my eye behind Grant and I swiftly shifted to my left. Something moved, but it wasn't in the cave. Something was already outside. I flicked my eyes back toward Grant. With only a few meters to go, he'd be safe behind Max.

There it was again. A shifting, fleeting movement out of the corner of my vision. I frantically scanned the area, but again, found nothing.

"You see that?" I risked a whisper to Max.

He nodded not taking his eyes off Grant. "It's fast."

As I turned back, Grant ran past me and stopped beside Max. His chest was rising and falling as fast as he ran the sweat glistening on his face and arms. We were just one man short now. With Remie beside us, we could turn this fight into our favor.

All our eyes were locked on Remie, but he didn't look back at us. He was squatting down, staring at the handguns in his gloved hands. I was searching his face, trying to read him, but the brim of his hat kept it concealed.

"What the hell is he doing?" Drew asked from above me. His legs leaned against my back as he bent around the corner to provide additional cover.

"I don't know," I replied with irritation. All he had to do was run to us, but he was just squatting there. "Run!" I whispered as loud as I could between gritted teeth.

I turned to Max, who was signaling Remie toward us, and growing as frustrated as I.

Finally, Remie turned to us. Relief flooded through me and I reached out my arm waving him toward us. We'll fight these demons together all he had to do was run like hell.

Remie lifted his hat and dropped it to the ground. Still watching us; his amber eyes spoke volumes as I stared into their depths.

Rembrandt wasn't going to run.

"Come on!" Grant shouted angrily. Remie shook his head.

Panic should have incapacitated me, but instead my resolve pulled me through. I knew what Remie was doing. It was reckless and incredibly dangerous, but I understood his determination. Something inside of him must have snapped. He was tired of running, tired of letting the demons decide how and where the fighting would take place, or how the rules would be applied. This is where Remie would make his stand. For once, the demons didn't call the shots. Remie was going to bring the fight to them.

I nodded at Remie, telling him that I understood. I had to make a decision, fast. Soon, Max, Grant and Drew would catch on too, and I didn't want them to stop me. Despite this being the time and place where Remie chose to make his stand, on his own terms, I'd be damned if I let him fight them alone.

I bolted out from behind the cover of the building and ran to Remie as fast as I could. My legs pumped violently; heat searing my muscles. I heard Max scream my name from behind me, but I didn't turn back. I couldn't. I was going to stand beside Remie.

Movement shifted wildly in the shadows of the mountain as I closed the gap between Remie and me. He was right. They were territorial and they didn't like me approaching any closer.

"What are you doing?" Remie asked sternly as I planted my back against the Explorer. I could see Max standing in the distance shaded by the building. I knew he was debating his next move. Right now, in his eyes, I was probably a crazy woman, but I hoped he understood. I'd never leave anyone behind, and I'd certainly never let anyone fight against these monsters alone. Not while I still had a breath in my body.

"Not going to let you have all the fun that's for sure," I said smugly.

"You know what you're doing?"

Remie eyed me up and down. He wasn't doubting my skill; he was making sure I knew what I was getting myself into. I did.

"Yeah." I cocked my shotgun letting the sound of it echo against the surrounding area and stood beside Remie. We faced the mountain and whatever was hiding in the shadows waiting to ambush us.

Max screamed for me to stop, but it was too late. There was no turning back now.

As Remie and I rounded the front of the Explorer, I hoped that Max, Grant and Drew were following behind us.

The closer we got, the more I could see the shadows growing frenzied with movement. We ran nearly thirty paces before the first demon scurried out of the shadows.

A spider demon.

Relief as well as fear consumed me. I'd fought them plenty of times before, and I knew how to defeat them; but spider demons never fought alone. Nor in small groups. No, they fought in swarms and if this was where they nested, we might be facing hundreds of them.

Suddenly, facing the demons became a very bad idea.

Remie and I both halted our advance. He too, was immobilized with surprise. More spider demons crept out from the shadows. Seeing them in the light of the late afternoon sun made them much more daunting. Before, I'd never noticed the varying shades of their spindly hair, or the fact that they came in dozens of sizes. The hum of their bodies swarming filled my ears and made the hair on my arms stand on end.

"What do you want to do?" I asked Remie clutching my shotgun. I planned to take out as many as I could before they got me. But by my count that wouldn't take long. Unlike their attacks on our compound, we couldn't sneak into their masses like we normally did. Not in broad daylight anyway, and especially with no way of distracting them.

"I wasn't expecting spider demons," Remie said sounding suddenly unsure. "I thought they were a flock of those demon birds or maybe hounds."

"We can't just stand here." Getting stared down by a myriad of spider demons with thousands of eyes unnerved me. Every flinch we made was being watched. I felt like they could even see the bead of sweat that rolled down my temple. I pulled the bottom of my shirt up and wiped my face.

I heard footsteps pounding the pavement behind me arousing the spider demons and making them grow more restless. They scurried further down the mountain toward us.

I swiveled around reluctantly turning my back toward the demons, but I didn't have a choice. "Stop!" I commanded softly so as not to create any echo in the area. These demons were on edge, but there was something preventing them from attacking us. I pushed up my hand to halt the trio behind me, and they obeyed. Panic was plastered on all their faces, but Max's eyes revealed something more. While Grant and Drew appeared to doubt our chances, I could see that Max was ready to kill as many demons as possible. He was already calculating how many he could slaughter before they got to him.

Remie, who was obviously unsettled, froze in place. I had to muster whatever strength was still inside me. I would get us out of this disastrous situation, somehow. Remie's resolve to make a stand obviously hadn't included the possibility of failure. No, he was hanging right off the edge of a cliff, and his rope was starting to fray.

"Back up," I ordered Remie as I retreated. He hesitated for a moment, but started to move, stumbling over his own feet.

"Damn it Rembrandt." I snatched his arm trying to guide him. He seemed to be in a trance. If we could back out quietly, we might stand a chance.

"Look!" Remie pointed toward the cave. I didn't want to look, but something snatched my eyes away from the task at hand.

Emerging from the cave of the mountain were smaller, baby spider demons. The situation had just become exponentially worse. "Holy shit!" I let go of Remie's arm and started to back away even quicker. They were defending their young! Despite my lack of knowledge regarding demon reproduction, I was smart enough to know that any creature with offspring nearby would defend it to the death. By backing away and showing them we weren't a threat; we might at least stand a chance.

I was almost ten feet before I noticed Remie wasn't moving. I turned to see Max another twenty feet behind me. I was torn. Although I swore never to leave any man behind to fight alone; Remie had totally snapped. He was just standing there!

Max was silently pleading with me to come to him. I took two more steps toward Max and stopped. I thought of Remie's daughter, and the way he looked when he talked about her. Maybe Remie hadn't just snapped. Maybe the depth of his losses had finally culminated to break him. He was an injured man, and I couldn't leave him behind.

I crept slowly to Remie's side. I didn't want the demons to think I was advancing again. Every step I took crunched against the dirt on the pavement no matter how silent I tried to be.

I made it to Remie's side and tugged on his arm. "Remie, let's go."

"I did this." He looked at me with pain in his eyes.

"What are you talking about? Let's go!" I tugged on his arm harder this time.

"I'm sorry, Zahara." Tears threatened to spill from his eyes.

I couldn't get him to snap out of it, so I did the only thing I could think of. I rounded on Remie, pulled back my arm, and slapped him hard in the face. My hand stung from the impact, but it seemed to work.

Remie blinked as if waking from hypnosis and stared at me. "Abby?" His handgun dropped from his hand and time seemed to freeze. I watched, wide-eyed, as it fell to the pavement and clattered noisily before firing into the mountainside.

The buzz of nearby spider demons erupted at the sound. There was no backing out now. They darted down the mountainside, crawling over and on top of each other to get to us. Their bristly-haired legs rubbed against each other and sounded like sandpaper being scraped on wood. Panic clutched at my heart. We had no other choice now, there was only one thing we could do.

"Run!" I screamed.

Remie, finally out of his trance, turned with me and ran back toward the museum. Grant and Drew were already doing so, but Max was still waiting for me. He wasn't going to run anywhere until I was by his side. It made my heart fill with love for him, but I wanted him out of danger. "Go!" I shouted at him on my approach. When I was close enough to him that he knew he could protect me if he needed to, he ran.

I didn't dare look back, even though my nerves told me the demons were closing in on us. I grabbed a pillar to hang onto as I catapulted around the corner. Slipping now would be the last mistake I ever made. With so many demons after us, I wouldn't stand a chance.

Max reached for my hand, but I didn't grab it. I might have looked ridiculous, but I needed my arms to keep my balance as I ran. I didn't trust my own legs. Sure, I was ready to go down fighting, if that's what fate had in store for me, but my body's reaction to the sensation of nearby demons caused me not to trust it.

Remie and Grant were holding the glass doors open as Max and I dove through. I dared to look then, as I crawled across the tiled floor in my retreat. Fortunately, our plan appeared to be working, but it didn't make me feel any better.

The spider demons had just rounded the corner, smashing together into one immense, writhing mass of darkness. Their bodies merged together as they struggled to reach us. Apparently, they didn't understand the concept of a single file line. Good for us. Spider legs jutted out like grotesque branches of dead trees. I imagined those spiders were stuck in place by the pressure of all the other bodies. Maybe if we were lucky, they'd even kill some of their own as they tried to get us.

"Push!" Drew grunted as he began to shove the massive greeting desk toward the entry doors. It wouldn't do much to stop the demons, but that wasn't the point. It was just one more object in the way, keeping them from full attack mode.

I jumped to my feet and ran behind the desk; helping to push it the remaining few feet just in time.

As the desk smashed against the glass of the automatic doors, the spider demons slammed into it on the other side. A web of cracks blossomed for mere seconds before shattering allowing them to push their legs in through the doors.

We were still reinforcing the desk against the demons, as their long legs groped over the top of it, blindly searching for us.

Remie and Max were tall enough that they could push against the far wall with their feet, while their arms helped support the desk. They wouldn't be able to do it indefinitely, but for now it was working. The desk was tall enough, blocking off half of the entrance; but it would only be a matter of time before the demons pushed through, and even less time before one squeezed through the still exposed top half of the doorway.

"What's the plan?" I groaned leaning against the desk. My arms were getting tired and I knew my muscles would atrophy soon. There would be no holding the demons back then. I'd be useless and there would be nothing for me to do about it.

"Shit!" Drew squirmed as a spider leg tapped the top of his head. They were reaching further in.

"Don't let go!" I screamed at him, but I could see in his eyes I was losing him. We needed everyone's last bit of strength to keep pushing against the desk. The mere fraction of a second that Drew faltered gave the demons another inch on us.

I looked at each of the men around me as I considered my options. Their faces were dripping with sweat, and the muscles on their arms and legs were shaking with fatigue. If any one of them yielded even in the slightest we'd be spider food. I was the weak link, but I was also the only one that could do anything to turn the odds in our favor.

Yanking out the knife on my thigh without even a blink, I sliced off the demon leg that was now fidgeting around Drew's chest. His cheek was rubbed raw from the coarseness of the demon hair. Stinky, yellow ooze dripped onto Drew's head as the stump of the severed leg retreated. A piercing arachnid wail was swallowed up by the hum of demons.

Drew looked at me, the fear evaporating from his eyes. I winked at him, with no time to explain my plan. I'd been in tight spots before, but not like this. Yet, I still had the same reaction as always. Demons were knocking on our door, literally, and I vowed to do whatever it took to stop them.

I let go of the desk, and the guys didn't weaken a millimeter. I was right; they didn't need my help supporting the desk, and now I was free to make a difference.

"Abby what the hell are you doing?" Panic contorted Max's face. I couldn't let him lose his concentration.

"Keep pushing Max," I ordered without the slightest hint that I doubted what I was doing. Max could read me like an open book, and I needed for him to see that I believed in what I was about to do.

He searched my expression frantically trying to find a crack in my facade, but my resolve was evident. I scurried around grabbing all the weapons from my friends. It felt wrong to take their guns and knives since they were our only method of defense in this world. But right now I was their primary defense.

None of them said anything as I took each of their hand guns, stowing two in the front of my pants and two in the back. I cut the strap from Max's rifle, not wanting to risk him removing a hand from the desk by unstrapping it. I tied the frayed ends around my neck and let it hang beside my shotgun.

Last of all, I crawled over to Remie and unhooked the ammo strapped across his chest. He refused to make eye contact with me, choosing to close his eyes tightly as I took his belongings.

"Get ready to run," I told them as I centered myself, squatting in the middle of the desk. Spider legs reached out for me as my head bobbed above the desk. They were only inches from touching me.

"No Abs," Max said simply. There was nothing else he could say, and nothing he could do to stop me, but I wouldn't put it past him to try. I knew Max wouldn't hesitate to let go of the desk and run to my side.

Before risking the thought popping into his head, I stood up. The view of writhing demon bodies was just as horrifying as it had been minutes before, but this time I was ready. This time, I was not afraid.

No, I might even enjoy this.

Clad in every weapon we had, I lifted my firearm of choice, my shotgun, and fired mercilessly into the center of the horde of spider demons. Shrieks rattled my ears causing me to fire faster. Each explosion of shells triggered a renewed eruption of high-pitched spider squeals getting louder every time. I dropped my shotgun on the floor when the ammo ran out, grabbing Max's gun without missing a beat. I unloaded into the horde again evenly spraying every inch of their bodies that I could. I needed to kill as many of the demons as possible. Then they'd have to back off to drag away their dead before they could get to us. If they were even smart enough to think of that. I hoped they weren't.

The remainder of Max's bullets didn't last long, and I let it drop to my side, hanging painfully on my shoulder. Where I usually winced at the familiar pain, this time I embraced it further fueling my rage. A demon gave me that wound, and I was going to make every last one of them pay for it.

I yanked out Drew and Grant's guns that were stowed in my waistband and aimed at every demon eye I saw. I knew these small handguns would do nothing against the body of a demon, but I could definitely shoot out their multiple eyes, and if they couldn't see they'd be no match for us.

Pus oozed from their hideous faces as each eye exploded. I was a damned good shot, Carter would have been proud. Of course, it wasn't too difficult, considering I was only a short distance from them.

Shooting out their eyes seemed to enrage them more than anything else, and only strengthened the force behind their pushing through the entrance. New, live demon limbs began to wiggle through the now motionless bodies before them. My plan wasn't working. I didn't dare look downward, toward the men at my feet whose lives were in my hands. I couldn't let them give up yet. As long as I could still breathe there was hope.

I dropped the handguns having used the last of the bullets in Remie's ammo strap, and brought out my knives. I chopped off the appendages of the demons as they wiggled around on top of the desk. I hacked at them like a butcher, not caring if the blade went all the way through or not. If I saw yellow ooze, I knew the cut counted, and right now that's all that mattered.

My arms burned as they became heavier and heavier I didn't know how much longer I could go on, but I kept pushing, while hacking and slashing. It was all I could do.

Sensing my exhaustion, Max placed a comforting hand on my calf. I willed myself to look away from the horror before me, but saw defeat in his eyes. His arms were slacking, no longer straining against the desk. He was giving up. I looked at Grant and Drew, and found they were both wavering in their resistance. They couldn't go on any longer either. But, Remie? Unbelievably, he still fought. He still had his eyes clamped shut, and the veins in his muscles still pulsated with effort, threatening to burst.

"No!" I kicked Max's grip off my leg. I wouldn't give up; I'd never give up. The demons would have to take me kicking and screaming. I lifted my knife to hack off another protruding limb that threatened to touch me, when a bright light soared in the air to my left. And then another. Scorching flames flared rapidly, clinging to the spider demons like sticky honey.

The fire caused them to make unimaginable sounds. A deafening volume of shrieks filled the air, and suddenly they stopped pushing. They were starting to retreat as another flaming ball of fire launched itself through the open doors, establishing a protective barrier of flames around us.

I stood there, frozen, like I'd never seen fire before. My breath pounded in harmony with my heart threatening to burst my rib cage. They stopped attacking, but they didn't leave. The spider demons were testing the flames shrieking every time one of them got too close. We weren't out of the woods yet, but for now we had a moment to collect ourselves.

It was Max's grip on my hand as he began to stand up that made me finally turn around. A young girl, around my age, and two other teenage boys were staring at us. One of the boys had a Zippo lighter, while the girl carried two dark bottles with rags sticking out of the tops. They made the Molotov cocktails. There was a familiar defiance in their eyes that I knew well.

"Thank you," Max said finally breaking the silence.

Their eyes roamed over Max inspecting him from top to bottom. I wasn't sure how much I liked that. The last time we met a stranger who looked at us like that it turned out very, very bad.

Max offered his hand, but neither of the three heroes took it.

"The fire won't hold them back for long," the girl finally said. "I'm Wade, and this is Matthew and Ben." She pointed to the two guys with her and they nodded, taking their eyes off the entrance for only a second.

I turned around and introduced everyone, while Max stood protectively at my side. "Where did you come from?" I asked curiously.

"We live here. Or at least we did," Matthew said disdain dripping from his voice.

"We couldn't have stayed here forever." Matthew rolled his eyes at Wade's response.

Ben lit another Molotov after pulling it from Wade's grip and chucked it at the entrance without blinking. His sudden movement roused us all to prepare ourselves for another attack. I saw Grant and Drew reach for their guns, only to realize they were no longer there. They knelt down and picked them up, placing them in the back of their pants. At the moment, the guns were useless, but they weren't willing to leave them behind. One never knew when bullets would turn up, and they wouldn't do us any good if we didn't have a gun on hand.

"We need to get moving," Wade commanded looking down at their last Molotov. She handed it to Ben who then lit it and threw it at our fire barrier.

The three of them turned and ran into the museum without checking to see if we were following. We all looked at each other unsure of what to do, but there were no other options. Staying here and waiting for the fire to die down wasn't a good idea.

Remie hadn't said a thing since I smacked him. I wasn't sure what was going on with him, but right now we had bigger problems. Max grabbed my hand and we took off running deeper into the museum. There were dozens of items on display, but I couldn't focus on them. I was certain that in the past they would have been terribly interesting, but now they were just dusty relics of a world that no longer existed.

6

Glass crunched under our feet as we dashed across the room. Ben stood waiting for us, holding open a door to a stairwell. He waved us in, and after we were all inside he slammed it shut with a bone-shaking thud. The echo of metal hitting metal vibrated through the stairwell, and I had to clench my teeth to keep my nerves intact.

Grant and Drew helped Ben drag a giant filing cabinet in front of the door. It scraped against the cement floor of the stairwell like nails on a chalkboard. With their makeshift blockade in place we began our ascent. Our footsteps pounded against the cheap steps. I grasped the cold railing trying to keep myself grounded to earth as my head began to spin. Everything was happening so fast. Just seconds before I was thinking I would most definitely die, and now I was fleeing deeper into the museum with three complete strangers. Who knew if they were sane or not? What if they were completely bat-shit crazy? What if they intended to sacrifice us to the spider demons? Like John tried to do with the giant demon hound.

I bit my lip. I didn't want to think about that. I didn't want to think about that night, or the last time we saw that demon, and heard him speak. It opened the door to indescribable horrors that I didn't want to acknowledge. I clutched Max's hand tighter, the sweat making our palms slide and threatening to pull us apart, but we still held on.

Ben led us out of the stairwell and then down a short hallway before he burst through a set of double doors. They opened into a small, indoor screening room. I imagined that it used to be a tiny theater, which the museum probably used when showing films. Most likely, movies about NASA and shuttle liftoffs, but now it was transformed into a safe house. One that we had just compromised.

The small group of people that lived inside the tiny theater were aflutter with activity. They packed frantically, casting wary glances in our direction. Ten people I counted in total. Ten lives that were in danger because of us. I hated the way they were looking at us, and I felt guilty. I wanted to help.

The guys stood at the door, while I sought out Wade. In my opinion, she seemed the most level-headed, and hopefully the least combative toward us.

"What can we do to help?" I asked Wade as she packed foodstuffs into a giant, plastic tub.

"You've done enough," she replied without looking up.

"Listen," I felt my tone rising, but I swallowed it down. "We didn't know anyone was living here, and we certainly didn't mean to attract the demons." She nodded her head and I took that as acceptance; while her eyes rolled at me. "Come and stay with us," I offered without even thinking.

I only half regretted saying it. I felt guilty for the trouble we caused, and offering to bring them back to the base was the only thing I could think of. Yet, it felt wrong knowing that we could barely care for the people we already had there. Especially after Max and Remie's revelation about the truth of our living conditions. Without a new generator, or at least generator parts we couldn't survive there for much longer.

That piqued Wade's interest. "Where are you staying?"

"On the base."

She looked hesitantly at the rest of my group like she didn't trust us. Could I blame her? We *had* just brought an angry horde of spider demons to their very doorstep. "There are lots of us. It's safe, or at least as safe as things can be in this world."

"How many of you are there?" she questioned warily.

"A few dozen," I admitted, even though I wasn't quite sure it was accurate.

"Just a second." Wade dropped an unmarked can of food into the tub and jogged over to an older woman who was shoving clothes into a large, bright blue duffel bag.

Not wanting to stare at them as they talked I decided to look around the room. Maybe there was something we could help pack or carry. Just standing around idly didn't feel right.

I noticed that all of them were in their late to early teens, except for the older lady that Wade went to speak to. They seemed an odd group, but nothing could be called normal anymore.

I saw two blonde twins crying and tying up their sneakers. They obviously didn't want to leave. Maybe they had it pretty good here? It only made me feel that much more guilty.

"What's going on?" Max sneaked up next to me. He surveyed everyone as they packed up their belongings, what little they owned that is.

"It's not safe here anymore for them." Max nodded like he understood. "I invited them to come back with us," I said flatly preparing myself for his reaction.

"Good. What did they say?" I should have known he'd be okay with it. That's the kind of guy he was. In fact, I doubted he was even worried about how we'd protect ten more people on the base. All he saw were people who needed our help. And even worse, people who needed our help because we had put them in danger. No matter the cost, we were going to offer them any assistance we could provide.

"They haven't answered yet." I nodded my head toward Wade who was still conversing with the old lady. They spoke for a few more minutes before walking over to Max and me.

"Abby?" Wade said hesitantly like she'd already forgotten my name in the brief interim since we'd met.

I nodded.

"This is Eleanor." She smiled kindly at Max and me offering her hand. Her wispy white hair swayed with the movement. I took her hand in mine, and was startled at how firm her grip was. I looked at her surprised, and she only winked at me.

"I'm not as frail as I look, child." I stifled a laugh. "Wade tells me you have offered us sanctuary."

"Yes," Max interjected. "We didn't mean to put anyone in any danger."

Eleanor waved him off. "Pish posh. These spider demons have been pestering us for weeks. This day was bound to come. We should be grateful we now have more assistance to help us survive," she spoke her last sentence loudly so that everyone could hear. "Had this happened with you not here I doubt we would have fared so well."

I found myself shocked by her words, and my mouth hung open emphasizing the fact. It was a long time since I had heard someone talk about the world the way she did. Seeing the silver lining in an abyss of darkness. She sounded like my father. Heck, she sounded like Taya!

"Now, let's get down to business." She guided Max and me to the corner of the room, while Wade went back to loading up the remainder of their food supplies.

We sat down in the first row of seats, and Eleanor dug into a bag, pulling out a knitted sweater. She wrapped herself in it tightly even though the room was rather warm. But, the danger and gravity of our situation could definitely send a chill down anyone's spine.

"Your three men over there." She pointed at Remie, Grant and Drew who still hung back at the entrance. I couldn't help thinking they looked more terrified than when they were leaning against the desk as the spider demons' legs reached for us. I suppose they felt as guilty as I. "Do any of them know how to work on cars?"

"Grant and Drew do, yes." I volunteered their names even though I wasn't quite sure of their abilities. Max looked in my direction, but didn't say anything. "They got the Explorer running." Maybe that wasn't an impressive feat, but it allowed me to think they could do it again. Maybe even more.

"Good. We've got a passenger van parked at the larger IMAX theater down the hill. If we can get there without being noticed, we can make an escape. Can't seem to get the damn thing to turn over though. If one of your boys would run down there with us?"

Max turned and waved the guys over. "This is Eleanor." Max introduced everyone. "She needs help getting their van started."

"I can do it," Grant said without hesitation. I was so proud of the confidence in his voice.

"Wonderful. Ben will take you there, and hopefully you can get that hunk of scrap running by the time we get there. Ben!" No sooner had she called his name, and Ben appeared at her side.

"Yeah?"

"Take...?"

"Grant."

"Yes, take Grant to the van. Help him get it started, okay?"

"You got it." He placed a reassuring hand on her shoulder, and she patted it lovingly.

"Such a good boy," Eleanor said to herself as Grant and Ben disappeared through a door at the back of the stage. "Now, what kind of situation do you have going on at this base of yours?"

"Situation?" I asked confused.

"Don't play dumb with me, child. No one comes way out this far unless they are looking for something. And to a museum, no less."

"We were hoping to find parts for our generator," Remie suddenly spoke up, and the sound of his voice nearly startled me. I'd forgotten how deep it was.

"Ahh. And what made you think you'd find such a thing here?"

"We didn't think we'd find anyone here, ma'am."

Eleanor nodded, like that made sense to her. She was quickly earning the title of the weirdest old lady I'd ever encountered.

"I suppose that's reasonable. A museum is a very unlikely place to find survivors." She met Remie's gaze without blinking. She was the only person I'd ever met that didn't find him intimidating at first glance. "That's why we chose it," she winked at him, but he didn't respond in kind. Remie still seemed to be suffering the effects of whatever internal battle raged inside him.

"So… do you have a generator here?" I hated to be nosy, but I was impatient. Who knew how much time we had until the spider demons reached us?

"Why do you want to know?" Wade asked suddenly standing nearby. I didn't notice her approach. She was leaning against the stage, her short, spikey bob accenting her angular features. I might have thought she was pretty, if she hadn't been glaring at me.

"I want to know, because we are going to need it to survive once we get out of here." I didn't hide the irritation in my voice.

She considered what I said, which only further tested my nerves. What was there to think about? I was desperate to get that generator, and even more desperate to get back to the base, to Carter, and to the little bit of normalcy and peace that we'd established.

"Calm down," Max whispered into my ear and squeezed my knee.

"How can I calm down when they are wasting time?" I whispered back at him through clenched teeth.

"And if we don't give you our generator?" Wade asked folding her arms and staring us down.

I looked from Wade to Eleanor, and she just shook her head. She and Wade were obviously in some kind of disagreement. Maybe Wade didn't trust us. If I were her, I probably wouldn't trust us either.

"Then we'll take you anyway," Max proclaimed as he stood up. "We won't leave you behind. I know you don't trust us, but what other choice do you have? You need our help just as much as we need yours."

"We wouldn't have needed your help if you hadn't come here trying to steal from us," Matthew interjected as he joined the conversation. He draped his arm around Wade's shoulders, but she shrugged him off.

I bolted up from my seat like a jack-in-the-box. "Hey! We weren't trying to steal from anyone. We came here because we didn't think there would be anyone here." I leaned into Matthew's face, ignoring his look of suspicion and distrust.

"Well, there are people here!" Matthew spat back at me. "And because she," he said pointing his finger at Wade, "talked us into saving your sorry asses, now we've got spider demons crawling all over the place!"

"Matthew Ryan!" Eleanor's stern tone boomed over all of us, and the glower she sent Matthew made him shrink back from me. "Stop blaming them for what happened. What do I keep telling you? We must fight the demons and not each other. If we do, then are we not just as bad as they are?" She raised an eyebrow at him, but his only answer was to roll his eyes. They'd obviously had this conversation before.

Max wrapped a protective arm around me as he stepped forward. "Listen, man. We didn't mean for this to happen, but just because you have to leave doesn't mean it is a bad thing. We've got a pretty decent set up on the base, and with the help of your generator, it can stay that way."

"Yeah, dude. We've got food, water... we've even got a projector that we show movies on once a week," Drew added, trying to quash Matthew's aggression.

"Really?" Wade asked suddenly interested. "What else? Showers too?"

I laughed. I remembered what it felt like to be dying for a shower. "Yep. They aren't the fanciest things you ever used, but it's definitely a step up from a sink bath."

Wade's smile softened her face and Eleanor wrapped an arm around her. We might have brought a demon attack with us, but I was starting to believe it was a good thing we had come.

"Matthew, show these nice boys where the generator is," Eleanor ordered in a softer tone than previously.

Max kissed my head and headed onto the stage to follow Matthew through the same door Grant used. Drew was hot on his heels. Remie stayed behind with me as I sat back down. The guys were getting things ready, so I decided it was better that I help formulate a plan.

"How long will it take for your group to be ready to leave?"

"Oh, honey, we won't be leaving 'til morning."

"What? Why?"

"They're more active at night," Remie said solemnly. "Especially, after today. They are going to be more alert. Eleanor is right, it's best if we wait until morning."

"What if we don't have 'til morning?"

"We should be okay for one night," Wade said. "They've always been super active at night. They hunt the bats that live in the caves on the mountain.

I simply shook my head. I hated the idea of having to stay here, but they had a point. I'd fought spider demons before, and they *were* much more active at night. They would definitely notice us if we tried to make a run for it, but I sincerely doubted they would forget we were here. Both options were terrible.

"We lock down fairly securely at night, child. As soon as the boys are back, you'll see. We will be safe for the night."

Eleanor and Wade walked away, leaving Remie and me to ponder the difficult decision. It didn't really feel like a decision to me, because I knew we didn't really have a choice. We'd have to stay here tonight. I just hoped we'd live through it.

Forty minutes passed and Max didn't return. Grant, however, came back with Ben, and both had triumphant looks on their faces. They managed to get the van started and even put it in neutral, pushing it closer so that we wouldn't have to run so far the next morning.

When I told Grant we were staying for the night, he didn't seem too surprised. "Yeah, I kinda figured that. Especially after what I saw outside. They've got pretty much the entire front of the building surrounded."

"How did you guys get past them?"

"Went out the back," Grant said like it was the simplest answer in the world. "The spider demons aren't very smart. I mean, they've got to be dumb if they are just sitting by the entrance waiting for us to come waltzing back out. Don't you think?"

"Yeah..." Although I did agree with him, I wasn't one hundred percent convinced that demons were stupid. "I just wish we had a way to get to the Explorer. We've got a lot of good things in there."

"I'm sure we'll be able to come up with some kind of plan," Grant said as he leaned against the wall and slid down to the ground.

I'd known Grant a couple months now, but until today I never felt very close to him. After what we'd gone through it was hard not to be. In a weird way, Grant and even Drew were the additional brothers I never had. I squatted down in front of him placing a hand on his knee. "We'll figure something out." He nodded but avoided my gaze. I could tell his hope was hanging on a thread, all of our hopes were. But, thread or not, there was still hope.

"Thanks for what you did."

"What I did?" His eyes were red with emotion, but contained no trace of a tear. "What are you talking about? I haven't done anything," he sounded disgusted with himself.

"For fixing the van."

"Eh," he waved me off and I took my hand off his knee. "I just needed to clean up the connections to the batteries and tighten the bolts. It wasn't a big deal."

"Stop it." I slapped his arm. I knew what he was doing. I had been known to do the very same thing to myself. Sure, fixing a car wasn't a big thing, but being able to use it now because he fixed it was.

"Stop what?" Grant fumed from the slap, but I knew he wasn't angry at me. He was angry at the world.

"Because you were able to fix that car we can get all these people out of here. You helped save all their lives. You should be proud of that."

"I wouldn't have been alive to do that if you hadn't held off the spiders to begin with." His tone sounded fierce and laced with anger, but it didn't reach his eyes. Maybe I was wrong, maybe he *was* mad at me for something.

"You say that like you're not glad I saved you."

He sighed heavily and clenched his fist turning his knuckles white. "I am glad, I just..." he looked at me then, his tone finally softening. "It should have been me saving you, or Max, or even Remie or Drew. We should be protecting women, not the other way around.

Seriously? That was his problem? He was pissed because *I* saved his life. Maybe I was wrong, maybe Grant wasn't the man I thought he was.

I stood up, not wanting to remain at his level anymore. It was quickly becoming too tempting to slap him in the face. "That's what your problem is?" Grant lifted his chin, like he was proud of the fact, which only infuriated me further.

"Well, maybe next time I'll just leave your ass behind the desk and save myself. Sound good to you?"

"Yeah sounds good," he sneered at me.

I turned on him, ready to flee the argument. I didn't have it in me to fight with him as much as I would have liked to considering how pissed he was making me. I eyed Wade across the room, fiddling with some kind of radio. Its wires were strewn out like spaghetti in her lap. I made a beeline for her. After the verbal assault I got from Grant, a little girl talk was needed. Even though I'd just met her, I got the sneaking suspicion we would get along fine if we got to know one another.

"He's not upset with you, ya know?" Remie caught me as I walked by.

"How would you know?" I didn't mean to direct my anger toward him, but it was still fresh. I bit my lip and tried to flee from Remie's knowing gaze. One argument was enough in one day.

I relinquished, too tired to fight. "A man can tell when another man cares deeply for someone." Remie's eyes rolled slowly toward Grant's slumped figure.

I suddenly felt my cheeks flush with embarrassment. Was he saying what I thought he was saying? "What do you mean?" I whispered the words fearing his response.

"Grant cares very deeply for you. I can see it in his eyes."

"Wha...? Wait..." I couldn't get the words out. Remie's proclamation sounded completely alien to me. I had never sensed any feelings from Grant, and I didn't feel any for him. At least, not in that way.

"Now, don't get all worked up. I didn't mean it like that." He placed a hand on my shoulder trying to calm what I was obviously not hiding.

"Well, how *did* you mean it?"

"Like everyone else, he lost someone he cared about, but I can tell it runs deeper than that."

"How do you know all this?"

He shrugged, looking as if he were contemplating whether or not to tell me. "Just don't be mad at him. The boy has got a mission to save someone, and he's chosen you. I think..." He looked up like the words he needed were written somewhere on the ceiling. "I think he feels it will somehow make up for what he lost, or perhaps what he couldn't save."

We both turned to look at Grant who was still sitting next to the wall tapping his head against it as he popped his knuckles. I suppose everyone handled their grief in different ways, and most of them I didn't understand. I didn't know why Grant chose me. Maybe he thought of me as a sister, or perhaps I reminded him of someone from his past, as I did Remie.

Grant must have felt us looking at him because he raised his head and stared looking confused at Remie and me. I gave him a weak smile, and the brief anger I felt toward him vanished. I was relieved that Grant didn't have romantic feelings toward me, but I felt guilty about how I handled our conversation. I shouldn't have snapped at him. I should have seen what was really wrong, but how could I? I wasn't even able to face my own grief, so how would I be able to recognize it in someone else?

Wade was still tinkering with the radio on her lap when I approached. "Hey," I said sitting down beside her.

"Oh, hey." She looked up at me from under the hair that had fallen over her brow.

"What are you working on?" I pointed to the mess of wires in her lap.

"Been trying to get this pile of junk working for days. I just don't have the tools I need here." She sighed in frustration tucking the miniature screw driver behind her ear.

I peered over into the innards of the radio with no clue as to what I was seeing. I never understood electronics. The extent of my knowledge was where to plug something in and how to turn it on and off.

"I bet we have something on base that you could use. I mean, it's a military base they've got radios ten times that size and probably a hundred times more powerful."

"Really?" Wade set the radio aside and turned to look me full on.

"Yeah," I smiled happy to have gained her interest. "My brother is a total computer geek. I mean whiz." I couldn't hold back my laugh.

"Me too. Kinda hard not to be when you're raised by a dad who builds computers for a living."

"What about your mom?"

"They divorced when I was really little."

"I'm sorry."

"It's okay. I don't remember her."

"My mom died when I was little. It was just me, my dad and my brother. I guess that explains why I'm such a tomboy."

"Nothing wrong with that," Wade smiled and started biting at her already short nails. A smirk popped onto my face when I saw she'd painted them neon green.

My ears suddenly started ringing, which rattled my nerves and made the hair on my arms stand on end. "You hear that?" I asked Wade sitting up straighter and trying to listening harder like that was something I could actually do.

Wade hadn't heard anything, but didn't doubt that I had. She jumped down from the stage listening to hear what I heard. I wasn't sure I even heard anything, but there it was again; a ringing in my ears that now traveled down my spine instead of my arms.

"That." I jumped down next to Wade grabbing hold of her arm. "Over there." I pointed to the door that Ben used to bring us through when we first got there, and my nerves began to buzz.

7

I hadn't taken a complete step forward before the door burst open and spider demons started crawling through. Three skittered in on the floor, while two crept across the walls and up to the ceiling. Again, they planted themselves firmly in place, taking defensive stances as they inspected us. Screams erupted around me, and for a moment I couldn't move. I was completely frozen in shock. These spider demons were acting very strange. I understood them attacking us, but creeping into our hideout just to watch us with their innumerable eyes didn't add up. They looked at us and we could see our figures reflecting off the dark pools that shone on their eight-eyed faces.

Wade's scream pierced my eardrums rousing me out of my petrified state. I slapped a hand across her mouth, silencing her as best I could. "Shut up!" I yelled at everyone who was shrieking in fear. All it was going to do was... well honestly, I didn't know.

I should have known none of the screamers would listen to me, but only increase their volume. They stumbled over their seats to back away from the five spider demons that skittered in. Watching us intently, their bodies swayed back and forth. I felt sure they were contemplating what to do with us; whether or not to attack, and how. Oh yes, they wanted to eat us, that much was obvious by the way their pincered mouths salivated.

An explosion of gunfire blasted through the screams. I turned and found Grant snagging a gun from one of Eleanor's shocked survivors. The strap of the gun was still partially around the girl's arm, and Grant fired again.

The moment of serene horror ended when the sound of gunfire prodded the spider demons into attack mode. The three on the floor lowered their bodies momentarily and sprang into the air like flying squirrels. Their legs were outstretched like wings, allowing them to soar through the small space of the indoor theater.

The others skittered across the ceiling faster than I could keep track. "Get back!" I shoved Wade behind me as I ran to the nearest spider demon, and pulled out the knife on my thigh. It had a group of girls cornered, and was herding them like weeping goats, while hissing at them. Attack was imminent, but I wouldn't let that happen.

Raising its massive body, the spider demon stood up and lifted its hairy front legs to crash down on its victims below. It was fully unaware of me, giving me the opportunity I needed. I knew how to take these monsters out, and this one just made it easy for me.

I dove between the demon and its helpless victims, slashing off its appendages before they drove into the flesh of innocents. Their legs cracked like toothpicks, falling onto the floor as sticky, yellow ooze spewed from their stumps, spraying us in putrid droplets.

"Run to Wade!" I shoved the girls in the right direction pointing to Wade before raising my knife again. The demon wasn't dead yet, only stunned.

Its shrieks of pain drew the attention of one of the spiders that was clinging to the wall. Like a bug, it slinked down the wall on my right, dropping down heavily in front of me. The thud of its landing vibrated up my legs. This one was bigger than the rest, *and* it looked pissed. Unlike the others, whose bristled legs and massive appendages were as black as a raven, this one was graying. Was it older than the others?

It hissed at me, oozing sputum from its twitching, pincered mouth. Its eight eyes were abysmal blackness and I saw my horrified expression in them. No, I couldn't be afraid I knew they could smell fear. Couldn't they? Damn, I wished Max were here.

I took a fleeting second to look at the battle raging around me. Grant was beating in the brains of a still twitching demon using the butt of the gun he snatched from the now weeping girl. Remie was fighting off one putting himself between Eleanor and them. But where was Ben?

I looked around again and found him. He was trying to draw away a spider that was threatening Wade and the rest of the survivors who were trying to hide in the corner of the small theater stage. Unfortunately, he didn't see what I saw. A demon from the ceiling right above him was about to drop. With sheer horror, my heart felt like it would burst in my chest. He didn't see it! And he wouldn't see it until it was too late.

In that split second, I had only two choices: kill the giant spider demon before me, or try to save Ben and those he was trying to protect. I guess it wasn't really a choice. I didn't know if I'd even make it to them in time, even if I ran. Either Ben would die, or the noxious, gray spider would kill me, before I got to him.

Drawing my attention back to what was before me, I blocked the demon's lunges, hacking off only the tips of its forelegs as it struck at me. This one was smarter than the rest. It saw what I did to the other one. It didn't want to give me the opportunity to do the same thing, so it pulled its limbs back just before I could hack them off.

Shit!

I charged at it, screaming with rage that billowed from my stomach. It didn't see that one coming and skittered a few steps back, bumping into its injured ally which was still struggling to crawl toward me, but its legs were gone.

This was my only chance. I took it.

Time seemed to freeze and I felt swallowed up by the silence as I spun one foot and ran toward Ben. He was still fighting the same demon completely unaware of the spider that was dropping down onto him. Its fangs dripped saliva from its mouth, while its body began to writhe in anticipation of devouring his flesh.

But not if I had anything to do with it.

Ben dropped from the stage pushing the demon back, but causing little damage. They were learning. It was pulling back on purpose, getting Ben into position, setting him up in the perfect spot for its creepy companion to attack.

I can't remember even taking one breath as I flew from the back of the theater to the side of the stage. Wade called out my name as I launched myself up the stairs and sailed off the edge slamming my body into the demon that was dangling from the ceiling. I should have played football in high school; I had no idea I could put so much force into a blow.

The spider demon's legs curled around me in a grotesque embrace as we tumbled to the floor and crashed into rows of chairs. Pain radiated through every inch of my body with agonizing intensity. I wasn't sure what I'd broken, but it felt like everything. I rolled over, feeling the urge to vomit, and ended up falling off a chair and onto the floor. I was in so much pain that I knew my fall should have hurt, but I couldn't tell. I was starting to go numb. Was I dying? Or was my adrenalin kicking in?

No, I wasn't dying. I could hear people screaming. I thought I could hear someone calling my name. I blinked and tried to sit up, but the world spun violently. I fell back onto the floor wanting so much to close my eyes, but something kept clawing at my arm. I batted it away, but only ended up hitting myself.

The urge to puke insisted that I obey, but I could only manage to flop my head to the side. Instead of the limited contents of my stomach, the metallic taste of blood filled my mouth. I choked on it when my tongue found something rattling around in my mouth. My eyes popped open in shock and I spat. A tooth tumbled out like a bloody die.

"What the fu...?" I wiped my mouth, the dizziness now being replaced with anger. Everything came flooding back into me.

Something clawed at my head this time, and I pulled away. A spider demon was reaching frantically for me from under the chairs. The tips of its legs were already digging into the carpet.

I heard it again, someone calling my name. I sat up, refusing my body's request to collapse from fatigue. I was going to do what I had to do whether or not every bone in my body was broken.

Blood dripped wildly from my mouth like a vampire who had just fed ferociously on a victim as I rose from the floor. There, towering above me was Grant. He was straddling three theatre chairs, pressing the seats down on top of the spider, to keep it from attacking me. His body jerked violently as the demon fought to rise from its temporary cage.

Ben was in the aisle; his clothes were torn and his face was scratched. He looked like he'd gotten into a fight with a lion, but he was alive. I saved him and now Grant was saving me; just like he intended to.

The demon that Ben was fighting lay on its back, its legs curled up and inward like every dead spider I'd ever seen in my life. I stumbled a few steps relying on the chairs to guide me successfully to the aisle until I reached what I needed. My knife was on the floor behind Ben. I picked it up, and avoided looking at myself in the reflection of its shiny steel. I shoved Ben out of the way, and in one smooth swipe I chopped off the spider's leg. It barely reacted; it was almost dead.

Grant looked at me like I was insane as I approached him, and I'm sure I looked like I was. Blood flowed from my mouth in throbbing gushes, spilling down my chin and across my chest, while I wielded a severed spider leg in one hand and a knife in the other. I probably looked like something from a horror flick, but I had something *special* in store for this demon. Something I hoped the others would learn from. A message that I wished they'd pass along... if they lived of course, which I knew they wouldn't

"Move!" I commanded Grant in a fierce tone. He obeyed without question hopping off the seats and jumping into the next row behind him.

As expected, the seats flew upward at his release, and the spider on the floor scrambled to turn itself upright. I leaned over and shoved the sharp point of the severed spider leg into the center of its abdomen, wiggling it back and forth. Ooze bubbled up around the limb, and it twitched for only a few seconds before curling up and dying.

I walked back into the aisle to find Grant and Ben, both with the same stunned expressions on their faces. "What?" I slurred, my tongue feeling thick and clumsy as I wiped the blood from my mouth with my forearm.

Ben just shook his head before running back toward Wade. I watched him go, confused by his reaction. I saved him, so what was his problem? "Something wrong with killing demons?" I asked Grant as I knelt down to pick up the gun that lay at his feet.

"Abby!" Remie's voice boomed as he called my name, but it was too late.

I looked up just in time to see the elder spider demon flying at full speed right toward me. There was no time to respond, or to even mentally register what was happening. I couldn't even form a complete thought before the demon slammed into me, sending my body flying backward.

I crashed into the wall with a skull-cracking thud, fresh blood seeping from my mouth again. I'd bitten my tongue, maybe even lost another tooth for all I knew. Gripping the knife in my hand, I was mildly surprised to still find it there, after being flung like a ragdoll. I lifted it before me. Like I said before, I would only go down swinging. I pointed it at the elder demon as it descended upon me. I was ready to die, but I wouldn't go out alone. No, I was going to take it with me.

A loud crack accosted my ears as the elder demon collapsed on top of me in an oozing, pulsating heap. I was crushed under the weight of the remains, but didn't have the strength to shove it off. It was a sobering thought to realize that this wasn't the first time I was stuck under a demon carcass, but I supposed it wouldn't be the last either.

Grant and Remie were quickly at my side lifting the corpse off me. As the steaming heap of blasted demon was removed, I saw Max standing in the aisle. He appeared to be in shock. He was holding a gun, and pointing it directly at me. His hand was shaking as tears streamed down his dirty face. He was alive, but what had he done?

I watched him fall to his knees as Grant put his head under my arm and guided me to Max who finally let the weapon fall to his side. He wept harder the closer I got to him. Grant lowered me down in front of Max, who pulled me into his arms as his whole body shuddered. Tears and blood soaked his shirt and I cried with him. I let it *all* out. Everything. All the tears and pain I'd been restraining came flooding out of me. I didn't have the strength to hold them back anymore.

Max pulled my head from his shoulder and held it securely before him. "I didn't know what else to do, Abs." His eyes were aflame with emotion, but all I could do was blink at him. I was still confused about what happened. Obviously, Max had killed the demon, but it was more than that.

"You did what had to be done, and you saved her life," Remie interjected from nearby.

Max shook his head, unwilling to agree. "No! I could have killed her!" Max pulled me into his arms again, but this time he snaked his arm under my legs and lifted me up. "I'm so glad you're okay," he said looking down at me.

"What happened? Where are we going?"

"We've got to get out of here!" Max ordered aloud to everyone as he jogged up the steps of the stage.

"Put me down I can walk," I said even though I wasn't sure I could. Max obeyed me, but kept a firm grip on my hand as he hefted a nearby bag over his shoulder.

I looked around as everyone rushed toward the stage. Wade was guiding people out of the room by the door, with a strange look on her face. Fear mixed with utter helplessness, and loss. But who had we lost? I wanted to save everyone, but I knew with an attack like that, there was no way. They took us by surprise.

Everyone in my group seemed to be fine, for the most part. They had wounds of course, but nothing they couldn't heal from in time. I, on the other hand, didn't know the extent of my injuries; but I was walking and alert so that had to be a good sign. Right?

It wasn't until I saw Remie and Matthew carrying a makeshift stretcher that I suddenly lost the tiny bit of control I had regained of my limbs. There was Eleanor, lying atop the stretcher with a giant spider fang protruding from her chest. Her fragile, old hands clung to it like it was a newborn child, and her eyes stared lifelessly at nothing; then her head dropped to the side.

"Eleanor!" I screamed her name and attempted to go to her, but Max wouldn't release me.

"We don't have time right now, Abby. We need to leave."

"We have time! We need to make sure she's okay." I didn't understand why he was in such a rush. We had killed all the spider demons surely we had time to tend to Eleanor's wounds.

"Abby!" he pulled me toward him forcefully. "If we don't get her to the base, I don't think she'll make it."

His words slapped me in the face, but I knew that's what I needed. He was right, and I was glad he was giving it to me straight. "You're right." I shook my head, disappointed at my own panic. I was always in control of my emotions, but I suppose everyone has a breaking point; and this was apparently mine.

We all stumbled hastily down the back stairwell carrying whatever we could. I knew we were leaving at lot behind, but there wasn't anything we could do about that. Max and I were the last to exit the theatre followed by Wade who closed the door behind us. It was sheer torture watching Eleanor being lowered down the stairs before us. All I could do was stare at the grotesque fang protruding from her body. It looked so alien against her angelic features. She wasn't even bleeding and I didn't know if that was good or bad.

Once we were outside, I noticed that it was later in the evening than I realized. Aside from the full moon that shone more brightly than ever before, we were in complete and utter darkness. Only the sounds of our labored breathing seemed to interrupt the silence of the night as we rushed down the hillside toward the larger theatre and our waiting van. I worried how we were supposed to get away in that, since there was no way we'd all fit. Luckily, my fears were extinguished when I saw the Explorer parked right next to the van.

"How did you get that here?" I asked Max as we stumbled onto the pavement at the far end of the parking lot.

"We were heading back after we loaded up the generator when we saw that all the demons were gone. I took that as our chance to move the Ford, but I guess I should have realized what was really happening. We should have gone back inside to check on you all first. All I could think about was that we needed another vehicle."

I could hear the disappointment in his voice. "You did the right thing. Those demons would have attacked us either way, and if you hadn't moved the Ford, we wouldn't have it to escape in right now. Would we?"

Max didn't answer, but I knew he wouldn't. I knew he saw the logic in my words, even if he'd never admit it to himself. He was stubborn like that, but then again I was stubborn too.

Once inside our getaway cars, we had to make the tough decision not to drive directly to the base. As much as we wanted to, we couldn't risk the possibility of the spider demons following us there. It wasn't like we hadn't withstood their attacks before, but we weren't exactly in tip-top shape. Besides, a far as we knew, the generator on base could have already gone out.

It was Eleanor's deciding vote that finalized our decision. She was surprisingly lucid despite her injury, but by the way she kept falling in and out of consciousness, I knew it wouldn't last long. We loaded her into the van, on the laps of her fellow survivors. No one said much, but the looks on their faces spoke volumes. The night had taken an ugly turn, and with Eleanor's current condition all our fates were hanging by a very thin thread. I immediately got the impression that she was like a mother to all of them, and if she didn't pull through this they would take it very badly. If I had to guess, it would be Matthew whom I'd have to worry about the most. He didn't appear to be the forgiving type.

We wanted to be sure we weren't being followed, but we didn't exactly have very much time either. No one knew what kind of condition Eleanor was in, but bringing demons back to the base with us definitely wouldn't improve her chances of survival.

Max took a few detours, with the passenger van following behind us. We drove toward the general direction of the base, which I thought was smart. We were still headed there, just taking... the "scenic route".

Wade was the only survivor of the museum who chose to ride with us. I wasn't exactly sure why, but if I had to guess I think it was very difficult for her to see Eleanor in such a state. I hardly knew her and it was hard for me. Eleanor had only shown us kindness, and honestly it was easy to like her because of it.

None of us spoke on the drive except for Max and me. I'd whisper directions to him when I saw a side street or alley we should take, but aside from that there was an uncomfortable silence. Our small scouting mission had turned out to be so much more than we could have ever imagined.

I leaned my head against the glass and was happy to find that the night had started to cool the air. I didn't realized how much my head was throbbing until now, but the cold glass offered me a small sliver of comfort.

Outside, in the dark landscape of the deceased town, a handful of orange lights flickered. They were the remnants of a civilization; the city's solar-powered streetlights. With no one left to maintain them, it wasn't likely they'd last much longer. I knew they would eventually die like everything else; and this tiny town would be snubbed out, engulfed by the darkness of a world destroyed by demons.

After what seemed like an eternity, Max finally pulled onto the main highway that led to the base. He slammed his foot on the gas and the Explorer roared instantly picking up speed. The movement was making me nauseous, but the realization that we would be back on the base in no more than thirty minutes provided instant relief. I knew Carter and Taya were probably worried sick, and if we were gone any longer they'd come out looking for us. I definitely didn't want that. No, I wasn't sure I ever wanted to leave the base again after tonight. At least not for a very long while.

We were pulling off the freeway and Max slowed down. Whoever was on watch tonight would see us coming, so Max started flashing his headlights; first twice, then three times. Then, all over again. It was our code that we were returning. Didn't want to be mistaken for demons and get fired on, not that demons could drive or anything, but better safe than sorry.

When the spotlight of the base glared through the windshield of the Ford and then blinked twice, we knew they saw us. The light pulled back and guided us around to another entrance of our makeshift compound. We didn't like to use it because it was so loud. However, we didn't have a choice. There was no way we'd be able to shove Eleanor underneath the stack of cars. No, there was a giant hangar connected to the back of our compound. Opening the door was like opening the world's largest squeaky garage door.

Whoever was directing the light seemed to know that was our only option. I had no doubt that they'd noticed we had a second vehicle with us and that could only mean one thing.

Following our lighted beacon, Max navigated the Ford down the roads before coming to a stop in front of the hangar doors. Then we waited. It would take them some time to get enough people together to pull the doors open. Using the power would soak up too much juice.

I saw Ben as he pulled up alongside us, his arm hanging out the window. He didn't even glance over at us. Maybe he didn't have the energy, or maybe he was still in shock; I wasn't sure. I'd never been in a situation like this before. Everyone we tried to help before wanted our help, but the survivors of the museum... they were a different story.

Grant and Drew jumped out of the Ford without a word. They obviously couldn't take the awkward silence anymore. I wasn't sure if I could either if it got any thicker, I'd probably choke on it.

"Where are they going?" Wade asked. Her voice was quiet, but I didn't think she was whispering.

Max simply shrugged his shoulders, slumping into the driver's seat. It had been a long night and I wanted nothing more than to crawl up next to him and sleep for a week.

Grant and Drew passed in front of the Ford's headlights before being swallowed up by the darkness, only to reappear in front of the van. If I had to guess they were probably going to try to pry open the hangar doors themselves. Normally, I would have found such a sight entertaining because it was pretty much impossible; but I found myself secretly hoping that they suddenly possessed super-human strength. The sooner those doors were opened the sooner we could go inside and this horrible night would finally be over.

8

I was just about to jump out of the Ford when a loud scraping noise pierced the still air. The hangar doors were opening. Finally! Max and Ben waited only until the doors slid open far enough before they pulled in. I jumped out of the Ford before he'd even shut the engine off. The hangar doors slammed shut, and I finally felt like I could breathe.

"Abby!" I heard Carter's voice call out from somewhere inside the hangar.

"Carter!" I ran in the direction I thought it was coming from. I saw my brother barreling toward me, bathed in the van's headlights.

"You guys scared the crap out of us! What happened?" Carter pulled me out of his arms and looked me over. "Jesus, Abby! What happened to you?"

"I'm okay." I pulled him into another hug and sighed heavily. Hugging my brother felt like home, and it was just the medicine I needed to regain a morsel of strength.

I turned around to find everyone crawling out of the van, and being greeted by those who came down to open the doors for us. Some of the faces I recognized well. Grant and Drew were unloading supplies and Max was working with Ben, lifting Eleanor out of the van.

Her eyes were shut, but the color of her skin told me she was still with us. Seeing her again, kicked my instincts into high gear. "Carter, wake up anyone here that has medical experience. I don't care if they've only ever stopped a bloody nose; I want them in the sick room like yesterday."

"Yeah, no problem. I'll get Taya on it. She's been pacing around here nearly biting her fingernails off with worry. She'll be happy to have something to do." Carter eyed Eleanor with a concerned look, and then took off toward the back of the hangar where the door to the compound lay.

"Steady!" Wade guided Max and Ben as they carried Eleanor. There wasn't much light in the hangar even with the car's headlights still on. Sure, there wasn't anything to trip on in there, but these men were so tired I wouldn't be surprised if they tripped over their own feet. In fact, I wouldn't be shocked if I did.

Candles and lanterns lit our way as we entered the main hallway of our compound. Doors slowly began to open as we shuffled past, curious faces peering out from behind them. I tried to smile like everything was okay. I was full of worry for Eleanor, but I didn't want *everyone* to go into a panic. We'd all made it back, so hopefully, that gave them some comfort.

No one was in the sick room when we lumbered through with Eleanor in tow. Ben and Max set her gently down on one of the open cots and stepped back looking completely clueless as to what they should do next. I didn't know either, but I couldn't stand around. I wasn't good at sitting still; especially not when someone was hurt.

"Get some towels and water!" I barked the orders directing them at whomever would follow them. The sound of multiple footsteps confirmed that I was being listened to.

I walked to Eleanor's side and grabbed her hand, Wade rushed up beside me. "Is she going to be okay?"

I didn't answer her. If I told her what I really thought she'd just fall into hysterics, but if I lied... well, I just couldn't bring myself to lie.

Max came back with what I asked for, dumping it at Eleanor's feet. I gazed up at him feeling as completely helpless as he looked. "Where's Carter?"

"I don't know. I haven't seen him," Max replied running a hand across his face.

"Find him." I snatched the bottle of water from the foot of the bed and unscrewed the lid. "Hold her head up."

Wade jumped at my command and lifted Eleanor's head lightly, careful to remain as far away from the protruding spider fang as she could. I tipped the bottle only slightly allowing only a small sip to pass her lips. Eleanor swallowed, coughed a little, and then seemed to fall right back to sleep.

"Abby?" Taya came stumbling into the sick room. Her arms were full of bandages and orange bottles of medication. Seeing that triggered my memory.

"Max!" He immediately stopped his frantic pacing and looked at me. I nodded toward the bottles that Taya was dropping onto a nearby counter and he shook his head in recognition. We managed to grab some medications from the Walmart pharmacy; maybe something in our duffle bag would help Eleanor. Within seconds, Max was out the door with Ben close on his heels.

"What happened?" Taya questioned her voice full of concern. Her small frame was engulfed by an oversized t-shirt and her hair was a frizzy mess on top of her head. Dark circles hung under eyes, glistening with recent tears. I guess she *really* was worried.

"She got hurt by a spider demon," I said flatly.

"A what?" Taya was looking at the dark mass on Eleanor's chest, but jumped back at my words.

"A spider demon," Wade repeated sniffling. She stroked Eleanor's cheek with the back of her fingers.

Of all the demons we'd ever encountered, I knew the spider demons frightened Taya the most. Maybe she had a fear of spiders before everything happened and seeing giant versions of them only maximized that feeling.

"Taya, this is Wade. Do you think you can find her someplace quiet to lie down?"

She eyed Wade who was silently crying over Eleanor's body. "Yeah, she can have my bed." Taya stood up and walked to Wade's side placing a comforting hand on her shoulder.

"I don't want to leave her," Wade blubbered through her tears.

Taya bit her lip, still resting her hand on Wade's shoulder. None of us knew what to do. Everything I could think of would likely kill Eleanor, even though I was becoming increasingly certain she was going to die anyway. Pulling the fang out would only cause her more pain, or kill her quicker. Wouldn't it be best to just let her fall asleep? Then she could die peacefully. In a world like ours, that seemed the best way to go. I wouldn't mind going that way myself.

I fell back into my seat and covered my face with my hands. They stunk of sweat and dirt, so I tried breathing through my mouth.

"Finally," Taya said in an annoyed tone. The room was silent aside from Wade's sobs, and even though Taya hadn't spoken loudly it blasted through the space like a church bell.

"Finally, what?" I groaned at Taya through clenched teeth. My body was starting to ache and my head was pounding. I hadn't been this tired since the night we escaped John. Or rather, the demon that he kept imprisoned in the basement.

"What kinda trouble have you kids gotten yourselves into this time?" a familiar voice boomed into the quiet sick room.

I knew that voice, didn't I? But it couldn't be, could it? I stumbled out of my seat in total disbelief to see Charlie marching through the room toward us.

He looked just as I remembered him. Though we'd only spent a short time together I couldn't have been happier to see him.

"Charlie?" My mouth hung open like a panting dog. "When...? How did you get here?"

"Hey, kid." He winked at me. "You don't look too good." Charlie inspected me visually before casting his glance over to Eleanor. "My God!" The whites of his eyes expanded to the size of golf balls.

"She was injured by a spider demon," Taya instructed Charlie as he walked closer to Eleanor's cot.

"I've yet to encounter these damned spider demons, but I can see they've got quite the nasty bite haven't they?" He directed his question toward Wade, who didn't respond. "I hear that's what all that mess was outside. They look pretty foul to me."

"What mess?" Wade asked curiously.

I shook my head, tacitly telling Charlie not to go any further with his explanation. Now wasn't the time to let Wade know that spider attacks on our base weren't a rare occurrence. Of course, they were never as bad as they were at the museum, but she probably wouldn't believe that.

"Can you help her?" I asked, trying to focus on the issue. I didn't know much about

Charlie, but I always felt he was the type of man who knew a little about a lot of things. Hopefully, one of those things included some medical knowledge.

"Well, let me see here." Charlie walked past me toward Eleanor's head. He folded his flannel sleeves up to his elbows and pressed his wrist against her forehead. The white hair on his arms glistened in the dim light. She furrowed her brow a moment, but then relaxed.

"She's got a fever. Taya get me some cold compresses."

"You got it." She scurried out of the room, her loose bun bobbing on top of her head as she went.

Charlie leaned closer to Eleanor and squinted at the fang in her chest. It was plunged right above her left breast, and just below her collarbone. I never paid much attention in health class, but I was fairly certain it probably missed her heart. I bit at my nails as I watched him study her. Even though I didn't know Eleanor well, in fact, she was practically a stranger. I didn't want to lose another person in this world again. There were too few of us left.

Charlie pulled at the top of Eleanor's blouse and Wade gasped. "I need to inspect the injury more closely." He looked back toward me as I continued to gnaw at my already too short nails. "I need some scissors."

I turned to find what Charlie asked for and Max came barreling into the room with our duffel bag dumping it onto the floor with a heavy thud.

"What do you need?" he asked already unzipping it.

"Scissors." I put my hand out before he even found them.

"Got 'em." Max held them up to me, and I took them hastily. I didn't give him a second glance before heading back to Charlie.

Wade looked up at me as I returned to the side of Eleanor's bed, scissors in hand. Her eyes were swollen to twice their size, and trails of dried tears ran down her face.

"She's going to be okay." I knew I shouldn't have said it, and I had to bite the inside of my cheek. But for some reason the sight of Charlie gave me hope. I don't know how or why, but I was grateful to have him there.

Charlie took the scissors and cut away the top of Eleanor's blouse, revealing the true horror of her wound. Wade choked at the sight, but held in her sobs. She was trying to be strong, and that was definitely something I could relate to. I walked around, and took her free hand in mine. It was the only thing I could think of.

Max brought over the soap we found and put it in a bowl with some water and a washcloth. He then returned to his pacing. Ben chose to squat in a corner, slowly knocking a closed fist against his head. I didn't quite understand what he was doing, but everyone handled stress in their own way.

Carter and Taya walked in as Charlie began the delicate job of cleaning Eleanor's wound. I noticed earlier in the night that she wasn't bleeding much, but what Charlie was cleaning was something entirely different. An almost neon liquid was slowly seeping out at the edges of the fang and a startling thought dawned on me. Was that venom?

"Lauren's on her way," Carter said as he peered over the top of the bed to see what Charlie was doing. Lauren was our resident school nurse.

"Good." I let go of Wade's hand and gently squeezed her shoulder before walking away. "Can I talk to you?"

"Yeah." Carter eyed Wade curiously for a moment, before walking with me to the far corner of the room. I smiled as Taya took over my post for me. She laid a cool rag on Eleanor's head before patting Wade's hand in support.

"Why didn't you tell me Charlie was here?" I whispered to my brother.

He pushed his glasses higher up on his nose only for them to slide down again. "Well, I didn't really get the chance. He only just got here a few hours before you did."

"It's good he's here. His timing couldn't have been better. I don't know what we'd do without him." I looked back toward Charlie, as he worked on Eleanor's wound under the watchful eyes of Wade.

"What happened out there?" Carter grabbed my arm to direct my attention back toward him. "You look like... some kind of victim from a slasher movie, Abby."

I completely forgot that I was covered in blood. My body and head were throbbing so badly I was either getting used to the pain, or choosing to ignore it. I wasn't sure which.

"It's a long story." I sighed grabbing an unused rag that Max left on the counter.

"We've got plenty of time," Carter's voice grew stern. He folded his arms across his chest, and glared at me through his glasses. He'd looked at me like this many times before, but since his injury his scowl seemed even more fierce. I knew he wasn't going to let me get away with not telling him tonight.

"Carter, I'm tired and I feel like crap. Can't it wait until tomorrow?" I knew he'd say no, but I had to try.

"You look like crap too." I glared at him appalled by his statement, which only made him roll his eyes. "You know what I mean. I didn't want you to go on this scout without me. I knew something bad was going to happen."

"This didn't happen because you weren't there."

"Then why did it happen?"

"It was my fault." Remie's voice rocked the room like an earthquake.

"What? No, it wasn't!" I shouted back at him, not sounding at all like myself, but rather an annoyed sibling. I was happy to have gotten to know Remie a little better, maybe even understand him more, but his new pitiful behavior was testing my nerves. He wasn't any worse off than the rest of us, and getting all *"woe is me"* wasn't going to help anyone.

"What did you do?" Carter stormed to face Remie nearly bumping chests. The sight was almost comical.

"Whoa! Calm down." Max stepped in-between the two before a fight ensued. Actually, I wasn't sure I could call it a fight because Remie was *allowing* my brother to snarl in his face. It felt crazy to admit it, but I thought for a second he might have even let my brother beat him up. Remie was twice Carter's size, and the idea of that even being possible was ridiculous.

"Carter that's not how it happened," Max said placing a firm hand against his chest trying to calm him down, and preventing his advance on Remie.

"What are you talking about? He just said it was his fault!"

"Well, *he* isn't thinking straight right now." Max gave an angry stare toward Remie that would rival any scowl I'd ever seen. I couldn't remember ever seeing Max angry before, and I knew *I* never wanted to be on the receiving end of it. "This isn't the time or the place," he nodded toward Eleanor.

We'd drawn the attention of Wade, Taya, and even Charlie; none of them looked very happy. There were more important things to be doing right then.

"Let's step outside," Max said and Remie immediately complied like an obedient schoolboy. When Carter didn't budge, I gave Max a pleading look and he tugged on my brother's arm. Carter pulled away from his grip and marched out of the room like a petulant child although I knew that wasn't the effect he was going for.

Remie was nowhere in sight when we reached the hallway and I was glad. We might have been out of the sick room, but I still wasn't ready to have this argument. Hopefully, Max and I could restrain Carter's anger long enough that he would let us tell him tomorrow after we had some rest.

"Okay, somebody tell me what the hell happened. Now!" Carter growled through gritted teeth.

"We all made it back safely. That's all you need to know right now," Max replied. Exhaustion drenched his voice making him sound as tired as I felt.

"Oh please, don't give me that horseshit." The lid above Carter's wounded eye started to twitch. "That old lady obviously didn't make it back safely; and Abby... I mean, just look at her!" Carter waved his hands at me like I was some sort of science experiment.

Max turned to look at me, releasing a heavy sigh. His chin began to quiver as he drank in the sight of me. I knew he was reliving what happened like a horror movie on a never ending reel inside his head.

I hated seeing him look at me like that. "Stop it!" I screamed at the top of my lungs certain that I'd probably woken up everyone in our entire compound. "Just stop it, Carter!"

He looked utterly confused by my reaction, and opened his mouth to speak. I shook my head at him, and he firmly closed it. I held his gaze and marched right up to him, grabbing his chin. "The only thing you need to know right now is that I'm alive, and it's because of him." My words doused the tension in the room as I pointed at Max.

Before he could say anything else, I released his chin and made my way down the hallway toward our room. "I'm just worried about you Abby," Carter called out pitifully to me. He sounded wounded, but I was too tired to care about his feelings, at least for tonight.

The truth was; I was worried about me too. How many close calls could one person survive? I was like a cat with nine lives, and fairly certain I'd used four or five already.

I somehow managed to get myself cleaned up before I went to bed. When I woke up, I was clean and still smelling of soap. Max pushed our beds together at some point during the night, but I didn't hear him. He was snoring softly on the bed beside me, still covered in the blood, sweat and dirt from the night before. I gazed at him for a while, noting that he was also wearing his shoes, and most likely fell asleep the moment he lay down. I wanted to fall back to sleep myself, but my body protested in discomfort. Every part of me was sore. My current level of exhaustion could have easily persuaded me to fall back to sleep, but the growling in my stomach prevented it. I could sleep through almost anything, except hunger pangs.

I sat up slowly, knowing that if I didn't a wave of nausea would assault me. I was right, but my slow movements helped nullify its intensity. The way my muscles screamed, and my joints popped with every movement I wouldn't have been shocked if someone had told me I got hit by a semi-truck last night. That's certainly what it felt like. A semi-truck with eight legs, and toxic fangs. Nothing four ibuprofen couldn't cure, right? I sure hoped so because I had never been very good at sitting still for very long. Even as a kid when I would get the flu I never wanted to stay in bed. I always felt that getting up and doing things, no matter how sick I was, was better than groaning in bed all day.

I pulled on a pair of cargo pants and some sneakers, trying to be as quiet as possible. Max looked like he could sleep through a meteor crashing into earth, but I knew he needed it, and didn't want to risk waking him. I resisted the urge to give him a quick peck, but gently laid a blanket on top of him. Then I soundlessly shut the door behind me and left.

I licked at the scab on my lip, and flipped my tongue across the new hole between my molars as I made my way down the hall. It was tender and felt a bit swollen. My stomach grumbled louder with every step I took, but I had one detour before I could comply with its demands. I wanted to check on Eleanor.

Heat radiated through the windows as I walked by, telling me it was late afternoon. I'd slept nearly all day, but it didn't feel like it. Only a few fellow survivors passed me as I made my way. They all commented how glad they were that we were back. I couldn't control the smile that stretched across my face, pulling at my raw lip. This compound might not have been much, but it was certainly home. It had been a long time since we had anything like it. A tear threatened to fall, but I wiped it away. I'd done enough crying in the last twenty-four hours; I'd have to save some for later.

The door to the sick room was only partially closed. Dead silence greeted me as I pushed it open with my fingertips. My sneakers squeaked across the tiled floor, so I tried my best to walk on my tip-toes even though my leg muscles protested achingly.

Charlie was sleeping on one of the extra cots, his arm hanging off the edge and his glasses clinging precariously to his fingers. I don't know what we would have done if he hadn't shown up. I couldn't wait to hear his story and find out what brought him down, and for which I was very grateful. He was pretty firm about staying at his house the last time we saw him.

Walking further into the room, I found Wade sleeping soundly at the foot of Eleanor's cot. Her legs were curled up under her and her head rested at the foot of the bed. Her dark eye makeup was smeared drastically across her face. She, no doubt, fought sleep as long as she could before it consumed her. I'd have done the same thing if I were she. If anything were to ever happen to Max or Carter...? Well, that was one thought I couldn't even allow to take root in my mind. As far as I was concerned, that was never going to happen, and I'd just leave it at that.

Eleanor looked the same as when I left her the previous night, only slightly paler. The spider fang still protruded from her chest. The gauze that surrounded it had turned a putrid yellow, and obviously needed changing. How much venom could one fang hold?

The chair beside her bed held a tray with extra gauze and tape, so I got to work changing her dressing. I could manage that much on my own; and Wade and

Charlie definitely needed their sleep. Taking a seat in the chair I placed the tray in my lap. Eleanor's chest rose and fell steadily. Aside from her injury, she looked like she was simply sleeping. I wished so much that were true.

Her old bandages peeled off easily, barely sticking to her skin. I held my breath as I tossed them into the trash can beside me. They had an odd smell - a rancid mixture of rotten fruit and fish.

When all the old bandages were off, I slid the trash can further away with my foot. My stomach was a little too sensitive at the moment, and I wasn't sure it could handle the smell for long.

A damp cloth sat in the same soapy water beside the bed. I grabbed it, squeezing out the excess liquid. The water was icy and felt good in my sore hands. Placing the bowl on the side of the bed, I went to work on cleaning the areas around the wound before adding new gauze. It wasn't oozing as much as before, but I didn't find that comforting. Hopefully, most of the venom had already seeped out of the wound, but that was doubtful. I was desperately looking for things to be optimistic about, but I knew I was grasping at straws.

Wiping away the slimy residue, I caught sight of something that made my hands tremble. Underneath the yellow venom, Eleanor's skin was starting to change color. It was ever so faint, and if I hadn't been looking at her so closely I might never have noticed. The edges of skin touching the fang were starting to turn black, almost as though it were charred.

One thought, and one thought only ran through my mind. We needed to get that fang out. Now!

I couldn't stomach looking at it any longer. Even with an empty stomach I still felt the urge to heave, and it was getting harder to fight it. I patted the area dry, and gently placed new gauze down.

Setting the tray back where I found it, I retreated from the cot leaving it as though I'd never been there. Cleaning the wound wasn't much, but I felt the tiniest bit better that I had helped. I wanted to do more, but what else could I do?

"We need to get that fang out of her," Charlie said sadly. I jumped in surprise and placed my hand on my chest to catch my breath. "I tried pullin' it out, but it caused her a lot of pain. The sucker is holdin' on in there." He rubbed the bridge of his nose before putting his glasses back on.

"What do you need to get it out?" I leaned against the end of his cot and crossed my arms over my chest. If he needed something to save Eleanor, I was going to get it. Remie might be taking all the blame for what happened, but he wasn't the only one who was guilty. Cleaning up Eleanor's wound made me think about what happened. Maybe if I hadn't slapped him he wouldn't have dropped the gun, and it wouldn't have misfired.

"I need medical supplies. A scalpel and suture needles... uh." Charlie rubbed his head while he tried to think, the fog of sleep still shrouding his mind.

"There's only one place I know of that we can get those things, and fast," I said. It would be a dangerous mission, but I'd already made a promise to myself. I was going to get what Charlie needed to save Eleanor. No matter what.

"Where?" Wade's voice was full of anticipation, but her appearance contradicted it. She looked like a drowned, emo clown. Her dark makeup accentuated the dried rivers of tears down her face, and her hair was plastered with sweat across her brow. The hems of her sleeves were tucked tightly in her fists and held at her sides as she stared hopefully at me. Her appearance might have been dark, but her eyes were bright and full of life. There was hope in them, and I knew I couldn't let her down.

"The hospital." I swallowed hard.

"Great! Let's go." Wade clapped her hands together and started walking toward the door.

"It's not that easy," Carter said ambling into the room. Had he been eavesdropping? Or did he just have impeccably horrible timing? He was going to put a kibosh on my hospital plan; the alarming stare he cast in my direction made that much unmistakable.

"Why not?" Wade took a challenging stance in front of my brother.

"Because it's in the restricted zone," I groaned rolling my eyes at my brother. Wade gave me a confused look. "You should probably take a seat." I pointed to a small table and chairs across the room. She thought about it for a moment before complying.

"So, what's the restricted zone?" she asked as I joined her at the table. Carter took a seat beside her, but not because he wanted to be near her. No, he wanted the perfect seat directly across from me, so he could glare at me while I explained. Charlie stood a few steps behind me and I told myself that he would take my side against Carter on the idea. Besides, Carter never much liked him... at first, anyway.

"When we arrived here there was a large section of the base blocked off by tall fencing."

"Okay, so what? You can't get past a few fences?"

I sighed. I didn't really have the patience for her to get an attitude with me. "The fences weren't the problem." I leaned back in my chair trying to think of a way to tell her without making her panic, but there wasn't a way around it. No matter how I worded it, it was terrifying.

"The warning signs stopped us."

"Warning signs?" Charlie jumped in his tone concerned.

"Somewhere inside those fences," Carter pointed toward the eastern wall like we could see what he was aiming at, "are a whole new breed of demons that we've never seen before."

"How do you know that?" Wade asked.

"The signs warn of smoker demons." As much as I wanted to forget I'd ever seen the signs I couldn't. They were a constant reminder of a lingering evil we had yet to face.

"Well, have you actually ever seen a smoker demon?"

"No."

"Then how do you know they're even there?" Wade's tone was starting to flutter with anger.

"How do we know they aren't?" Carter challenged. "All the descriptions I've heard about every demon that anyone on this base has encountered do not portray anything that could be called a smoker. But they do account for dozens of other kinds. Who knows how many there really are?" He pulled his journal out of his back pocket and slapped it on the table. His eyes met Wade's in a strange gaze like he was expecting his journal to be the only evidence she needed to believe him.

I, on the other hand, understood what was really bothering her. She didn't think we would risk crossing those fences to get the supplies we needed for Eleanor. I wasn't particularly ecstatic about the prospect of having another demon encounter, but I'd never been the kind of girl who shied away from danger when something important needed to be done.

"So, what are you saying? You aren't going?"

"No," Carter answered, and I shook my head at him.

"Yes we are." I refused to meet my brother's eyes choosing to look at Wade instead. "I'll go."

"Like hell, you will!" Carter jumped from his seat and sent his chair sliding across the floor with an eardrum-shattering screech. "You barely survived the last scout, Abby."

"I'm going Carter, and there's nothing you can do to stop me." He bit his lip, ready to spew every threat he could fling at me, but I knew the one thing that could simmer his temper. "And you're going with me."

"Now hold on," Charlie raised his voice taking a seat in the last empty chair. "You kids aren't serious? You don't know anything about these... these smokers."

"What choice do we have Charlie? She isn't going to make it if you can't get that thing out of her." Panic flickered in Wade's expression, but she quickly hid it. I knew I hadn't said anything that everyone else wasn't already thinking. I was just the first one to admit it out loud.

"That settles it. I'm going too." Wade pounded her fist once against the table to emphasize her point.

"No, you're not," I replied.

"Who the hell do you think you are?" Her face turned a livid red.

"Someone needs to stay behind and look after her. This is our base, and our compound, and we call the shots. What do you think your chances are of actually surviving an attack from a demon no one knows anything about?" Her angry expression was fading to defeat, but I stayed on the offensive. "Are you really willing to risk the chances of her survival on your fighting abilities?"

Although she held her own during our fight against the spider demons, Wade was too emotionally compromised. She'd either get herself or someone else killed, and I wasn't willing to risk that. We'd seen first-hand the results of someone being emotionally unstable, and were currently arguing because of it. If Remie hadn't been distraught with memories of his daughter, if Carter hadn't wanted to play hero to save Norah, if my father hadn't been so worried about our neighbors... things might have ended up very differently. The memories should have made me sad, but instead they fueled my rage. And right now, I was taking my anger out on Wade... I could be a real jerk sometimes.

She was giving me the same hurt look that Carter gave me when I told him he was too much of a liability to go on our last scout. I always believed that giving the truth straight was the best option, but the way people kept looking at me made me feel like a big bully. Was I big bully? Did I really have the right to tell them what they could or could not do?

"Listen," I turned to face her hoping to better convey my sincerity. "I'm not trying to be a jerk, but this is a risky enough mission as it is. Our best chances are to go into this with the best possible group. Anything less..." I was at a loss for words.

"Anything less would be the same as not going at all," Carter added although it didn't sound entirely like he was agreeing with me. More like his inner nerd, refusing to let an unfinished sentence dangle.

"Don't even think you can tell me I ain't goin', kid," Charlie announced when I made eye contact with him. "I know what supplies I need and I'm not gonna let you kids go in alone. Not when there's smokin'... smoker demons around."

I simply nodded my head. I'd never dream of telling Charlie what to do, except maybe to stop calling us all "kids." I suppose though, compared to him, we kinda were. It was endearing and annoying at the same time. I certainly wouldn't let anyone else get away with it.

Wade stood up without a word heading back to Eleanor's bedside, and leaving the rest of us to sit in uncomfortable silence. I didn't want to be the first one to break it. As soon as I did, I knew that would give my brother the green flag to start his barrage of verbal attacks. Telling him he was coming with me had only temporarily distracted him.

"So, when are we going on this little excursion?" Carter asked with agitated sarcasm.

"Soon." Before he could say more, I slid off of my seat and out the door. I wouldn't be able to do anything more until I got something to eat.

To my surprise, Carter didn't chase me down. I knew I wouldn't be able to avoid him for much longer, and sooner or later he and I would need to have a talk, but for now I savored the silence. We'd been getting on each other's nerves for a while now, and we really needed to get through this rough patch. We were both only trying to look out for one another, but by doing so we were driving each other crazy. It had turned into a vicious cycle of sibling fighting, and it was getting old.

"There you are!" Taya shouted from the end of the hallway. She speed-walked to my side. "I brought you some food."

"Thanks," I said suspiciously.

"Don't look at me like that." She drew her eyebrows together wrinkling her forehead at me, and shoving the tray of food at my chest. "I don't know what stick you have up your butt, but you should really have it extracted."

"Still hating me, I see." I took the food and ate it as I walked. I wasn't sure what it was but I was swallowing it faster than I could taste it.

"I don't hate you. I just hate how you act sometimes. Like you're mad at the world, and you take it out on everyone. News flash, Abby! *Everyone* is mad at the world right now."

I swallowed hard and the bite of "mystery meal" lodged in my throat. I stopped to lean my back against the wall to brace myself as I coughed violently. With my lungs surprisingly in place, I stared watery-eyed at the scrawny girl standing before me. She was a thorn in my side, and we'd been at odds for a while, but she really hit the nail on the head. Who wasn't I at odds with lately?

Taya was calling it out as she saw it and a smile perked up my lips. She and I were becoming more alike. Or maybe we always were, but I was just now realizing it.

She folded her arms across her chest. "Don't look at me like *that* either." I expanded my grin against the protests of my split lip; and despite herself she smiled back at me.

"So... I wanted to ask you something."

"Ahh that explains why you brought me food!" I said feigning surprise.

"Fine, I'll take the food back then!" she tried to snatch the plate from my grip, but I was too quick for her.

"I didn't say you couldn't ask." I scooped up the last globs of food in the plate and shoved them into my mouth. There was no way anyone could take that food away from me before I was finished with it. Not with how starved I was.

A smirk sneaked onto her face again. I got the feeling that she wasn't truly mad at me anymore, but she was too stubborn to admit it. I'm sure it didn't help that I teased her sometimes. Then again, she was like the sister I never had, and I just couldn't help it. Plus, I missed the times when we *did* get along. They seemed so long ago.

"I wanted to know if you'll still give me a shooting lesson?" she asked hesitantly sounding much like a little sister asking to borrow her big sister's clothes.

I forgot that I promised her I'd give her a lesson. After the amount of ammo we used up the night before, the type of lesson she wanted wasn't going to be an option. We couldn't waste what few bullets we had left, but there was another alternative.

"There's nothing I'd rather do."

Taya sneered at me for a second until she realized I wasn't being sarcastic. As tired as I was, a little one-on-one time with a firearm would do me good. Even though I was only shooting BBs, and it wasn't a real firearm, shooting was shooting, right? I hoped so. Since my dad died my shotgun had turned into an unusual sort of security blanket for me. It helped calm my nerves, clear my head and gave me the comfort of knowing that I could use it to take out any demon that tried to attack me.

I was out of shells for it, but that was a fact I was trying to ignore. Last night was a nightmare that I did not want to relive, or recall how close we had really come to... I didn't even dare think it.

"Really?" Taya beamed.

"Yep. Meet me in the hangar in twenty minutes?"

"I'll meet you there in five!" she squealed with excitement turning on her heel before I could protest. I was still going to meet her in twenty. She'd just have to wait for me. There was something I had to do first.

9

To my disappointment Max wasn't in bed when I returned to the room. I didn't want to wake him up, but I knew I'd have to if I expected to be the one to tell him what was going on. I thought it best if he heard it from me first, but that plan backfired.

He was probably getting an earful from Carter right about now, which would only make him less likely to be on my side on the decision. If I had been able to talk to him about it myself I would have been able to appeal to his sense of duty. We had brought the spider demons to the museum, and it was our fault that Eleanor was in her current state. I felt like it was our responsibility to do everything we could to bring her back to health.

With a groan of frustration, I sat heavily atop Max's cot rubbing my face in my hands. My subconscious sensed my close proximity to a bed, washing a wave of exhaustion over me.

I could easily have fallen back asleep, but it would only have made matters worse. Sure, I'd sleep for another eight hours, but I'd wake up even more tired than I was right now. Besides, the noise in my brain was currently so loud I knew my sleep would be restless, which was even worse. No, I needed to clear my head and relax. There was only one way I knew how to do that. I decided to find Max later, or let him find me. Either way, we needed to talk.

Taya was impatiently awaiting my arrival in the hangar. The passenger van and Ford we commandeered during our scout were still parked where we left them.

Taya was looking inside them like there was something interesting to see. There wasn't; everything had already been unloaded.

"If we got this thing cleaned up, it might actually be pretty cool," she said pointing her finger toward the Explorer.

"Why does it matter?"

She shrugged. "I don't know. Something to do, I guess."

"We've got something to do." I walked over to the supplies that were stacked against the wall and picked up one of the BB jugs, rattling its contents.

"What the heck are those?" She squinted at me, placing her hands on her hips.

"Unlimited ammo," I beamed at her, waiting for her to explode with alarm like Grant, Drew, and I did. Discovering that BBs were all that Remie managed to scavenge from the Walmart didn't go over particularly well with us at the time, but now I could see the logic in it. Sort of. All the practice in the world wouldn't do any good if we didn't have real bullets to shoot when the time came to put our training to the test.

Taya, in her usual fashion, didn't respond the way the rest of us did.

"Cool!" Taya snatched the tub from me, shaking it; and staring at it in wonder as if it were a wrapped Christmas present. The neon yellow pellets popped around like uncooked popcorn kernels.

"Cool?" I scoffed at her picking up two BB guns. I should have known I wouldn't get a reaction out of her. I'd forgotten she had the uncanny ability to completely ignore the horrors of the world around us and focus herself on finding amusement in the little things.

Actually, maybe that wasn't such a bad idea. I could, no doubt, learn a tip or two from Taya. Perhaps if I did I wouldn't be so much on edge all the time.

"Let's go."

I headed out a side door to the outside and was instantly slapped with the brightness of the afternoon sun. Squinting did nothing to lessen the penetrating rays. Sweat immediately began to bead on my brow as I led Taya to our improvised courtyard. It was once a parking lot, but was now being used as our training grounds; among other things.

The cars were positioned along the borders of the small lot, forming a wall around it. Empty tables were set up, scrap wood was piled in a mountainous heap, and giant rolls of barbed wire clung to each other. Drew had gathered up more than we had initially required, but with the arrival of all our new survivors, I imagined we needed to expand. Our small, three-building compound wasn't large enough anymore and we couldn't expect people to double up and have to share rooms. One of the biggest inspirations for this compound went beyond safety – it was to provide some semblance of normalcy. To give these people back a tiny bit of the lives they lost. If we started cramming people in together like sardines it just wouldn't work.

I snapped out of my inner monologue to watch Taya setting up her first target. I suppose she really was eager to practice. I was still a little incredulous since it appeared so out of character for her. Something must have happened that was making her take this much more seriously than I'd seen her take anything in a very long time.

She was propping a large piece of Styrofoam atop a scrapped couch that we found near a dumpster. It wasn't anything anyone wanted to sit on, ever, but it was perfect for target practice.

"How's that?" Taya shouted from a distance.

I opened my mouth to shout that it was fine realizing that my mouth was dry. I knew we should have brought some water. I gave her a thumbs up, and she jogged over to me.

"Okay, do you know how to load one of these?" I handed her the BB gun, unscrewing the lid on the jug.

"Yeah, these are easy. It's the real guns that are hard." I only nodded my response recalling how sore my fingers were when I first learned how to load a gun.

"Why are we using these?"

"We don't have the ammo to waste on practice. Plus, the noise probably isn't a good idea right now."

"Yeah..." She eyed me curiously for a moment before she went to work loading the plastic BB gun. She finished in record time and plopped down in one of the plastic lawn chairs.

"Ow!" she jumped back up, rubbing her butt. "These chairs are hot."

"Well duh," I smirked at her, and we broke into fits of laughter until tears began to fall from our eyes, which was actually refreshing considering how hot it was outside.

"Oh wow, I needed that." I sighed, feeling out of breath, but much more at ease. Our giggles seemed to disperse some of my stress.

"Abby?" Taya asked drawing a serious expression onto her face. "What happened out there?"

I knew this was coming. I would have to explain it to someone, and as much as I didn't want to talk about it speaking to Taya would be a lot easier than telling my brother.

I pulled over another lawn chair, and sat carefully on the edge of it not anxious to burn *my* backside. Taya chose to lean against the table unwilling to singe her rear again.

It took me a quick ten minutes to spew the horrible details of what had happened. I didn't stop to breathe the entire time, and had to gulp mouthfuls of air when I finished. I wouldn't even pause to let Taya ask a question, and when I was done she just stared at me dumbfounded; unable to speak the questions I prevented her from asking.

"Aren't you going to say anything?" I said wiping the sweat off the nape of my neck.

"I... I don't know what to say." Her tone was almost apologetic like she felt she was required to ask me a ton of questions. For the first time since we'd met, Taya was speechless.

"What are we going to do now?"

"That's the tricky part." I stood up and walked toward the target pumping the cheap gun so I could take my shot.

"What's tricky about it?" Taya walked up beside me cradling the gun like it was a baby doll.

"I'm crossing the fence," I said flatly, firing at the target. A tiny popping noise confirmed that I landed a shot, but it was difficult to tell where. "Your turn."

I stepped behind Taya and helped her raise the gun. She moved woodenly, obviously unnerved by what I just revealed. "You don't mean the restricted fence?"

"Yes." I braced myself for her rebuttal, but there was nothing. "Now, prop it up against your shoulder here." I adjusted her arm to correctly bear the weight of the gun as if it were a real one.

"Spread your feet out a little bit. You shoot like that and you'll fall flat on your burned butt." I tapped her thigh and she obliged.

"I'm not really going to fall down Abby, and you're avoiding my question."

"If this were a real gun you'd fall down. You need to pretend it's real, or you aren't going to learn anything. And I answered your question."

I lifted the muzzle of her gun; she was pointing too low.

"Well... you didn't answer it to my satisfaction," she fired back at me.

"Okay. Close one eye. No, don't squeeze it shut like you're a pirate!" I giggled at her and she sighed noisily.

"Abby!" she groaned as I swallowed my last snigger.

"I want to go to the hospital to get Charlie what he needs to save Eleanor. To do that, I need to cross into the restricted area," I explained without giving her any warning.

"But those *things* are in there." She lowered the gun and looked at me. "The... the smokers."

"I know." I avoided her fearful gaze as I lifted her gun. "Get back into position." I walked around her, eyeing her stance and position. "Steady your breathing and focus on the target. Are you ready?" Taya nodded her head. "Don't move your head!" I chuckled lightly at her.

"Sorry," she said with a smile.

"When you're ready to fire I want you to hold your breath and squeeze the trigger. Don't pull." I stood back to watch her in action, and the BB gun clicked in response. With a tiny puff of air, the BB flew out of the barrel and hit the back cushion of the couch; causing a wisp of dust to curl into the air, and disappear.

"Darn it!" Taya stomped her foot as she quickly fired again. She hit the couch a second time.

"Relax." I patted her shoulder. "You need to focus."

"Okay, okay," she expelled a heavy breath and fired again. The Styrofoam popped in response.

"I got it!"

"Nice job!" She beamed at me and an overwhelming sense of pride tugged at my heart. I never taught anybody anything before. It felt pretty good. Plus, it was even nicer that Taya and I were really getting along.

"Now, just keep doing that, and you'll be a pro in no time." I smiled again and joined her, firing at the target.

For a good thirty minutes and multiple BB refills, we unloaded our toy rifles into the pitiful Styrofoam target, pretending it was a demon. It felt good. Not as good as a real gun, but good all the same.

"Wow, now I know why you carry your shotgun everywhere you go," Taya said dropping her body into a chair. I did the same. We'd been outside long enough that the plastic felt cool now, instead of burning hot.

"This is nothing compared to the real thing." I dropped the plastic gun onto the table. "Don't you remember when you shot all those little demons at the cabin?" That was right after we found Taya, just a handful of weeks ago, but since then she'd grown from a mere wisp of a girl to a strong, young woman.

"Yeah, but I was scared out of my mind. I hardly remember picking up the gun in the first place," she admitted.

"Scared or not, you saved us that day. It took a lot of guts to do what you did."

"Thanks," she looked embarrassed. Did I ever thank her for what she did that day? I couldn't remember.

"I'm not going to tell you that I think you shouldn't go. Is that what you're waiting for?" she asked suspiciously.

I toyed with the jug of BBs like it was something interesting. It wasn't. "That's not what I'm waiting for. You're actually the first person to agree with me." She didn't look surprised.

"Guys think differently than women do." She shrugged like it was the simplest fact in the world. Maybe it was. "All they can focus on is the fact that you'd be putting yourself in a very dangerous situation, which challenges their role as the protectors."

"What do you think?" I asked suddenly eager to get some confirmation that I was doing the right thing. *I* knew I was doing the right thing, but garnering some support would be nice.

"I think..." she held my gaze without blinking, "that I would be surprised if you did any less."

Much of the weight lifted off my shoulders, and I breathed deeply. An unusually cool wind danced across my sweaty body easing the intensity of the heat. "So... you agree with me then?"

She nodded. "I know you'll do whatever it takes to help save Eleanor." She swallowed hard. "I know that's what you've always done... for everyone."

I blinked at her and she looked away suddenly finding the current state of her fingernails to be very appealing.

Was she trying to apologize? Taya had long blamed me for the deaths of Norah, Judy and Savannah. I tried to ignore how much her anger bothered me, but now that she appeared to be on the verge of forgiving me, I wanted it and badly.

"What are you saying?" I scooted closer to her, placing my hand on her knee.

She groaned with frustration and wiped at her eyes. She was fighting something inside herself and I didn't know what. Either she didn't want to apologize, or it was hard for her to say she was sorry.

Her eyes finally met mine after what felt like a lifetime. They were brimming with unshed tears, and her face was red with simmering emotion. "I'm sorry Abby." She barely got the words out before she started sobbing.

"It's okay." I pulled her into my arms and together, we put on quite a waterworks show - two girls crying their eyes out.

"I'm so stupid," she shouted at herself pulling away from me. "I should never have been mad at you, but I just needed to be mad at something."

"I know, I know." I suspected that all along, which was why I tried to shrug off all her anger. It wasn't really me she hated; and if she needed someone to use for her punching bag; I was willing and able.

"All you do is look out for everyone else, without any care for yourself." Her unbridled, pent-up feelings were suddenly overflowing. "I mean look at you!" She pointed at me as a new wave of tears washed down her face.

"What?" I wiped at my face no longer crying.

"You're a mess Abby," she snorted through the last of her sobs.

I looked down at myself and didn't see anything that I didn't always see. Scuffed up shoes, dirty cargo pants and a t-shirt. "What do you mean, 'I'm a mess'?" I didn't share her amusement.

"Your poor face." She reached up to touch my lip. "Does it hurt?"

"I'll be all right." I pulled away and licked at my lip; feeling the scab.

She put her hands on her hips and frowned at me. "See! This is what I'm talking about. Have you even looked at yourself?"

I wrinkled my brow. "Well, no. So, what?"

"Abby," she said exasperated, "let's go inside and get you cleaned up. If you aren't going to take care of yourself then I will!" She assumed an authoritative tone that I never heard her use with me before. For a girl her size, it was almost comical until I saw the stern look on her face.

I smirked at her and followed her lead as we cleaned up our mess and headed inside.

Since she broached the subject, I felt entirely different now when walking inside our compound. I wasn't certain everyone was staring at me just because they were glad I came home, or maybe they were; but apparently my face was something pretty startling to see. Maybe even scary?

I was never one to stress over my looks, but if I looked like a walking punching bag I suppose that might make it a different story.

We deposited the BBs and guns on a table as we walked to our room. I found myself avoiding eye contact with everyone; becoming more self-conscious with every step. I regretted not spending a little more time on basic hygiene after I woke up.

"Go sit down on the bed," Taya ordered as she shut the door. I obediently complied eager to get off my feet, and let the exhaustion wash over me again. If it were possible, I might even fall asleep sitting up.

I slipped off my shoes while Taya rummaged through a footlocker 'til she found what she was looking for.

"What's all that?" I asked as she upturned a small purse onto the bed beside me.

"Just stuff I've been saving," she said poking through the small pile.

"Whoa, where'd you get this?" I snatched a tube of Neosporin.

She snatched it back. "I took it from that nice house we stayed at."

"Sticky fingers." I smirked at her.

"Yeah? So?" She sneered at me and unscrewed the cap. "Now be quiet so I can work."

"Yes ma'am." I held back a snigger. It felt as good as ice cream on a sunny day to be civil with Taya again. I didn't realize how much I missed her friendship.

"There!" Taya announced when she felt she adequately bandaged up my injured face. It wasn't too painful, except for the part when she had to clean up a cut on my cheek. That part hurt like a son of a... you know what I mean.

"Will I live?" I jested.

"Outlook not so good," Taya said sounding like a Magic Eight Ball. We both tittered with laughter.

"I'm glad you're not mad at me anymore."

"Me too," she admitted. "Now go check yourself out in the mirror."

I approached my reflection while Taya cleaned up her supplies. When I finally saw myself, I was grateful that Taya wouldn't let me look until she fixed me up. I looked leagues better than I imagined I could. No more scary Abby.

My bottom lip was still split and slightly swollen, but it no longer looked as bad as it felt. A long cut on my cheekbone was turning pink around the edges, held together by two butterfly bandages. Seeing them brought back memories of my shoulder, when Max applied them to my wound.

I pulled down the collar of my shirt, and traced my fingers over the old scars. They were less pronounced than before, but still very visible. I could never forget they were there, especially since they never stopped hurting. It became a dull ache. I was getting accustomed to that pain, but every now and then I'd move wrong or hit it and the pain would stab through my body like a knife.

I gripped the sink and closed my eyes; trying to fight a sudden headache that sneak-attacked me. With no warning it burst into my skull. If I thought I could fight the urge to sleep before, now I was definitely unable to.

"There you are!" Max broadcast in a loud tone behind me. I squeezed my eyes shut even tighter. He sounded as loud as a train horn.

"Shh!" Taya chastised him. "Can't you see she has a headache?" I felt her shove something into my hand. "Take these and go lie down."

I popped the pills into my mouth, grabbing the cup of water she offered me. It was old and tasted like it was sitting around for a couple days, but I didn't care. My mouth was dry and relished the moisture. I held a big gulp in my mouth and allowed my tongue to swim in it before swallowing.

"I got you," Max said more softly this time as he walked me to my cot. I kept my eyes closed, but could still see that the light in the room was turned off. They were so bright they shone through my lids.

I heard the door shut and assumed Taya had left. I was so grateful that she wanted to take care of me, but even more that we were friends again. No, we were more than that; she was like my sister. I didn't know what I'd do without her.

"How are you feeling?" Max asked lowering me down into the bed.

"Tired," I answered with a yawn. I pushed off my socks with my toes and wiggled out of my pants to get more comfortable.

Max draped a light sheet over me and started stroking my hair as I nestled into the cot. That was one of my favorite feelings in the world, and we both knew sleep would soon claim me if he continued. While I was still semi-conscious I wanted to talk to him.

"I need to tell you something Max."

"I know," he said without missing a beat.

"I want you to go with me."

"I wouldn't let you go without me."

"Good." I was glad he wasn't fighting me on the subject or maybe he wanted to, but was waiting for after I slept to rebuke my plan.

"Abby?" he asked softly.

"Mhm?" I was scarcely awake.

"We aren't going until you're all healed up," his voice sounded as if it were etched in stone.

"Okay," I sighed feeling heavenly. My headache was easing away and I was terribly comfortable. Sleep was effortlessly seducing me and I embraced it. Max didn't snub my plan, and though he never said yes; he didn't say no either. For now, that was enough. Score one for my team. Or was it two?

10

I woke up in a haze. My eyes fought my need to open them and I practically had to unlock them from my lashes. My body was stiff and objected to every movement.

I managed to roll over only to find Max's cot empty. Disappointment lapped at my heart. I wanted to curl up with him and fall back to sleep, but noting his absence my heart willed my body to get up.

Taya was sleeping quietly in her cot, so I tiptoed around not wanting to wake her. I crept past her and dug into my footlocker looking for a clean change of clothes. Pulling on a loose pair of jeans and one of my favorite t-shirts, I slipped out the door without causing her to so much as stir in her sleep. I guess I could be pretty darn stealthy when I wanted to be.

The halls were empty as I made my way. The cool, tiled floor felt like heaven on my feet. Summers in New Mexico were nothing like back home. I was slowly adjusting to the heat during the day, but still found it difficult to sleep at night. Waking up on the hour, and being covered in a sheen of sweat every morning wasn't exactly desirable, especially since we didn't have any A/C. But, things could definitely be worse, so I always enjoyed the little things when I could. Like the dramatic cooling effect of tile floors, and the fact that Max hadn't stomped on my idea of going into smoker territory.

I brushed my hair through with my fingers, tugging violently on the knots. Perhaps, I should adopt a more manageable hair style. A demon apocalypse doesn't really permit much time for such things. Maybe I should cut my hair like Wade's? I bet her short bob felt extremely cool in this heat.

The thought of Wade made me change my direction. I wanted to check on her and Eleanor before facing down my brother. I needed to be a little bit more awake for that, and still felt slightly sleepy. The fog of sleep hadn't entirely lifted yet.

An orange glow outlined the doorway to the sickroom giving the hallway a strange luminescence. If the light was on that meant someone was awake. At least, I knew I wouldn't have to worry about startling anyone. That was a relief. Tiptoeing around was making my feet tired not to mention creating a burning sensation in my calves. Was I really so out of shape?

Wade was leaning back in a chair with her sneakered feet propped up on top of the table. Her legs were covered up to her knees in rainbow-colored socks and her short hair was separated into two funny looking pigtails. Her bright red shorts, rock band t-shirt and newly applied black eye-shadow completed her unique look. She looked like an emo Rainbow Brite. Oddly enough, it fit her perfectly.

"Hey." I smiled at her and pulled out a chair for myself sighing as I sat down. Yeah, I really was out of shape. Then again, I did get my butt kicked by a demon.

Either way, I was hobbling around like an old lady. Speaking of old lady...

"How's Eleanor?" I asked fidgeting with some of the magazines strewn haphazardly around the table. Teen and beauty magazines; they must be Taya's.

"I'm not sure," Wade said looking up. She was picking at her already frighteningly short nails. She stared at the ceiling like she was trying to solve an impossible math problem in her head. "She's awake... ish." She brought her head back down and grabbed a magazine off the table. She obviously wasn't ready to talk or didn't particularly want to. Seeing her suddenly enraptured with a magazine that she held upside-down in her lap was all the evidence I needed.

I decided Wade probably needed some time to compute all the craziness of the recent events. I got up and walked to Eleanor's bed. To my surprise, she was sitting up and Lauren, our resident school nurse, was feeding her spoonfuls of what looked like broth. I should know; we had a nearly limitless stock of the watery stuff. Apparently, when the demons first attacked us, and people started hoarding supplies, no one thought that bouillon cubes were worth taking. Worked out pretty good for us.

Lauren spooned some broth into Eleanor's mouth and wiped away what dribbled down her chin. She beamed at me as I approached, and oddly enough it didn't make me feel happy. I only felt more guilt. Sure, she was finally awake and well enough to be eating, but she never would have had to endure any of this if it weren't for us. If it weren't for the fact that we brought a horde of spider demons down on them.

"Hello, child." Her voice wasn't as soft as before. Now she sounded like a woman who had spent the better part of her years chain-smoking like a chimney.

"How are you?" I knelt down beside her bed. Lauren was sitting in the only available chair.

"Oh…" she patted my hand and allowed Lauren to feed her more broth. She swallowed hard. "I'm doing much better, my dear."

I nodded like I believed her. How could she be better? The spider fang was still lodged in her chest!

I sat with her quietly while Lauren finished feeding her. A few droplets of broth trickled down her chin, so I grabbed the towel to wipe them up. Some slipped down her neck, so I mopped them with the cloth to avoid leaving a sticky trail. As I gently patted it away, I noticed that the blackness that I first observed around the edges of her wound had now traveled up her neck and become a web of black veins.

I bit my lip straining to hold back my instant reaction. If I freaked out at the sight of them Eleanor might get scared, and it didn't appear that she knew they were there. Lauren caught my eye and shook her head, answering my question. It was probably best not to let Eleanor know, for now. No doubt Wade had seen them, and they were probably what had her so muddled. Or more accurately, freaked her the heck out.

I squeezed her hand needing to direct my attention elsewhere. "We're going to get you all better," I said and I meant it.

"I know, dear." Her eyes were getting droopy. She must be sleepy. "Charlie tells me you have a plan?" She rested against her pillow, and kept her eyes closed while she spoke.

"I do. We just need some supplies and then Charlie can fix you up good as new." What was I, a used car salesman? Who was I trying to convince: her or me?

She nodded with a little wobble of her head then sighed heavily. Sleep was her only escape and I thought it best to let her rest. She didn't need to know the scary details of what we really were going to do. All she needed to know was that we were going to do what needed to be done to take care of her.

Remie was sitting at the table with Wade when I walked away from Eleanor's bed. He bolted out of his seat at the sight of me, and stood at attention like a drill sergeant. I didn't know whether to roll my eyes or smile at him, so I did both.

"I was just telling Rembrandt about your plan," Wade said peeking over the magazine in her lap that was now facing upright.

"Were you now?" I raised my eyebrows at her incredulously. I forgot how quickly word traveled around on the compound.

"I'm going with you," Remie said defiantly. "I feel I owe it to Eleanor, to Wade and the rest of their group." His voice was picking up speed.

I raised my hands up. "Whoa. Calm down. No need to get all worked up, Remie. I never said you weren't going. I was going to ask you anyway." And I really was. Despite everything that happened Remie was probably one of our best fighters and I trusted him in any battle. He just had a little... hmm...? What would you call something like that? A momentary meltdown? Everyone was entitled to at least one of those. I hoped his was over.

He seemed to calm down a bit at that and relaxed in his chair. "Good." He nodded to himself; without making eye contact with either of us.

"How long do you think it will take?" Wade asked.

"No more than a few hours I think." That was my best guess. I really didn't know. I suppose it would depend on whether or not we ran into any of the smoker demons.

"When do we leave?" Remie asked joining in on the conversation.

"Yes, when are we leaving?" Carter asked from the doorway.

Great, here we go again.

"Soon. Maybe tomorrow." I didn't know for sure, but I didn't think Eleanor's odds would improve if we waited longer than that. Especially not if those black veins continued to spread across her body.

"Then we have a lot to do to get ready. Let's go."

With that, Carter turned around and strolled down the hallway. Was he seriously not going to fight me on this anymore? Maybe telling him that he was going with me was what did the trick. I'll have to remember that in the future – annoying big brother easily placated by letting him tag along and play his role as big brother.

Remie swirled out of his seat and headed out the door after my brother. I had only one guess where they were going, but I wanted to talk to Wade before I went there.

"We're going to take care of her. Okay?" She looked away from me, her eyes red and brimming with tears. "I won't give up until she's healthy. You understand me?" My voice was stern and commanding.

"You promise?" She looked at me with more fierceness than I had thought she could muster. She was fighting desperately to stay strong.

"I promise."

****

The guys all met up right where I thought they would. We were gathered together in the locker room that we used for our... well, I suppose it would be called a war room. All the gear and weapons we used for scouting or fighting against demon attacks were kept here. In the center stood a large table covered in maps and dozens of notes. Pretty much anything we ever came across on the base regarding demons was brought to this room. It was the living brain of our operations.

Remie, Max and Carter were huddled around the table all of their focus zeroed in on a map of the base. No doubt they were trying to find the best route to the hospital. Get in. Get out. That was my plan, and I hoped it was theirs.

I pulled up a seat and squeezed in next to Max. I wanted to be near him; to feel the strength that always seemed to radiate from him. Perhaps I could cling onto some of it and use it for myself.

Max's hand stroked my back while I tried to see what plans they had already managed to come up with. Knowing Carter, every step of the way had already been accounted for. Hell, he probably even outlined everything we'd be wearing. Okay, scratch that; that's a little exaggerated but... that's kinda how my brother was. Sometimes it was a good thing, and sometimes it was super annoying.

"Where's Grant and Drew?" I was surprised to find the dynamic duo missing.

"Haven't seen them since they started working on the generator," Max said dismissively.

"Hmm..." I exhaled and went back to looking at the map trying to locate the hospital. I had thought Grant and Drew would be going with us, but maybe our last little excursion was something they preferred no to relive. No doubt heading into the lion's den, also known as smoker demon territory, seemed more like flirting with death.

Whatever the heck these smokers were I wished we knew at least one small detail about them. Then maybe we'd have some tiny clue of what we were getting ourselves into. Not like that would stop me anyway. When it came to demons; I was always a "shoot first, ask questions later" sort of girl.

Carter kept pointing to specific points on the map, and Remie nodded his approval. "Is that where we're going in?" I asked him hoping he was still over fighting me on the subject.

Apparently he was. "Yep. Right there on the eastern side. It's closest to the hospital, which gives us less of a run to and from. The less time we spend on that side of the fence, the better."

"It shouldn't be a problem. There can't be too many of these... smoker demons. If there were, we'd have seen some by now," Remie said flatly like he was talking about something as common as a bird sighting. Oddly enough it gave me an idea.

My eyes widened as the light bulb in my brain began to burn brightly. "What if there aren't that many of them?"

"Then that's a good thing." Carter looked at me like I was a nutcase.

"Duh! That's what I'm trying to say." It took me a minute to wrap my brain around the idea that was rattling inside. "Let's just wipe them out and reclaim this entire area!" I traced a circle around the area of the hospital. "Things are getting crowded around here. We could use the space and the supplies."

"Whoa, whoa Abs!" Max spoke up pulling my hand away like I playing with fire.

"Yeah Abby! Are you crazy? Or do you have some sort of death wish?" Carter's eyes burned into me like red-hot pokers, and he yanked the map away from me.

I pulled my hand away from Max suddenly enthralled with my idea. It seemed brilliant to me. Why couldn't they see that?

"Don't be so dramatic Carter. Think of what we could do if we had that hospital at our disposal! It is probably filled with supplies! It's been fenced off for who knows how long? And if just a handful of smoker demons are guarding it, then why don't we just get rid of them?"

He scoffed at me shaking his head unable to speak. I looked at Remie hoping he would back me up, but his chocolaty eyes looked away.

"What's wrong with you guys?" My great idea was suddenly not feeling so great. Why was everyone looking at me like I was a leper?

"Abs." Max placed a hand on the back of my head urging me to face him. With his fingers in my hair it was hard not to obey.

"Let's just focus on getting the supplies we need for Eleanor first. Okay?" I sighed. I wasn't ready to give in yet. For some reason the idea of having the hospital in our possession seemed like it would make everything better.

"Our first concern is to get her healed Abby." Remie's voice was deep and austere echoing through the room. "Once we have done that then we can make preparations to seize the hospital."

"What?" Carter was near hysterics. "You're all losing your friggin' minds!"

"He's right," Max added.

"Thank you!" Carter breathed a sigh of relief and quit his frantic pacing. Ever since the night in the basement of the fanatic, John, Carter just wasn't the same. In fact, he seemed to be on edge about everything, afraid of everything. I was starting to miss the man Carter used to be. Sure, he was always my overprotective big brother, but flipping out over every little thing wasn't doing us any good. Maybe his allotted freak-out was overdue, and he needed to get it over with.

"I meant Rembrandt," Max corrected him. Carter groaned. "Just hear me out man," Max pleaded leaning forward against the table. "Stop focusing on how dangerous it is for a second, and try thinking about having the full advantage of a hospital at our fingertips. Hell, we could move our entire compound into there."

Remie nodded his head in agreement and I repressed the smile I was feeling inside me. If I let it spread onto my face it would only piss Carter off. We needed for him to agree with us on this. We needed for him to see reason and stop being... well stop being Carter.

"He's right Carter. We would have a much more secure location than where we are now. Having everyone in one defensible building as opposed to several is much better."

"Let's just worry about getting the supplies we need for now." I could tell by his tone that he wasn't ready to admit we were right.

"Deal." I smiled at my brother, but he didn't return it. Instead, he pulled his lips into a thin line and directed his attention to smoothing the map back onto the table.

"Do we have a list of what supplies we need?" I asked Max who was running his fingers through his hair. We had been planning our point of entry for nearly an hour and were all getting tired.

"We don't need a list. Charlie is coming with us," Carter answered for him.

"Good." The thought that Charlie was coming somehow made the trip not seem as bad. I don't know what it was about the old man, but he always made me feel safe. Well... safer. Perhaps having an older man around reminded me of when my dad was still alive.

I pushed the thought of my father to the back of my mind before it sent the tidal wave of grief crashing down on me. No amount of time could heal that wound. Ever.

"We will leave in two days' time then?" Remie questioned.

"Yeah," Max replied.

With that, everyone got up and stretched their arms and legs before heading out the door. To my surprise Carter left without a word, but it was just as well. Neither of us had the energy to talk things out.

"How are you doing?" Max started massaging my neck and I closed my eyes in response.

"I'm okay, I think." I turned around and planted my cheek firmly against his chest. "Be honest with me Max. Do you think this whole thing is a bad idea?"

He remained quiet for a moment before answering. "Is it a dangerous idea? Yes. But a bad one? I can't say. You know me Abby. I'm going to do whatever it takes to help Eleanor. To help all the survivors. Besides, I really feel like it's kinda our responsibility."

"Yeah..." I felt the same. I should have known from the beginning that Max would support me in the plan. We were so much alike in that way. We were willing to do whatever it took to protect those we cared about.

"Abs?" He kissed the top of my head and I burrowed deeper against his chest. The sound of his heart beating thudded in my ears. "What happened back at the museum..."

"You saved my life. That's what happened." I pulled away and looked into his eyes. Exhaustion hung heavily on his features.

"No." He shook his head, and tore his gaze from mine when tears threatened fall. "I risked your life."

"I don't believe that for one second." I really didn't. That spider demon would have torn me apart. I was sure I was going to die.

"That bullet could have flown right through that demon, and straight into you!" His tone was angry, but the expression on his face spoke of a different emotion. Raw, unmasked fear.

"But it didn't!" I couldn't stand to see the man I loved feeling so tortured. I was alive now, and that's all that mattered. Not how close I came to meeting my end.

He shook his head and ran his hands through his hair. The sight of him was tearing at my heart and I couldn't stand it any longer. I launched myself into his arms, bringing my mouth to his.

His lips were soft at first, but my fervent kissing brought him up to speed. His mouth was warm and inviting. As our tongues mingled wildly. Max ran his hands through my hair and around my waist, pulling our bodies closer together. His heart began to beat rapidly, in time with my own, and I could feel it pounding in my chest as I pressed against his.

He tugged softly on my bottom lip as he pulled away and began planting soft kisses all over my face. Shivers ran across the length of my body, until they turned into a burning desire.

Max's hand rested on either side of my cheek while he planted supple kisses onto my pouting lips, and then onto my cheeks. I didn't want him to stop kissing me. Not ever.

"God, I love you so much." His breath tickled my neck.

"I love you too."

He lifted me effortlessly and positioned me atop the table. The map crunched under my weight and adjusting my body I shoved it away with my fingers. All the while, Max's lips were on mine; his breath hot and rapid.

Were we really going to do this? I couldn't think of anything else! Just the thought of being with the man I loved sent ribbons of passion rocketing through me. I loved Max. I'd been in love with him all my life.

I tugged at his shirt, lifting it up as I wrapped my legs around him. His muscles flexed with the effort and he hoisted the shirt up over his head dropping it on the ground by his feet.

The sun did wonders to his expansive chest. His tanned skinned only further defined his muscles making the light dusting of hair stand out on his pecs. He was the most beautiful creature I had ever seen.

I leaned back against the table while he just stared at me. His chest was heaving, and his eyes full of desire. I was ready. I wasn't scared or nervous. As much as I wanted to tell myself everything would be okay someday, maybe it wouldn't be. No one knew how much time was left. That colossal draining hourglass loomed in the back of my mind. I didn't want to miss out on any moment that I *could* share with Max. I could see in his eyes he felt the same. The thought that he nearly lost me opened the floodgates of our desire.

Max leaned forward and I closed my eyes expecting him to lustfully kiss my neck, but instead his hands lodged under my armpits and he hoisted me upward.

"What's wrong?" My eyes popped open the heat of my desire quickly dissipating.

He brushed a strand of hair from across my face. "You deserve better than this Abs."

"Better than what?"

"This." He waved his arms around the room. "Do you really want your first time to be in some dirty locker room?"

"It's not a locker room. It's our strategy room." Was he really choosing *now* to be noble? I folded my arms across my chest.

He smirked at me. "You know what I mean." He placed a kiss atop my forehead, but it lacked the hunger he previously displayed.

An unexpected whimper escaped me. "No, this isn't how I pictured it, but the *where* isn't what matters Max. It's the *whom*. And as long as I'm with you it doesn't matter to me where we are."

"I know, but I just feel like you deserve better than this. You deserve something special."

I had to give it to the guy for wanting to be a gentleman and chivalrous, but we were living in a dang demon apocalypse. How special could anything be?

"Max, look at the world we're living in!" I pulled myself off the table and onto the nearest seat. "We're alive, we have food and water, and for the time being we're safe. This is about as special as it's going to get."

In one quick movement Max snatched me from my seat and had me wrapped in his arms. "No, Abs. Someday things will be better than this. You'll see."

I didn't want to argue with him on that one. He sounded hopeful, and hope was definitely something in short supply. I buried my head into the crook of his shoulder and let myself be carried out of the room. By the time we made it to the hallway, sleep had already clamped massive weights onto my eyelids. I wrapped my arms around Max's neck and allowed my body the rest it so desperately needed.

11

"Abby!" A whining voice was tickling the edge of my senses, but I refused to let go of the thick blanket of sleep that still cloaked me. My arm instinctively swatted at the pesky sound, but whatever it was swatted back.

"Abby, wake up!" The voice hissed urgently at me.

"Why?" I groaned pulling the covers tightly over my head. I slept like crap and felt like it too.

My visitor, whoever it was, wasn't going anywhere. They planted themselves heavily at the foot of the bed, the weight jostling me further out of my slumber. I could hear heavy breathing. Was the intruder getting pissed off that I wouldn't wake up? After everything I'd been through didn't they think I deserved a little sleep? It wasn't too much to ask as far as I was concerned.

I was about to resign myself to give in, forfeiting the precious sleep I so urgently fought for, when I heard my visitor whimper. It was a pitiful sound, and it cut straight through me with more power than any alarm clock could. Someone was in pain and it went against every fiber of my being, and my genetic structure not to bolt out of bed and help them.

"What's wrong? Is everything okay?" I pulled myself up to a sitting position yanking the blanket off me before even recognizing who was sitting on my bed. But whom I found, was not whom I was expecting.

"Wade?"

Her face was buried in a cocoon made by her hands, and she wobbled a nod at me in response. Only one thought came to mind that could possibly have gotten her so upset. Eleanor must have died.

I scooted toward her and pulled her against me. Losing someone never got easier. Even though that had become the norm in our new world of horrors, I would never get used to it. I could never steel my nerves against that pain. Nothing I could say would comfort Wade, but I tried my damned hardest anyway. Of all the people in the compound she could have gone to she chose me. Not the people she was living with at the museum, but me.

"Wade..." the words caught in my throat while I stroked her hair. Maybe it was best I didn't say anything right now. She probably couldn't even hear me through all her weeping. Instead, I just let her cry; her tears soaking my shirt and dripping down to my bare thighs.

Time passed slowly or quickly I wasn't quite sure. It was just the two of us in the room. Her bawling slowly shifted into sniffles and then to silence. I kept rocking her slowly certain that she must have cried herself to sleep, but every once in a while a tiny sigh would escape her and I'd start rocking her again.

I felt deeply sorry for Wade, not just because she'd lost someone, but because she was trying so hard to be such a strong girl. Or at least, she used to want to be, but the cruel reality of our lives had broken her. I couldn't help but wonder if I would someday fall apart too. No one could stay strong forever, could they?

The bedroom door bumping against the wall startled me out of my trance, but Wade didn't even stir in the slightest. Carter's frazzled expression greeted me when I looked up at him. His eyes flicked to Wade and then back to me, and he sighed with relief.

"I've been looking everywhere for her," he said squatting down beside the bed.

"She'll be okay. She just needs time," I answered for her continuing to rub her back.

Carter shook his head in disbelief. "I don't know." He pushed his glasses up with his finger only to have them fall down again. My brother always had an air of stress about him, but the way he kept clenching his jaw made me think that the level had risen substantially.

What made him so upset? Was he still pissed at me? I was hoping we were past that.

"What's up?" I kept my voice as low as I could. It was obvious now that Wade *did* cry herself to sleep. Carter eyed Wade's motionless body nervously. "She's asleep. What's going on Carter? You're starting to freak me out."

"The old lady..."

"Yeah Eleanor," I finished for him. His skin started to pale, which only confused me. Why was he so upset about her death? I mean, as far as I knew, he'd never even spoken to her. Sure, it was sad when anyone died, but he looked like...

well he looked like he was either going to start weeping uncontrollably like Wade did, or throw up. I wasn't sure which.

"Out with it Carter." He stopped squatting, and fell onto his butt on the floor.

"Something's happened to her."

"Carter," I said his name flatly like a parent reprimanding a child, and he shook his head at me holding up his hand as if to shut me up.

"No. You don't understand."

What was there to understand? People die. No one could escape it. If either of us should have been upset about Eleanor's death it would have been me, not him. I was the one who promised to make everything okay. I wanted to scream at the top of my lungs, and kick a few things. And *really* hard. But I couldn't do that. I needed to stay strong for Wade. If I lost my cool, it would only make her feel worse.

"What don't I understand? Eleanor's dead. We should be strong for the people who cared about her and not... not acting like that," I said as I waved my free hand at him. He looked like he had just run over someone's dog.

"What?" Wade was suddenly awake as if the simple mention of Eleanor's name broke through the walls of sleep.

"Nothing go back to sleep." I tried to push her onto the bed behind me, but she pulled away.

"She died?" She looked at Carter and fell to her knees before him.

What the hell was going on?

Carter locked eyes with me and disappointment was written all over his face. "No Wade. Eleanor didn't die."

"But Abby said..."

"Abby doesn't know what she's talking about. Why don't you go splash some water on your face while I have a little chat with my sister?"

Wade nodded and followed his finger when he pointed to the bathroom. When she was out of earshot, I darted from the bed to face my big brother head-on.

"What the hell is going on Carter?" I asked through clenched teeth.

He placed his palms on my shoulder and pressed me down onto the bed. I winced as the pressure grazed my wound causing me to gasp.

"Sorry," Carter apologized taking a seat on the bed beside me. "I keep forgetting."

"Mhm," I half accepted his apology and gently rubbed my shoulder. Not only did it hurt, but every time I felt it again it seemed to set off something inside me. Some untapped well of rage that remained dormant and out of reach otherwise.

I was about to start spewing everything I could at my brother. Everything he'd done in the past few weeks that pissed me off, but when his arm wrapped around me my anger instantly vanished.

"We have a problem."

My heart dropped and nausea threatened to start an attack on the contents of my stomach.

"What kind of problem?" I asked not sure if I really wanted to know the answer.

"That, I don't know. You should probably come see for yourself."

"She's infected," Wade said with severe loathing and disgust as she wiped a towel across her face.

"Who's infected?" As soon as I said it I knew who they were talking about. "Eleanor...?" her name hung onto my lips. They both nodded. The image of the black veins creeping across her skin flashed violently in my mind's eye. If my life were a horror movie that part would have definitely made me jump out of my seat.

"Well, is she sick? Do we have to leave for the hospital now? What are we doing?" I didn't see the problem. As far as I was concerned, our mission remained the same.

"I don't know Abby," he said standing up.

My brother always seemed to have an answer for everything. The fact that for once he didn't really freaked me out.

"I'm still going to the hospital. We're still going!" I shot a challenging look in his direction daring him to oppose me. He didn't. I softened my expression before turning to Wade. I wanted her to know that I wouldn't give up. I still intended to keep my promise. But she wouldn't look at me. Instead, her eyes were fastened to a spot on the floor.

"What aren't you telling me?" There was obviously an elephant in the room, and I didn't like it.

Carter took a deep breath. "That fang is doing something to her," he said with finality, but that didn't explain anything.

"Yeah, I've seen it. It's turning her skin black. As soon as we get it out the infection can heal. That's why I've been so adamant about getting to the hospital."

"It's more than that. It's spreading," Carter added before looking at Wade. Something in the way he gazed at her a moment longer than necessary hinted there was something between the two. But I couldn't wonder about that right now. No, right now I needed to understand what was happening to Eleanor.

I could feel that tingling sensation start to wiggle its way through me, but I shelved it. I knew what it was. It was fear and doubt, and I wouldn't let it get under my skin like some burrowing insect.

"Then let's just take the fang out!" It sounded like the simplest and most logical solution to me.

"They can't!" Wade spoke up suddenly. She looked surprised by the tone of her voice. I knew she was stronger than she realized. One day she will know that she can face anything. Maybe that day was today. Wow, I was starting to sound like Max.

"Charlie has tried, but the thing has... it's imbedded in her." He had a pained look on his face. It told me that he actually witnessed Charlie trying to remove the fang. It must have been a horrific sight. I was glad I wasn't there. Just trying to clean her wounds was enough to make my stomach churn.

"Okay, so I'll go the hospital now and get what Charlie needs." The solution still seemed so simple. Charlie needed medical equipment. So we go to hospital to get medical equipment. Then Charlie heals Eleanor. The end. Why couldn't it be that easy?

I ran over to my footlocker to start dressing for the task ahead of me. "I can be ready in fifteen minutes!" I shouted back at them as I pulled on a clean shirt. "Tell Remie and Max to be ready and meet me in the hangar. Okay?"

When no one answered, I turned to find them both staring gloomily at me. "What?" I pulled the tank-top over my head and walked over to them. Wade was standing closer to Carter than before.

"There's more," she said like a guilty teenager admitting to her parents of her previous night's misdoings.

"Okay..." I wanted to scream for them to just come out with it. I hated when people hedged information and didn't just give me the truth straight on. I could take it! All the what-ifs in my head were driving me crazy.

"She's..." Wade tried to speak, but lost her voice. She looked at Carter for help and he latched onto her hand. I had to bite my lip to keep my chin from dropping to the floor. They liked each other! It was blatantly obvious. If it weren't for the ominous report they'd just given me I'd be jumping for joy! Carter needed a strong woman in his life, and I had the sneaking suspicion that

Wade was a very strong woman underneath her sad persona.

"She's not herself," he said sounding stronger than before.

"What do you mean?" The ominous feeling was replaced by confusion.

Carter pushed up his glasses with his index finger. "God, how do I put this? I think she's infected, Abby."

"Yeah... you said that already. Get to the point. Whatever you're afraid to tell me just come out with it. I can take it." Were they scared I would freak out? Or was it really that hard for them to say?

"I... I... I think she's turning into a demon!" Wade screamed. My eyes went wide, and this time my chin *did* drop to the floor. Tears streamed down Wade's face and her hand flew to her mouth as she ran to the bathroom. The sounds of her retching filled the room.

I felt my knees buckle, but I kept myself firmly planted to the floor. *This* truth was a lot worse than I was expecting. In fact, I doubted even my mind could have tortured me with this kind of what-if.

"You can't be serious? Are you sure?" I didn't want to believe it was true.

"I think so. I can't fathom any other explanation Abby." Carter seemed to be at his wits end. He yanked out the demon journal from his back pocket and starting slapping it against his palm like the answers would somehow fall out.

"I need to see her." I didn't want to believe what they were saying was true. It was just too horrible. Could fate really be so cruel? I'd been seriously injured by a demon so why didn't I get infected? Or maybe I did? Maybe that's why my wound never fully healed. The dreadful tsunami of what-ifs came tumbling down on top of me leaving my emotions staggering in its wake.

"I don't think that's such a good idea." Carter put his hand on my arm, but I slapped it away.

"I'm going to see her." Before he could say anything more I was out of the room storming down the hallway barely resisting the urge to expel the contents of my stomach. I didn't even realize I was crying until my eyes started burning like fireballs.

Turning down the hallway of our sick room felt like walking smack into a wall of fear. There was something in the air. It was a thick cloud of dread that saturated everything. Residents of the hallway were poking their heads out of their rooms, their anxiety visible in their features. I pulled myself together, and told them everything was okay. They didn't believe me; hell, I didn't believe me, but they shut the doors all the same which was just as well. Whatever was happening to Eleanor... the fewer people who saw it the better. The fewer people to panic about the situation the better as well. The last thing we needed were people freaking out with worry. There was enough of that going around already.

Apparently, that was what Matthew had done. He was sitting on the floor, his head tilted against the wall drenched in perspiration. Lauren, our appointed nurse, was wrapping his hand in a bandage. Several large holes in the wall revealed the evidence of his reaction to Eleanor's condition. I had no doubt that was what made everyone peer cautiously from their doors down the hallway. I hadn't seen Matthew since leaving the museum, and those few days didn't do anything to improve my feelings toward him. I clenched my fists as I approached, fighting the urge to punch his face rather than the wall like he chose to do. He'd been nothing but a complete jerk since we'd met him. I knew he blamed us for what happened. I didn't despise him for that because I already shouldered the blame for what happened too; but it was the way he handled the situation that pissed me off.

Seeing Max step out of the sick room immediately clamped my mouth shut. I was ready to lay it out on Matthew. He needed to get his anger under control or we were going to have serious future problems. If he needed to hit something he could go outside and hit himself for all I cared, but I wasn't about to let him cause a scene with frightened onlookers. There were over a dozen other survivors in our compound, not counting everyone we brought from the museum, and I'd be damned if I let him scare them unnecessarily.

I was ready to ask Max to step back inside and check on Eleanor for me, anything to get him to leave me alone with Matthew for just a few minutes. I desperately wanted to give him a piece of my mind.

Lauren stood up and headed back into the room leaving the three of us alone in the hallway. I couldn't tear my eyes away from Matthew. If I could have possessed any super powers right then I would have chosen Cyclops' optic blast, and burned a hole right through the smug expression on Matthew's face.

Being the smartass that he was, he turned to face my venomous countenance head on. As much as I knew he wanted me to, I didn't turn away. I stared back at him without blinking using my expression to speak the volumes in my mind.

He shifted, allowing a stream of light from the window in the exterior door to cast a glow across his face. Dried blood was crusted under his nose and the left side of his face was battered, and bruised. Maybe the wall was a tougher opponent than he expected? I had to bite my lip to keep from smiling.

I turned to Max to ask what happened and he shook his head. My eyes darted to his hands and I saw that his knuckles were raw and slightly bloodied. It appeared they'd gotten into a fight. I expelled a heavy breath and closed the gap between us. With that, Matthew headed out the door, shoving it so hard it slammed shut loudly behind him.

"Don't." Max pressed a finger against my lips when I opened my mouth to speak. "I took care of it."

He released his finger and I folded my arms across my chest. "Okay." That might suffice for now, but he better tell me later. One way or another, I was going to find out what happened. For now, however, I needed to know more about Eleanor. "What's going on with Eleanor?"

Max shook his head, the muscle in his jaw flexing as he clenched his teeth. "It's not good Abs."

"Yeah, so I gathered. Carter said he thinks she's turning into a demon."

"I don't know what's happening to her, but it looks that way," he said starting to pace.

"I want to see her." I headed for the door and placed my hand on the doorknob as Max pulled me away.

"Trust me. You don't." There was fear in his eyes.

"I need to. I need to tell her I'm not giving up." I held his gaze trying to drain the fear from his. "I'm still going to the hospital. I don't care how things look in there," I pointed toward the sick room. "I won't give up on her. I promised. I can't break that promise." I realized then that the promise I made wasn't just to Wade, but to myself as well. I wasn't willing to accept defeat. No matter what Eleanor's condition was I refused to believe there was no hope left for her.

I don't know what I was expecting when I entered the room, but complete silence definitely surprised me and I found it oddly jarring. My wild imagination had me prepared for some grotesque scene like from the movie "The Fly." But instead, I entered an eerie hush that froze every hair on my body causing them to stand at attention.

Charlie was sitting in a chair about two feet from the edge of Eleanor's bed. He was just staring at her; studying her like a motionless statue. Not even our entrance caused him to stir in the slightest. Lauren, however, seemed grateful at our arrival which was her cue to leave. She practically tripped over herself trying to get out the door quickly.

I smiled politely at her as she rushed out, but she avoided my gaze. I couldn't blame her really. If I allowed myself to feel how afraid I really was I'd never have made it through the door to begin with.

With a few more steps, I was far enough into the room to see past the sheets that hung around her bed for privacy. I did the best I could to steel my nerves and not falter. I didn't want to show any fear when I saw Eleanor, or any hesitation. The best we could do for her right now was to show her we still had hope. I wanted to assure her that everything would be okay, and I wouldn't ever give up. For now, that was the only treatment we had for her.

Max's fingers touched the small of my back as I closed the distance between Eleanor and me. Just that slight touch from him gave me the courage I needed. With him standing beside me I knew I could be as strong as I wanted to be. And I needed every bit of it for Eleanor.

Tears spilled from my eyes when I saw her. But not for the reason I anticipated. For someone who was supposed to be turning into a demon, she didn't look as bad as I expected. I mean... she still looked human, so to me that was a good sign. Her skin though, was a different story. The black veins had infiltrated the entire left side of her body. They jutted this way, and that like black lightning bolts branded into her flesh. They stretched across her face, just barely grazing her cheek.

Sure, it was jarring to say the least, but there was no metamorphosis happening that I could see.

Max, obviously not wanting to come closer, chose to stand next to Charlie while I took a seat beside Eleanor. She was sitting up, but her eyes were closed. Her nose sniffed the air as I approached, and her eyes snapped open. I couldn't muffle the small gasp that escaped me, but I tried to hide it by smiling back at her.

They still looked like her eyes, just a little cloudy, like someone who had just woken up from a drug-induced sleep.

"Hi, Eleanor." I reached for her hand, but pulled back and rested my fingers on the edge of the bed instead. Something inside me ordered me to run away, and every nerve inside me warned, "Danger!" but I wouldn't listen.

She sniffed at the air again, and cocked her head to a neck-cracking angle before flicking her eyes to Max. He shifted nervously taking a step back with a worried expression. He could fight giant spider demons fearlessly, but when it came to little, old Eleanor...

"How are you feeling?" I was trying my best to remain calm and casual, but there was something off about her. Nothing she'd done so far told me that she was turning into a demon, but she was most definitely not herself anymore.

"Abby," she said my name in a voice not her own; almost robotic, like a person gets after a laryngectomy. Except it was somehow multiplied.

It wasn't just one voice, but many mixed together all speaking in synchronization.

Her eyes met mine and there was a flash of recognition, a brief moment of Eleanor coming fully through the haze.

"Yes, Eleanor, it's me. We're going to make you all better. I promise. Okay?"

I looked to Max and Charlie for encouragement. I wanted them join me and tell her that everything would be okay. If she knew we all felt the same maybe she'd be able to hold on that much longer. But they didn't say anything. Charlie just sat there like he was lost in thought and Max... well, I'd never seen him look so uncomfortable in all my life.

I turned back to find Eleanor smiling at me, but it didn't ease my nerves. She didn't seem to have the foggiest idea what I was talking about.

"I feel just fine, dear. Where's Wade?"

I was almost relieved that she asked for Wade. It had to mean that all hope wasn't lost. Right? She had to have some of the old Eleanor about her still.

"She just went to get some rest, but she'll be back later."

She nodded then lay her head back onto her pillow, closing her eyes. I allowed my gaze to travel her body again, surveying the extent of the damage. It appeared to be consuming her body at an alarming rate. We didn't have much time.

"I'll be back soon, Eleanor. I'm going to make sure you get everything you need." I stood up, still grasping the side of her bed when she latched onto my hand with a vise-like grip. Her eyes remained closed as her fingers constricted. There was more power behind her grasp than there should have been much more than anyone her age, or someone in her condition could have managed.

I tried to pull away, but it was like trying to extricate my hand from dried cement. Charlie darted up and yelled for Eleanor to stop. His voice boomed, and vibrated my eardrums. Max ran to my side, momentarily forgetting his fear of Eleanor, and began tugging on my arm.

"She won't let go!" Fear riveted me as tightly as her grip. The authority I had over my panic was immediately shattered giving it full rein to terrorize every cell in my body. I had to fight back, I couldn't let it win. She was only holding my hand down. Granted, she seemed to have the strength of about ten men, but she wasn't exactly hurting me... much. I started chanting to myself inside my mind, *she's not a demon, she's not a demon.*

"Danger in the west. The light is bad," she said and her eyes ripped open. Her voice was completely devoid of any resemblance to what it used to be. Instead, it sounded like a thousand insect-like noises all at once. A constant humming, like static electricity remained in the air. If someone had recorded the sounds of every insect on the face of the earth, and compiled them into one tape, that was what it sounded like.

God, if the world ever returned to normal I would never watch another episode of Animal Planet ever again.

I wanted to tear my gaze from her, but I couldn't. Her stare was penetrating, boring into my soul. Neither the paralyzing fear, nor the horrifying truth of what was happening to Eleanor could break our eye contact. The one thing, the one tiny, silent thing that drew my attention away from her moved only a mere inch. Had I not been looking at her, I may have never noticed it. The vein that had previously stopped spreading on the bridge of her cheek now crept further, reaching just a hair's breadth away from her eye. Then it spilled into her eye like ink being poured into a bottle.

I couldn't hold back any longer and began to panic, my internal chanting lost in the hum of her voice... or rather, voices. I tugged on my arm, certain I was going to rip it off, but no longer caring since I could not tolerate being beside her bed any longer. Charlie seemed pretty handy in the medical field, perhaps he could sew it back on for me. No, that was crazy, but apparently so was Eleanor and I wanted to get away from her A.S.A.P.

Something about the inhuman pitch of her voice made me feel like a million bugs were crawling across my skin. The sensation of countless insect legs tickling my flesh and wiggling through all the tiny hairs on my body tortured my mind. The horror of it soon became etched into my brain. I knew I was tough, and that I should be strong, but the touch of any demon was my kryptonite. I couldn't deny the truth any longer; Eleanor wasn't one hundred percent human anymore.

I looked at Max as he worked on prying Eleanor's fingers loose. With any normal person their fingers would have been broken by now. Max would have cracked their knuckles like measly toothpicks. Eleanor didn't budge. Charlie had gone so far as to shake her, but I could see the fear in his face. Just touching her was almost more than he could stand. Her voice evidently had the same effect on everyone.

My breath was catching in my throat and I thought for sure I was on the verge of hyperventilating. Dizziness rocked my brain and clouded my vision. But just as quickly as she clamped her death grip onto me, she swiftly released me.

"Is she sleeping?" Max asked cradling my arm and pulling me toward him as if expecting Eleanor to bounce up like a jack rabbit.

"She appears to be," Charlie said calmly. His nerves seemed to have settled. How he was able to do that so quickly I didn't know, but I envied it.

We backed out of the room letting Eleanor or whatever she had become get some rest. Max retreated farther away choosing to lay his forehead against the small framed window in the exterior double-doors. I knew him well and I understood the emotions that were no doubt raging inside him. It was Charlie though that had me dumbfounded.

"This isn't the first time she's done that. Is it?"

He looked up with pain in his eyes. "No kid, it's not."

I held back the series of curse words I wanted to spew. I hated it when people didn't give me the whole truth of what was going on. Maybe if I were warned beforehand, I wouldn't have been scared to death when "Demon Eleanor" decided to come out and play. I supposed maybe they had tried, but I just wouldn't listen.

Carter could have told me in the room, "Hey, sis, I know I told you we thought Eleanor is turning into a demon, but she's almost acting like she's possessed by the devil, and speaks like the mother of all insects. Just thought you should know." Okay, maybe not those words exactly, but some kind of caution was warranted. Hell not just for me, but for anyone that entered that room. No wonder Lauren ran at her first opportunity.

"How many times?" I demanded planting my hands on my hips.

"Several." Charlie looked defeated, which tugged at my heart. I was grateful he came, but now I kinda felt bad for him. He was perfectly safe back at his home, but since coming here it appeared we'd invited him into our little shop of horrors.

"You should get some rest. I'll keep an eye on her." I laid my hand on his shoulder, which startled him. Apparently, his nerves weren't as much under control as I assumed.

"No, no, no. I won't let you kids stay alone with her. I'm fine. I've gone days without sleep. I just need some caffeine." He waved me off and reached for the door handle, but I intervened.

"You need sleep," I said challenging him to say no again. I wasn't going to allow it.

"I'll keep my distance from her, don't worry."

He opened his mouth to protest, but I cut him off. "You aren't going to be any good to us when we get the supplies if you're half asleep. Now rest."

He nodded in agreement then turned to head down the hallway. He paused after making it only a few steps. "You're still going to the hospital then?" his voice was almost a whisper.

"Yes," I said with finality. I saw Max spin on his heel out of the corner of my eye obviously ready to argue with me. "There is still a part of Eleanor in there." I pointed beyond the door. "I believe we can still save her, and I won't give up. Not until we've done everything we can." I crossed my arms over my chest.

Charlie didn't have any response to that, and continued down the hallway. I wasn't sure if he agreed with me or not, but at least I stood up for what I believed was right. At least I was keeping my promise even though I was more horrified than I could let on.

"You know you're almost as crazy as Eleanor, right?" Max said sounding half annoyed and half worried.

"She's not crazy. She's infected." I frowned at him for being so insensitive. The root of this whole crazy mess was our fault.

He reached out to me holding me at arm's length and looked me squarely in the eyes without blinking. "She's dangerous Abby." I turned my gaze from him not willing to admit he was probably right. He sighed in exasperation. "Let me see your arm."

I handed him the appendage in question too busy twirling thoughts in my head to realize it was actually throbbing until Max squeezed a sensitive spot and I yelped.

"What the heck?" I pulled my arm away and inspected it. My skin was darkening in a ring around my arm. I didn't bruise easily, so seeing it there was a bit of a shock.

"How bad does it hurt?" Max asked pulling my arm toward him again.

"It's just fine as long as you don't go poking at it," I grumbled at him.

"What happened?" Carter asked rounding the corner. I prepared to defend my decision. Once my brother heard what happened he'd be even more insistent that I not go to the hospital, but seeing his demon journal gave me an idea.

"Let me see that thing." I tried to snatch at his journal, but he pulled it away.

"Why?"

I rolled my eyes at him. "What do you have in there about spider demons?"

"Why?" he asked again, but this time he was fiddling with the pages. I knew I could reel him in. The wheels in his brain were turning, and that's just what I wanted. If I could keep him focused on the idea that there was something incredibly valuable to learn about this situation then maybe I could keep him distracted long enough to complete the trip to the hospital and back. Heck, maybe I could even persuade him to get fully on board.

"Yeah, why?" Taya piped in from behind Carter. I didn't know she was there. I smiled at her and she returned it, but still looked confused.

"I think there's more going on than just her turning into a demon," I said. I pulled that one right out of my you-know-what not knowing what else to say. I needed something that would hook my brother like a trout.

It apparently worked.

Everyone's mouths dropped to the floor, and Carter's eyes grew wide. Even his wonky eye abandoned its usual sag and stretched to its limits.

"Like what do you mean?" Carter was already flipping through his pages frantic for information even though we didn't have a clue what we were looking for.

What did I mean? I didn't know what I meant. I was hoping he would just run with it, but now he wanted me to give him more theories? I was terrible at that kind of thing. I chewed my lip, trying to think of where I was going with this. I honestly believed now that Eleanor was indeed turning, but if I told him that I knew he'd stop searching for clues. And I needed him to be focused entirely on his journal.

"Yeah Abs like what?" Max chimed in. The expression on his face revealed that he was onto me. He knew I was scamming my brother, but he didn't say anything. The corner of his lip pulled up into a slight smile.

He was enjoying watching me squirm! That little twerp!

"Let's talk somewhere else," I said trying not only to buy time, but also to pursue this conversation elsewhere. I was either going to get away with my little ploy, or Carter would eventually figure it out and a screaming match would surely ensue. The latter didn't need to happen here these people had had enough disturbances already.

"So, what happened between you and Matthew?" I asked Max changing the subject, and trying to make him squirm a little too.

"Something happened between you and Matthew?" Taya chimed in curiously. "Did you guys get into a fight?"

Good ol' Taya. She hit the nail right on the head. I had to hold my breath to keep from laughing.

"Something like that yeah," Max answered evasively.

"How can you be in *something like* a fight? Did you, or didn't you?" Taya peppered him with her questions, and I was loving every minute of it. Max kept avoiding answering as I knew he would, but Taya was relentless as I knew she would be. Carter had his nose buried in his journal as we walked. Everyone was finally distracted enough for me to think of what the heck to tell my brother.

I led our small group to the strategy room. Carter nearly tripped over a chair trying to find a seat without taking his eyes from his journal. I grabbed a chair at the same table opposite him propping my head up on my hands. I was never very creative in the story department, and it was giving me a headache, but I thought I had something interesting enough.

"Well, then what happened to your hand? Did you forget that, too?" Taya was still nagging Max as they entered and sat down. She took a seat beside me and bumped me with her shoulder in greeting. When Max sat next to Carter she stuck her tongue out at him.

"So, what's going on?" Taya directed her barrage of questions onto me.

I pulled my head from my hands and laced my fingers together on top of the table. "Carter," his head snapped up giving me his undivided attention. "You told me that you thought Eleanor was turning into a demon."

"Yeahhhh," he dragged out the word waiting for me to continue.

"What notes do you have about our night at the museum?" he started looking through the pages for the information I requested.

Max sat up, his eyebrows drawing down into a scowl. "Where are you going with this?" he asked worried.

"Just hear me out," I said the wheels in my mind slowly turning. Suddenly, my thoughts didn't sound like some ridiculous story. The random pieces were fitting together in my head, but I needed to say them out loud to confirm they actually made sense. Or, at least, offered the tiniest ounce of possibility.

"Not much, no one feels like talking much about it yet," Carter said disappointed.

I nodded. That was a very difficult night. It wasn't surprising that no one dared to relive it by retelling their version to Carter for the sake of updating the notes in his demon journal.

"They were acting differently than we'd ever seen them act. Actually, differently than we've ever seen any of the demons behave before," I said trying to describe what was foremost in my head

"How were they acting?" Taya asked softly placing her hand gently on mine.

Flashes of the spider demons on the mountainside ran through my mind like a horror movie reel. The way they moved in unison, and seemed like they were protecting their young, how they swarmed us and sent "soldier spiders" to remove the threat.

"They were acting like... like organized insects," I finally said shaking the images from my mind and squeezing Taya's hand in comfort.

"Huh?" Max and Carter both asked in unison.

"Abby they're demons," Carter corrected me sounding as though I had been on the moon for the past several months.

"I know that, but that doesn't mean they can't share the same characteristics as other creatures on this planet. Does it? Don't you remember your theory? That they might work like an ant colony or something?"

"You think she can hear what they're saying?" Taya asked silencing us all.

"Holy crap," Carter gasped.

Hearing it out loud turned my world into a spiraling tunnel. Eleanor was changing, but that also meant she was able to link into the demon network. That was why she sounded so terrifying when she spoke; and why she sounded like a million insects rolled into one.

"That's what all those voices were huh?" Taya asked in a small, scared tone. "There must be millions of spider demons."

"She spoke to you too?" I asked suddenly frantic. I could only imagine how terrified she must have been when it happened. I knew I was.

She nodded.

"What did she say?" Carter asked a pencil at the ready.

"She told me to stay out of the west. The dangerous spirit is in the light. Something like that."

"That's like what she said to me too."

"What do you think it means?" Taya directed the question toward Carter who was writing furiously in his book.

I risked a glance at Max expecting him to be upset with me, but instead his eyes were full of concern. Our situation was becoming more dire.

"I don't know what it means, but I'm going to find out." He stood up from his seat and headed out of the room.

"Where are you going?" Taya called after him.

"I'm going to have a talk with Eleanor."

Taya shuffled after him, leaving Max and me alone.

"Do you really believe all that?" he asked after moments of silence.

I shrugged. I didn't know what I believed anymore. "Do you?"

"I don't want to." He got up and moved to a seat closer to me. "We'll leave tomorrow."

I looked up at him hesitantly. Was he really still willing to go to the hospital? I was clinging onto hope. I desperately wanted to keep my promise, but at what cost? To save a demon?

"Hey," Max stole my attention by placing his hand on my cheek. "Don't give up. Remember, there is still a piece of Eleanor in there somewhere, right?"

"Right." I buried the torrent of emotions rolling inside me, locking them up once again. "So, tomorrow then?"

"Tomorrow."

I scooted my chair closer and allowed him to tuck me under his arm. I could spend forever listening to the sound of his heartbeat pounding against my ears. He stroked my fingers as they lay motionless on his thigh. His knuckles were raw and starting to scab over.

"What really happened?" I asked touching his wounds gently.

"We got into a fight."

Well, duh! "Why?" I questioned in a tone that ignored my frustration. I hated it when he hid things from me. Especially something so inane as a fight with Matthew. In fact, that was something I'd pay to see.

Mainly because I knew Max would beat him effortlessly, and frankly Matthew deserved it just for being a jerk.

Max breathed heavily ruffling the hairs on the top of my head. "He wanted to kill Eleanor."

"What!" I jumped out of his arms bumping my head into his chin.

"Ow." Max touched at his chin, while I rubbed the top my head. "Geez, you have a hard head."

"Don't change the subject. Matthew wanted to kill Eleanor? Why?"

He rubbed his palms on his jeans. "He said she wasn't Eleanor anymore. That keeping her alive was cruel and that killing her was the right thing to do."

"What a psycho!"

"Well..." Max shrugged clicking his tongue.

"You don't agree with him now, do you?" I asked somewhat appalled.

"Would you want to live through that Abs? Being trapped inside your own morphing body? Watching and feeling yourself turn but not being able to do anything about it?"

"No, but I wouldn't want you to kill me either!"

"I'm not saying I agree with him. I'm just saying I can see his point."

I couldn't believe what I was hearing. "So, if you're on team Matthew, then why did you two get into a fight?" I couldn't keep the bitchiness from my tone.

"'Cause at the time, I didn't agree with him."

"What changed then?"

"You did, Abs!" He shouted at me in annoyance and I pulled back. Max had never raised his voice at me like that before, and I didn't like it one bit. "Seeing her grab you like that, the fear in your eyes..."

I understood now. He was afraid of losing me. I couldn't be angry at him for that. "It's okay." I scooted back onto his lap and wrapped my arms around him.

"If she continues to change... she could really hurt someone. I won't let that happen Abby."

"And neither will I, but we still need to try and save her. If we don't, then how are we any better than the demons?"

12

Minutes passed, but it could very well have been hours. My stomach growled loudly, shaking us both from our silence. We were sitting, utterly lost in our thoughts as we tried to navigate the prickly mess of a situation we were in. I hadn't come up with any more solutions, but I was still adamant that we go to the hospital. Regardless of whether or not removing the fang would save Eleanor, relocating our operation to the hospital was still the best option for everyone.

"Let's get you some food," Max said standing up.

"We should call a meeting," I told Max as I followed him out the room. We went through the exterior doors of the building we used for housing. The sun was on the verge of setting, but the heat of the day was still viciously clinging to life.

"Yeah, I was thinking the same thing. People are going to start panicking if we don't let them know what's going on."

"Should we tell them about Eleanor?" I looked up at him shielding my eyes from the sun.

Max stopped and thought on it a moment. "Probably not."

I nodded in agreement. As much as I hated lying, I knew he was right.

The assembly room was filled when we entered. A long line stretched out beside the serving table, while a group of women ladled out the night's meal. I wasn't sure what it was, but it smelled heavenly. A moment of silence derailed the hum of chatter as everyone looked at us. I shook off a temporary wave of nerves and got into line.

I snagged a plastic bowl from one of the stacks and cradled it against my stomach as I waited my turn. My stomach was screaming for food, but the line didn't bother me at all. It was surprisingly peaceful to be doing something as normal as waiting in line. It seemed like a long time since I'd had any bit of normal. Max and I chatted aimlessly about anything other than what was really on our minds, and even made bets on what was on tonight's menu. From the heavy aroma of spices, I guessed something spicy, but Max swore it was the usual "Mystery Mash."

I extended my bowl when it was my turn to be served. "What's on the menu tonight?" I asked hoping I could win the bet between Max and me.

"Vegetarian chili," the cook answered from behind the giant pot.

I recognized her voice and peered around the huge pot that stood as tall as I on top of the table. "Beverly?"

Beverly stepped out from behind the pot beaming at me. "Abby! I heard you were back sweetie. How are you feeling? Rumor said that you got hurt pretty bad."

I waved her off. "Nah, I'm fine."

"Give me your bowl." Beverly grabbed my bowl and filled it with another scoop. "You need to rebuild your strength."

"Thank you." My heart swelled with her kindness. Beverly was our resident mother hen. The miracles she worked in the kitchen were beyond everyone's expectations. It never ceased to amaze me how high a good meal could lift a person's spirit. It suddenly dawned on me how much Eleanor reminded me of her. I silently prayed that Eleanor would get better; I had no doubt that she and Beverly would become quick friends.

She wiped her hands on her apron and handed both of us a biscuit. "Ah, looks like you finally got that outdoor brick oven working Bev." Max winked at her popping the biscuit into his mouth.

"Oh, yes, thank goodness." She started ladling chili for the next people in line. "Go on, go eat."

I smiled appreciatively and headed toward the crowd of tables, looking for an open spot. I spied Carter, Taya and Wade across the room in the back corner. Taya saw us coming and waved us over with an excited expression.

"You know," Max mumbled with a mouthful of food. "If she keeps cooking this good, I don't think I'm ever going to leave this place."

I looked around at all the happy faces talking animatedly over their steaming bowls. "I think everyone here feels the same way. I'm glad

Drew was able to build her that oven." I recalled seeing him working on it the week before we left for the scout. It made me proud to know he finished what he started. We had a strong group of people here. Everyone helped out and did what they could to make the best of our situation.

"I talked to him this morning. He had just finished it and was already going on about building a larger one. He even said something about a wood-fire barbeque pit."

"Sounds like a lot of work." I didn't relish the idea of having to work out in the heat. I didn't know how Drew could stand it. But the idea of having more home-cooked meals made my mouth water.

"I think he likes to keep busy. Keeps his mind off other things."

"Now that I can understand," I said as I set my bowl on the table beside Taya.

"Understand what?" she asked.

"Nothing." I shoved a spoonful of chili in my mouth and it was piping hot. My mouth was burning, but it tasted so delicious I didn't care.

"Juice?" Taya asked seeing my eyes water.

I nodded.

She grabbed a chipped coffee cup from the center of the table and filled it with the watered down juice from the pitcher beside her. She handed me the glass and I gulped it down, enjoying how it cooled my tongue and filled my mouth with its sweetness.

"How'd it go?" I asked Carter swallowing my slightly cooled mouthful. He was scribbling in his journal, so I assumed he must have learned something of interest.

"Well, we've got two theories. Neither of which everyone agrees on," he replied setting down his pencil and spooning the remainder of his chili into his mouth.

"Let's hear 'em," Max joined in sounding more hopeful than I knew he felt; but at least he was trying.

"There's no doubt that she is... uh..." he looked nervously over to Wade and she nodded at him before he continued in a hushed tone, "changing. That we all agree on, correct?" We looked at each other and nodded quietly.

"Were you able to talk to her?" I asked curious as to what my brother could decipher from her crazed demon voice.

"She kept repeating several of the same phrases. The more I thought about it the more I could only come up with two possible conclusions."

"Okay, so what are they?'"

"I think your theory holds true. She *is* connected to a "demon network", but what we can't decide is the meaning behind her words. Either she's able to listen in on what the demons are communicating to each other, and trying to warn us; or..." he looked around to make sure no one was eavesdropping on our conversation, "or she's just repeating what she hears."

"I'm confused," Max said. "What do you mean 'she's just repeating what she hears'?"

"That confused me too," Taya added.

"She is either trying to warn us of a dangerous demon in the west, or she is repeating a warning the demons are spreading that there is a danger to *them* in the west," Wade explained answering for Carter.

No one spoke for a long moment while we processed the new information. I wasn't sure how to take it. On one hand, if there were anything the demons feared that could be very good for us. On the other hand, if it were some horrific demon that we hadn't encountered yet... well, that could be very, very bad.

"How are you going to tell which it is? I mean, whether she is warning us, or not?" I chewed more of my chili while everyone considered my question.

Carter started flipping through the pages in his journal and sighed heavily. "I have an idea, but..."

"But what?" I asked wiping my mouth with a napkin.

"We all think he is crazy," Taya interrupted.

"Not crazy," Wade corrected, "just farfetched."

I rolled my eyes. They obviously didn't know my brother like I did. His far-fetched ideas were usually spot-on, and if he thought it might be true it usually was. "Let's hear it." I gave my brother an encouraging smile.

"No one else seems to have heard it, but I swear I heard her... or one of her voices, whisper something about five spiritual points. That got me thinking." He held open his journal and handed it to me, pointing to a specific passage.

"Norah described her dream to visit the five most spiritual places in the U.S. before the apocalypse happened. The nearest is Sedona, Arizona. Despite my

protests, she says she plans to travel there after we make it to the base. She believes the mystical energies will protect her from the darkness of the demons. I can't say I trust in such things, but maybe it gives her comfort to think there is such a hope. I pray to whomever might be listening, if anyone still is, that she changes her mind."

I swallowed hard, remembering the exact conversation Carter was referring to. It brought to mind the memory of Norah, and a twinge of guilt bolted through me. We rescued her from the demon in John's basement only to lose her in the white sandy desert of New Mexico just before getting to the base. It took Taya weeks to get over her anger about all those whom we lost that night. It wasn't just Norah, but Judy and Savannah too. They didn't deserve what happened to them.

Max pulled the journal from my fingers and read through what Carter was indicating. "So, you think she's referring to one of these spiritual places that Norah mentioned?" he asked.

"Yeah. Sedona is one of the most spiritual places in America."

"I thought you didn't believe in stuff like that?" I asked him.

"I don't, but now it's the only thing that makes sense," he argued growing frustrated that no one was on his side.

"You knew her best." I looked at Wade. "What do *you* think she's trying to say?"

"Dude, she's not Eleanor anymore, so I wouldn't know." Her tone was surprisingly angry.

"I think we can worry about deciphering her later. I'm sure the crazy train will be here when you all get back."

"Back from where?" Taya asked.

"We're leaving tomorrow."

Wade challenged me by locking her eyes on mine as I answered. She was trying to appear strong about the situation, probably so I wouldn't be upset with her bitchiness. She was acting like she didn't care, but I knew that all she really cared about right now was whether or not we were still going to at least try to help Eleanor. I needed her to know we were, so I met her gaze without blinking.

"Cool. I'm going to go find Matthew." She jumped up from her seat leaving her empty bowl behind. I had opened my mouth to make a comment about Matthew, but telling her he recently voted Eleanor off the metaphorical island probably wouldn't go over very smoothly.

"She's weird," Taya commented absentmindedly.

"Nothing wrong with weird. It makes things interesting," Carter said doing a terrible job of acting like he was engrossed in the last lonely bean at the bottom of his bowl. I knew my brother, and it was obvious he wanted to run after Wade. No doubt the idea of her running off to Matthew drove him crazy.

"Whatever," Taya replied with disinterest and I gulped down some juice to keep from smiling. She vehemently denied still having feelings for my brother, but I knew there was still a tiny spot that held affection for him.

"Okay, so we'll head to the hospital tomorrow and you'll continue trying to figure out what Eleanor is saying?" Max asked Carter.

"I guess that sounds like the plan. Who is going with you?" I could tell Carter wasn't exactly thrilled with not going to the hospital, but the mystery of Eleanor was too hard for him to resist, and too important to be left unsolved.

"It'll be Max, Remie, Charlie, and probably Grant. Drew is busy building a barbeque for Beverly and I think he needs some time," I looked to confirmation from Max and he nodded in agreement. "I think it's best if we don't have a huge group. The less attention we draw to ourselves the better."

"Good idea," Carter agreed seemingly satisfied with my answer. "I'm going to try and get some sleep." He shoved his journal into his back pocket and grabbed Wade's and his dishes before leaving.

"Me too," Taya chimed in.

I jumped up after her before she'd gotten a few feet. "Hey, Taya, hold up."

"Yeah?"

"Can you do me a favor?" I asked pulling her away from a group of women who were loitering by the dirty dishes bin.

"Sure."

"Will you look after Eleanor tomorrow while we're out?" I knew Lauren could no doubt handle the job, but she was so frazzled the last time I saw her that I couldn't be sure she wouldn't go running from the room at the first chill.

"Yeah, I can do that. Is something wrong?"

"No, I just want someone whom I trust completely in there."

"Abby?" Taya planted her hands on her hips and looked at me with a scowl. "I'm glad you trust me, and of course I'll look after her, but you gotta tell me what's going on. It's written all over your face, so don't tell me it's nothing."

"I just don't want anyone knowing what's going on with her. There's no reason to get the whole compound panicking just yet."

"Good point. Don't worry about Eleanor. Just get whatever we need from the hospital and hurry back. Okay?"

"Okay." I smiled back at her, before another thought came to mind. "Taya!" I called out her name when she'd already made it across the room. "Take Drew with you."

She looked at me curiously; then nodded. *Better safe than sorry*, I thought. I wasn't only concerned with people finding out what was going on in the sick room, but I also didn't have time to worry about Taya's safety. Plus, who knew what Matthew was up to? He was a wild card, and wild cards never sat well with me. I didn't trust him, and wouldn't be surprised if tried something while we were gone.

****

I woke up for the first time in a long time without feeling like a zombie. Maybe it was the sound of Carter scribbling in his notebook that somehow lulled me to sleep, but whatever it was I was grateful. I actually arose before everyone else too, which never happened.

She'd never admit it, but I was certain it was the scent of hair gel that woke Taya up. I would swear on a stack of Bibles that no sooner did I pop open the bottle and squirt it into my hand when she suddenly snapped from dreamland.

"Why are you looking at me like that? Do I have slobber on my face?" she asked groggily, dragging her feet toward the sink.

I shrugged my shoulders unable to remove the smirk from my face. "Nothing."

"You nervous about today?" She sounded more alert after having splashed water onto her face.

"Nah," I lied.

"Well, I am." She twisted her long hair into a massive bun that made her small face look even smaller. "Don't get me wrong. I like Eleanor and I want her to get better, but... she gives me the heebie-jeebie's." Taya shook her body wildly like a ghost just walked through her.

I started laughing uncontrollably causing toothpaste to dribble down my chin. "You're crazy. The two of you should get along just fine," I said sarcastically.

"Hey! I'm not *that* crazy," she said feigning injury.

I left Taya in our washroom after promising to be safe and hurry back. The hallways were their usual noiseless passageways it being so early in the morning. I didn't see a single soul, which was fine with me. I enjoyed the quiet. In fact, I hardly ever got a moment to myself, so any opportunity I got was a treat. Plus, the fewer who knew we were heading past the fence line the better.

Ever since people began to arrive at the base after we turned the radio signal back on there was talk about what lay beyond the fence. Up until now, the warnings were enough to deter us from chancing a trip over the other side. But they also created an uneasy air of awe and dread. Knowing there was an unknown demon lingering somewhere so close to our sanctuary kept everyone constantly on edge. I knew crossing into there was dangerous, and if anyone found out they'd surely panic; but it had so much more potential to be a good thing. We could destroy whatever demons we found there, or pleasantly learn that they were already long since gone. I had to focus on those two possibilities. Having the hospital at our disposal would be very good for us, and I wanted to do nothing but concentrate all of my positive thinking on that. Like my father always said, *"If you want something good to happen; you need to believe it will happen."*

"Morning," Grant called out to me as we arrived at the entrance to the strategy room at the same time.

"Morning," I replied back with a smile. He held the door open and I stepped in. "How are you doing? I haven't seen you around."

"Yeah..." he scratched his head avoiding my gaze. "I needed some space." Grant headed to his locker and pulled out a backpack.

"I know what you mean, but I'm glad you're going with us." I pulled open my own locker and found my shotgun leaning inside; a full box of shells sitting beside it.

"Whoa, where'd these come from?" I pulled out the box and opened it; tracing my fingers along the tops.

Grant came up behind me. "Those are from me," he said looking almost embarrassed.

"Where did you get them?" I pulled my shotgun out of the locker glad to use it again.

Grant sat down next to me, bouncing his knee nervously. "I went past the fence." I froze. *Did he really just say what I thought he did?* "Don't look at me like that. I went alone, so the risk was mine to take." He put his hands up like that was going to stop my verbal assault.

"You could have gotten yourself killed Grant!" I said sounding like an angry parent, but I didn't care.

"We need ammo."

"We always need ammo. That doesn't mean you should go on a suicide mission to get it!" Sure, I would willingly risk my life crossing the fence into smoker demon territory, but never alone. That was the one rule I refused to break.

"I needed to do it Abby," he pleaded with me, his face turning red with emotion and the vein in his forehead pulsing.

"Why?" My anger had already dissipated. I couldn't really stay mad at him for what *could* have happened. He'd obviously survived his little secret excursion, *and* brought back ammo for us to boot.

"I don't know. I just felt like I needed to do something. Something that would make a difference." He stood up and walked back to his locker. The sound of him loading a gun broke the deafening silence of the room.

I didn't say anything. There was nothing to be said. I knew exactly how he felt. Nothing ever seemed to be enough. We got all the parts we needed for the generator, but we endangered the lives of everyone at the museum. We helped them escape, but not before Eleanor was critically injured. Then we promised them shelter and safety, while allowing a demon to develop under the very same roof! Now we were entering dangerous territory that could only end in one of two ways: either save a life or get ourselves killed. It was a never ending vicious circle, and the only thing that seemed to abate the chaos was continuing to try to do more.

Save more people, and kill more demons. That was the only way any of us could survive.

Remie walked in minutes later uncharacteristically chipper. He tossed a steaming hunk of bread at Grant and me. He had obviously made the rounds this morning and must have passed Beverly at her brick oven baking her loaves of bread for the day. I tore a chunk off with my teeth and savored its warm flavor. Bread never tasted so good. Charlie and Max followed in not long after.

We all got ready in silence except for the numerous questions as to where the ammo came from. Saving Grant the trouble, I waved everyone off and told them not to worry about it. We had much more pressing matters at stake. It seemed to work, and they went back to getting ready.

With my shotgun loaded and extra shells shoved tightly into a leather strap across my chest, I leaned onto the center table and surveyed the map again. I didn't really need to see it; I knew where I was going, but looking at it gave me some sense of order.

Fifteen minutes later, we were marching out of the building past our perimeter fence, and toward the unexplored barricade that housed a large region of the base. It was also the closest part of the barricade surrounding the hospital. Get in, get out; that was the plan.

A dirty sheet clung ominously to the wires of the fence flapping in the weak summer breeze. Black paint was smeared in bold letters; *KEEP OUT! Smoker Demons!* A strange feeling of anger boiled inside me at the sight of it. I tugged the knife out of the sheath on my thigh. After today, we'd either discover there were no more smoker demons, or we'd kill them all. Either way, I didn't want the sign hanging up any longer. I raised my knife and slid it down the center of the makeshift banner; ripping it apart in one solid stroke. No one said anything, and Grant tugged down one piece as I did the other, throwing them onto the ground.

I nodded at him in thanks.

Remie pulled out a pair of wire cutters and went to work on snipping enough of the fencing to allow us passage. After the last cut the fence rolled away and we crept through. I knew I was crazy, but the air felt different on the other side. My body tingled like it sensed I had just passed some magical barrier. Perhaps it was telling me I was where I shouldn't be, but I pressed on. Nothing was going to stop me, especially not my own body.

13

Loose sand twirled at our feet on the pavement as we silently made our way. If I didn't know better, I'd have guessed we were taking a stroll through a ghost town. An eerie sensation, along with the awareness in the back of my mind, said that something was watching me and it wouldn't go away. I sniffed the air as we walked out of nervous habit, but I didn't smell anything. At least that confirmed there were no demon hounds around, and there were definitely no demon birds. They tended to make themselves known whenever they were in the vicinity. Besides, they hadn't posed any problem since we started regularly supplying them with spider demon dinners.

Remie signaled us to stop along a building. I scurried over and pressed my back against it enjoying the brief moment of shade even though it didn't offer much relief in the way of cooling me.

"Ready?" Remie asked in a whisper. We nodded. There was no turning back now, not for any of us.

Remie dashed out and disappeared behind the corner, followed quickly by Grant, and then Max. Charlie took a step forward to go before me, but I slapped my arm across his chest shaking my head.

"You stay behind me," I ordered. He looked at my shotgun, and then back at my face before nodding. We all agreed that Charlie would hang back in case something happened. He was too important to us and we weren't willing to take any chances on his safety. Heck, I never would have agreed that he come along if not for his knowledge of the supplies we needed. It would have been all for nothing if we survived our excursion only to get the wrong surgical implements to save Eleanor.

I cursed myself for not checking on her before leaving. I took off around the corner before Charlie thought better of letting me take the lead. He wasn't very keen on the idea, but I tried to convince him of our logic.

The hospital stood prominently a half block down the street. Huge trees shadowed the entrance with their skeletal branches. I imagined that at one time it was probably quite beautiful. Something about the exquisite architecture of a huge brick building with white-framed windows, and lush landscaping was incredibly familiar to me. It seemed to sooth me. Of course, now the landscaping was dead, and the grass crunched beneath my feet like shattered glass.

Dozens of cars littered the lot, while several were parked in the grass, and a motorcycle leaned up against one of the trees. It was covered in a thick layer of dust, waiting for an owner who would probably never return. I wiped my index finger along it as I passed by. It was once a bright, cherry-red color. I'd always secretly wanted a motorcycle, even though the thought of riding one terrified me. Maybe that's why I wanted one so badly. They were scary, fast, and sexy too. The thought of Max riding it made my cheeks blush.

He caught me eyeing the bike and smiled before waving me toward him. "Nice bike, huh?" he asked as I squatted down next to him.

I nodded watching Grant and Remie pull apart the automatic doors to the hospital entrance. Once opened; they propped them in place by pulling a bench in front of each one, giving us a clear path to walk through.

I held my breath as we entered expecting to inhale a blast of rancid odors. Hospitals smelled bad to begin with, but add months of neglect, demons, and death and that's a recipe for a putridly noxious stench. I tried breathing through my mouth as long as I could, but gave up when I saw that no one else's face was covered. They were all men, so of course bad smells weren't quite as offensive to them as they were to me; but if they could handle it I supposed I could too.

Surprisingly, I wasn't gut-punched by the smell of death, as I expected. The hospital smelled dusty and old, much like I remember my grandparent's attic.

The sun was unable to penetrate through the thick layer of dust that clung to the windows making it darker than I would have liked. I wasn't scared of the dark, but I honestly didn't like it much.

Remie and Max flipped on their flashlights, so I quickened my pace to catch up and share their light. Papers skittered across the floor with the sudden gust of my movements, creating an unnerving rustle that echoed throughout the hospital lobby.

Grant branched off from our group and made it to the tall windows of the waiting room. Max directed his flashlight toward Grant, who grabbed a cloth from the ground, and wiped off the window. Dark dirt flaked off like ashes, allowing rays of sunlight to fill the space. Remie joined him, clearing off a few more windows bathing us in more natural light.

I scanned the walls looking for a directory, and spotted one across the room next to a set of elevators. Careful of my steps, I made my way toward it avoiding piles of clothes, abandoned wheelchairs, papers, and various other items littered there. I swore I saw a bed pan out of the corner of my eye, but I chose not to turn back and confirm it.

Charlie followed me toward the directory and ran his finger down the list of offices. *Pediatrics, Family Medicine, Radiology, and Pharmacy*, among several others. His finger stopped at Pharmacy. "We will need some antibiotics." He looked at the map and slid his finger to where it was located.

"Okay. Where else?" I wanted us to at least have some idea as to where we would be headed instead of wandering around aimlessly.

"There." He pointed to another area of the map. "General Surgery. We should be able to find everything else we need in there."

I traced my finger along the map from where we were standing to the Pharmacy, and then to General Surgery. The hospital was designed in an unusual shape, and it reminded me of the game Tetris. I never liked that game. I groaned, and decided to stick to main hallways; assuming that the least amount of turns we had to take the better. That meant we had to go straight down the end of the hallway, make a left through the first set of double doors, then follow those down make the last left, and then we'd be at the Pharmacy. After that, we'd follow the same hallway, but make our fourth right, go up the stairs to the third floor, and make our third left. I did my best to burn those directions into my memory before waving Max over. He, Remie and Grant were standing over a large pile of clothes, looking at it curiously.

"Know where we're going?" he asked as he approached the map on the wall and studied it.

"Yeah. Let's do it." Things were exceptionally quiet so far, and I wanted them to stay that way. No reason to make our presence known by loitering around for too long. We could worry about scoping the place out later.

Remie took the lead again as I followed behind whispering directions. Grant pulled up the rear, which made me feel a bit safer knowing he had my back. No offense to Charlie. As always, Max stayed by my side his pace matching mine step-by-step. I felt confident in our group. We were cohesive and stealthy.

The pharmacy looked like a tornado struck it, but considering the amount of pill bottles and boxes on the floor it was still amply stocked. Charlie called off a few different kinds of drugs for us to keep our eyes open for as we sorted through the mess. I found a few items that were not on the list, but stuffed them into the bag on Max's back anyway. It couldn't hurt to grab a little extra.

Remie ended up finding the antibiotics we needed, as well as some powerful painkillers that I'm sure Eleanor would be very grateful for in the end. Demon metamorphosis or not having a gigantic fang excised from your chest definitely wouldn't tickle.

We slowly made our way back into the hallway. Some bottles scattering at our feet which sounded deafening in the absolute silence of the hospital. We held our breaths before moving forward. It was hard for me to hear anything over the sounds of our breathing and the thumping of my heart. I was calm on the outside, but inside my instincts were screaming at me. They were telling me I was a careless moron and should immediately run to safety. Every sight, smell and sound associated with the hospital made my body resist any further voluntary movement, but we were on the home stretch now. All we had to do was get to the General Surgery room, and we would be home free.

As we got deeper into the hospital and away from windows, it became much darker. Max and Remie flipped their flashlights back on, but the light didn't do much to penetrate the thick darkness and heavy coating of dust particles that hung in the air like smoke. After seeing Grant pull the collar of his shirt up over his mouth and nose to filter the air, I followed suit. It seemed the further we got into the hospital the thicker the dust became, and the harder it was to breathe. If it weren't for the absence of flames I might have thought the building was on fire.

I was relieved to find that the stairwell wasn't what I was expecting. I feared an enclosed stairwell, and my claustrophobia threatened to shatter what meager control I was managing. Luckily for me, that wasn't the case. The stairs opened to the hallway, and were wide enough for several people to walk abreast. I wanted to run up and into the surgery room, happy to get this finally over with, but doing so could jinx everything.

Commanding my feet to obey me and resisting the urge to go stampeding up the stairway like a wildcat, I followed behind Remie woodenly. Those were the longest three flights of stairs I've ever climbed. The air was dense with smoke which seemed to increase at every step. By the time we made it to the top it was impossible to restrain the urge to cough. I succumbed to a fit of choking while tears streamed down my face.

We each struggled to control our bodies' violent reactions to inhaling the smoldering air, but even the cloths over the bottom halves of our faces proved mostly futile. Max patted my back hoping to knock some of the smoke that polluted my lungs, but to no avail. I disregarded his urgent pleas for me to go back and wait outside for them. We'd all made it this far, and I had no intention of heading back now.

With a thick tar lining our lungs, we pushed on. None of us could cease our coughing, but we tried to restrain our reflexes as much as possible to keep the noise down. I could feel the blood vessels filling in my eyes, and hot tears fell as my throat burned with every shallow breath. A sliver of sunlight sliced through the window frames of the third floor. I wanted nothing more than to smash the glass to allow fresh air to vanquish the smoke that assaulted us. Could this be what the signs were referring to? All this smoke? Did people stay away from the hospital simply from fear of choking to death? The sound of Remie and Charlie's wheezing coughs nearly answered that for me.

A particularly rough cough racked my chest and throat as we made our final turn down the hallway toward General Surgery. I placed my hand over my mouth to muffle the sound, until I felt a slimy wetness coating my fingers. Great, now I'm a snot monster too?

Max stopped as I wiped at my mouth and shone the light on my hands. What we illuminated made me wish I *was* just snotting all over myself. Black ooze dripped from my fingers like thick, murky blood.

"What the hell is that?" I said holding back a gag. I smeared my fingers on the wall to remove the offensive mucus.

"I don't know," Max said holding back a cough for only a second before it sprang out of him like a jack rabbit. Small droplets of black splattered the wall like freckles.

"We need to hurry up and get out of here," I said stating the obvious. He nodded his agreement through the dirty tracks of tears on his face, before turning to jog up to the rest of our group.

I followed close behind him trying to hold my breath for as long as I could. My logic was if I didn't breathe I wouldn't cough. It didn't work too well for me. I gasped for breath when I thought for sure my face was turning blue. I inhaled a mouthful of smoke only to cough it up instantly in a sticky, phlegm-like eruption.

I kept walking, not wanting to stop for fear of another fit of coughing. The sooner we got this done, the sooner I could be outside again breathing the wonderful, hot, clean desert air.

A tug on my arm pulled me through a doorway and into General Surgery.

We'd finally made it.

Charlie and Remie were violently tearing through drawers, cabinets and anything and everything that was lying around. They were in as much of a rush to get out of here as I was. There were only a couple items on Charlie's list that I could identify, so I set to work on my own, scouring the spacious room hoping to find what we'd come for.

Grant stood guard at a set of double doors at the far end of the room. He kept peering in through the small, inset windows like he was expecting something to come barreling through at any minute. His antsy movements were making me nervous. He was tapping his foot like he had to pee, and I wanted to shout at him to stop, but I didn't dare waste my breath and inhale more smoke.

Piles of dirt, and ash mounded as high as my knees like massive anthills were dispersed throughout the room. I dug through them, pulling out clothes and random objects that I only inspected long enough to discard into another pile of rejects that I'd already gone through.

Max joined me and we kicked up even more dirt, smoke and ash, but at this point we were so frantic to find what we needed and then get out I didn't think either of us noticed or cared. Whatever this smoke was doing to us, we weren't dying; or at least, I hoped we weren't. And as soon as we got some fresh air, we'd be fine. If we just toughed it out for a little while longer it would all be worth it.

My gaze landed on Max's face briefly and I saw tracks of black dripping from his nose and down his chin. I felt the same warm trickle spreading down my own face. I dragged my hand across my mouth when a dribble of black phlegm slid down my chin. It fell into the mound of dust and I pulled out what looked like a clipboard. Something sharp sliced my thumb and I withdrew with a sudden jerk, falling onto my backside.

"Ow!" I inspected my throbbing finger and found a ribbon of blood flowing purposefully done my hand. Crap!

"Are you okay?" Max grabbed my finger to see the wound.

"Don't touch it." I squirmed out of his grasp not wanting him to get his dirty fingers all over my fresh wound. Not that it wasn't already dirty. I didn't want to get an infection. And a small part of me was afraid of becoming like Eleanor. Who knew what kind of demon germs lay around everywhere? I was surprised the little, gremlin demon at the cabin hadn't already infected me, but maybe only certain demons were poisonous or infectious?

Max lifted up his shirt exposing the clean whiteness of his undershirt, and held it out to my finger. I nodded and waited as he tore off a strip before carefully wrapping it around my thumb trying not to touch the cloth if he could help it. He tied a tight knot at the tip, squeezing the inch of torn flesh together as firmly as he could. He topped it off with a soft kiss for good measure. I whimpered and bit my lip to keep from yelping. It probably needed stitches, but we didn't have the equipment for that. I'd heard somewhere that superglue worked, and we *did* have that. I made a mental note to have Charlie fix me up MacGyver-style when we got back.

"What's in there?" I asked myself after Max bandaged me up. Something sliced me pretty good, and I wanted to know what it was.

"Careful," Max warned poking the area with a broken piece of crutch. Something silver tumbled out of the pile and landed down by my knees.

"What is that?" he asked as I reached for it.

"I found the scalpel." I held up the surgical tool in triumphant glory, channeling my inner She-Ra.

"Great job, kid," Charlie beamed. His teeth were shockingly white against his ash-covered face. "That's the last of it then. Let's get the hell outta here!"

"Amen to that!" Grant agreed.

A thunderous snap assaulted my ears as it filled the room. My body froze, not just from fear but from something else. Anger. These demons were never going to give us a damn break, ever.

I answered the electric call of the mysterious smoker demon with a call of my own. The sound of loading a shell into the chamber of my shotgun. This was one human they were going to wish they never messed with.

This time, three rapid snaps sparked around the room leaving us all wide-eyed. The hair on my arms stood at attention. Max and I pressed our backs together to cover ourselves in all directions, while Remie shoved Charlie into a corner and stood guard before him. He and our medical supplies had become our precious cargo. Absolutely nothing could happen to them.

I nodded to Remie letting him know I was ready for whatever came our way. He held my gaze without blinking.

The air cracked harshly the next room over. All our eyes flicked to Grant as he peered through the windowed door into the next room.

"Nothing. I don't see anything," he said turning back as he used his forearm to wipe the murky discharge from his face. He managed to thoroughly smear it. The stuff was too sticky to get off without soap and water.

We took the opportunity of silence to shuffle out of the room. Remie led, with Charlie at his heels; the bag of supplies now strapped securely to his back. I still held the scalpel in my hand, but there wasn't time to stop and throw it in. Right now, we just needed to focus on getting out of this hell-hole alive.

We filed out into the hallway when another pop fractured the silence. But this time, we didn't just hear it. A swirling ball of smoke materialized at the end of the hallway in front of Remie and Charlie. In mere seconds, it disappeared and became a spiraling eddy, like a black hole was invisibly behind it.

Whatever these smoker demons were; they didn't want us to leave the hospital.

"Did you see what it was?" Max asked Remie in a whispered panic.

"It's just smoke," he replied without any hint of unease in his voice. How could he stay so calm? Even I was freaking out a bit, and I was known as the "Ice Queen." Well... only according to Carter.

"Screw this!" Grant shouted. "I ain't fighting these things in the dark." He stomped across the hallway, lifted his foot and kicked the window out like he was the Karate Kid. Mr. Miyagi would have been proud. The glass shattered allowing a beam of light to wash over a portion of the hallway. It was blinding, and I shrank back covering my eyes until they adjusted to the optic assault.

A barrage of thunderous cracks resounded from every direction. I didn't know anything about smoker demons, but my guess was... they were pissed.

Grant held his ground, standing in the sheet of light ready for whatever was coming. I suddenly felt uncomfortable in the dark, almost naked. Before I knew it, I thrust the butt of my shotgun through another window. Dust and ash sucked out of the hallway like a vacuum. Another onslaught of snaps erupted; only this time, they were everywhere. Spirals of smoke popped here and there, all around us. They each merged and swirled into an undetectable vortex moments later. I was sure, without any doubt, that sunlight must piss them off and breaking the windows was probably tantamount to kicking the proverbial hornet's nest, but it felt right.

No, I was allied with Grant on this one. We might be fighting these demons on their turf, but I'll be damned if I make it easy for them. If they hated sunlight, then sunlight was our weapon.

As if reading my mind, Remie and Max both broke another window filling nearly the entire corridor with glorious early afternoon sunlight. The New Mexican desert was suddenly starting to really grow on me. Maybe ninety degree temperatures at nine in the morning weren't so bad after all?

I peered out the window curiously. Three stories up. Could we survive a fall like that? I hoped we could if we needed a quick exit. I gulped at the thought. That was definitely not the way I planned to die.

The world zapped back into focus, like it was being shocked with a massive defibrillator. This time, the smoker demon didn't swirl into a void. A shifting darkness darted in the shadows beside Grant. He fired at the specter, but missed. It moved as fast as a hummingbird.

Another similar massive shock resounded at the other end of the hallway, followed by two more.

They were surrounding us. Suddenly, a quick drop out the window seemed like our best option.

Max knelt down and began firing on the figures that glided in the darkness near Remie and Charlie as they joined in. I watched. Bullets seemed to have no effect on these demons. Was that why they barricaded this section of base? Because they couldn't find a way to kill them? How do you kill something made of smoke?

Static electricity dashed painfully across my skin when a smoker demon popped right into the sunlight beside me. I swallowed the urge to let out a blood-curdling scream, and instead turned my shotgun on it shooting it squarely in the face.

I might as well have been shooting a balloon. The demon burst into a ball of smoke and sucked itself back into nothing.

The demons continued their bombardment; popping in and out for what felt like hours. They were toying with us. Playing with their food.

Another demon splintered the air beside me for the millionth time. I shrieked as the sensation of a thousand rubber bands being snapped across my flesh battered my senses. I was starting to think it was the same demon every time. Maybe it liked hearing me scream?

I fired again, but only managed to hit the wall behind it. Even the sunlight was failing to be effective. In fact, it was probably more of a nuisance to them than anything. Damn, what I wouldn't have given for a Proton Pack right then.

"Abby!" Grant screamed my name. His voice was hoarse, yet crazed.

I turned to find a smoker demon in its full smokin' glory, bearing down on me. This one was different than what was taunting us. It was pulling in the smoke around it, forming into a visible apparition before me. Blackened bones with sparkling embers were revealed beneath a soot-covered cloak. It was a burning ember of a being, flaking off ash as it moved, but retaining its form.

I stumbled backward, tripping over my own feet. These smoker demons looked like grim reapers. Hell, they could have passed for Dementors too. Last time I checked, I wasn't a wizard, so how the hell were we supposed to kill these things? Expecto Patronum wouldn't do the trick.

Max let out a war cry beside me shoving me away and vaulting for the skeletal demon beside me. It whizzed to the right letting Max fall to the ground where it previously stood, which was now a fresh pile of scorched embers.

His body jerked violently, then ceased. He didn't get up.

I dove for Max's motionless body, but the demon's shriek rang through the air with the icy hardness of steel, freezing me in place. My eyes drifted toward it, as much as I didn't want to see, but I couldn't stop myself.

Clutched in its boney fingers was a three-foot-long spear, deadlier than any spear I'd ever seen or could even imagine. It was *all* blade. There was no wooden handle to grip, just sharp steel. The hollows of its eyes lit up with blue flames; and if it were possible for a skeleton to smile, it definitely smiled at me.

I looked at Max in panic. He still wasn't moving and that scared me more than the wraith-like demon hovering before me preparing to eat my brains, or whatever it planned to do. I wanted to call out for help, but Grant was struggling with another smoker demon that lingered in the darkness beside him. It wasn't in its full form, choosing only to reshape its arms so it could strike out at Grant as he tried desperately to block its blows. Remie and Charlie were in much the same quandary, so it was up to me.

I directed my attention toward the monster in front of me, and not a moment too soon. The bladed spear flew straight at my face. Either by instinct or sheer fear I dropped to my knees. The blade landed in the wall behind me, just inches above my head.

That was way too close for comfort.

There was no way I could yank the demon's spear out of the wall to use it; I'd only end up slicing my own hand in half.

With no need for a weapon to make minced meat of me, the smoker demon clawed at me like a rabid raccoon. I rolled to my left; allowing his razor-sharp, boney fingers to slash at the ground where I lay. I didn't dare look at the damage it did. I didn't need to have the mental image of its rage terrorizing me anymore than I already was.

It slashed again. This time, I rolled to my right. We were playing a horrifying version of stop, drop, and roll. Only when I rolled back toward my left after its bony fingers grazed my arm; did I realize how right I was. The ground where its blow landed was scorched from the heat of the contact. I could have very well been rolled into a blanket of hot coals.

I screamed out as the heat exploded over my flesh like napalm. The smoker demon reared back and shrieked a bone-curdling cackle. It seemed amused by my pain, by my screams! That was all I needed to fuel my rage even further.

I tumbled into the sunlight of Grant's window, pulling myself into a crouch, and firing a shell right into the smoker demon's chest.

Its laughter stopped.

The fire in its eyes burned brighter, spilling out of the sockets like it was alive. I cocked my shotgun ready to fire again when Grant flew past me. I lifted my finger from the trigger just in time to avoid emptying a barrage of pellets into him.

The smoker demon was too focused on me to see Grant until it was too late. He landed on the demon like a star linebacker. Clay Matthews would have been proud. I had Max to thank for my love of football.

I didn't have time to gawk and wonder at what Grant planned to do to stop that demon, but I hoped he knew something I didn't. I ran to Max and shook his body, begging him to wake up. He didn't so much as twitch, and I rolled him over with a grunt. He was heavier than I expected.

"I got him," Grant said triumphantly holding up the skull of the smoker demon. He stood there, looking like a character from Mortal Kombat, and I half expected to hear the announcer shout, "Fatality!"

Grant stepped over the demon's smoldering corpse, carrying the skull like a scene from "Hamlet." I risked a glance at the skeletal remains, but they weren't moving. Did Grant really kill it?

Somehow sensing my doubt, Grant looked at the remains and then back at the skull before chucking it against the wall. It smashed like a snowball; and the body immediately followed suit deflating into another pile of ash like the many we'd already encountered inside the hospital.

So, that was it. Remove the head, and you kill the smoker demon. At least, now we knew they *could* be killed.

Grant helped me drag Max out of the mound of ash that was just starting to cool. I could feel the tendrils of panic binding my heart and squeezing. I couldn't lose Max. If I lost him, I... I wouldn't be able to go on.

"What happened?" Grant asked as we placed Max in the sunlight of my window. Remie and Charlie were still fighting at least two smoker demons, and I wanted to help them, to tell them how to defeat them, but I couldn't speak. The words caught in my throat like a stone, and my only concern was for Max.

A layer of thick mucus clung to Max's face. How had it gotten there? I didn't see the demon touch Max. Maybe something was in the ash?

Realizing it didn't matter how it got there, at least not right now, I started pulling it off. It clung like sticky glue, but it was coming off. Grant looked half confused and half freaked out, but he soon joined me in tearing the mask of demon sludge from Max's face.

"Max! Wake up, please!"

I pulled the last piece off his nose, praying he would start breathing. My tears dripped onto his face as I screamed his name, violently shaking his body.

"Don't leave me here!" I pounded on his chest with my fists to no avail.

"Abby," Grant spoke softly as he laid a hand on my arm, which I slapped away. "He's gone."

"No! Get away from me!" I wasn't willing to accept what Grant said. I wouldn't leave Max; not as long as I still had a breath in my body. I didn't know CPR, but I had a vague idea from watching TV shows and movies, so I got to work.

I pressed my lips firmly against his, and expelled as much breath as my tiny lungs would allow. And then another, and another, until my head grew fuzzy. My heart twisted in the barbed wire of panic at the feeling of his dead lips against mine.

Finding his sternum, I locked my hands together and began compressions on his chest; screaming for him to come back to me with each effort. His body shifted slightly with my movements, playing tricks with my mind, and my heart. I kept thinking that any second he was going to wake up.

He didn't.

"Abby." Grant placed his hand on my shoulder this time, and I collapsed into thunderous sobs. "We need to help the others." A shout of pain erupted from Remie in response. They were losing the fight, and they needed our help.

I felt Grant's hands under my armpits as he lifted my body up without any help from me. We were halfway across the hallway before I realized it. I was in complete shock.

The next thing I knew, right in front of us were Remie and Charlie fighting for their lives. Remie had three slashes streaked across his head, and Charlie's hands were red with blood. He had, no doubt, tried desperately to stop the bleeding on Remie's head while still fighting the demons at the same time.

My legs turned into lead and I anchored myself in place, watching them like a silent movie as the world around me dissolved. I wanted to help them, I knew they needed my help, but I couldn't give up on Max.

Tearing from Grant's grasp, I twirled around and ran back to Max's body. I refused to give up. Death would be denied today, because I wouldn't allow it to lay claim on him.

"You come back to me, dammit!" I blew air into his lungs until mine began to burn; then slammed compressions on his chest with all my weight. I kept repeating my technique, over and over fully unaware of how much time had passed. I couldn't hear Remie and Charlie fighting, and Grant never came back to pull me away. For me, all that existed were Max and I.

Something skidded to my feet and I looked down and saw a bladed spear. Grant was scrapping with another demon, but managed to break off its arm sending its weapon clattering to the floor. I saw the fear in his eyes as he fought, but he kept on giving everything he had with each block and blow. Like the one that attacked me, this one had embodied its full form and I knew it could now be killed - if we could just detach the head.

I removed my hands from Max's chest and kissed his forehead. "I'll be right back." His head fell to the side and his lifeless eyes fell onto Grant. It was utter torture to leave him there, but I couldn't deny myself the revenge I wanted, no needed so badly. These demons would pay for taking Max from me, and the price was extremely high.

I snatched up an abandoned shirt from the floor and wrapped it around the center of the blade. The steel cut through my hand nonetheless as I grasped it, but I hoped I wouldn't have to hold onto it for long. Warm blood dripped from my fist and in-between my fingers, but *that* pain was irrelevant. The only pain that I felt was seeing Max inert on the floor, his lifeless lips pressed against mine, and the absence of his heartbeat that once drummed in time to my own.

These smoker demons could claw my legs off for all I cared. Nothing would be more painful than what they'd already done. I had nothing left to lose.

14

Undaunted, I charged at the demon. Grant saw me coming, and hope lit up his face like a wildfire. He purposefully threw his body backward, tumbling to the ground so the demon would turn its back to me, and give the advantage that I needed. I ran the few steps between us as the demon raised its boney fingers to make its final strike on Grant. I rammed the spear into the back of the demons skull and snapped it off, leaving a piece of its spine still dangling precariously.

I dropped the blade to the ground, and stomped on the skull; disintegrating it into dust.

The body, which remained standing and fixed in place, collapsed into a heap of smoldering ash at Grant's feet.

"Holy shit!" Grant scampered to his feet, and lifted my makeshift weapon off the ground. His fingers slid on the blood, my blood. "Are you okay?"

I shrugged without emotion. I'd never be okay.

Grant yanked off his leather belt and wrapped it around the middle of the blade. I pushed the weapon toward his chest when he tried to offer it to me.

"Help them," I said pointing to Remie and Charlie.

Grant nodded and the whites of his eyes grew wide before going completely black. His body stiffened, and that's when I saw it. Singed, black claws were wrapped around Grant's throat. I screamed my rage like an Amazon warrior at the demon standing right behind Grant. Its eyes ignited with excitement, revealing itself in the darkness of the shadows.

Within seconds, Grant's entire body was burning from within. His skin grew murky and the intensity of a blue flame was visible in the shadow of his eyes. Still holding onto the spear, Grant's last act was to shove it toward me with all the strength he had left. Then the flames of the smoker demon consumed him.

I clutched the spear as I watched Grant disappear into ashes at my feet. Turning my eyes onto the demon, I knelt down knowing he would come for me next. The flames in its eyes were flaring out of control; nearly consuming its entire skull like it was Ghost Rider. It was enjoying its kill. When it tilted its head back to roar with victory I took my opening. I sprang up from the floor and shoved the spear right under the smoker demon's chin. I popped its head off just like a cork from a champagne bottle. The skull spun on the edge of the spear, twirling around like a crazed bobble head.

I hated bobble heads.

"Die!" I screamed with furious wrath flinging the skull out the window. It shattered on the concrete below like a terra cotta pot. Hot tears streamed down my face and I let them flow. They were mixed with misery, agony and the delicious taste of revenge. Killing demons could never completely fill the void in my heart, but I had to admit it felt damn good doing it.

I glanced toward Remie and Charlie before heading back to Max's body. They were gathering up the contents of Charlie's pack, which had spilled all over the floor. We'd be leaving in mere moments... well, they would be. I wasn't going to leave Max here. If it took me until next week to carry him out, I would.

Carefully stepping over the dusty mound of Grant's former body I choked back a sob. Thoughts of Drew streaked through my mind. How would I tell him what happened? How would he take it? I didn't want to see Drew go through that kind of pain. Grant didn't deserve to die. Heck, no one did.

I couldn't focus on losing Grant when there was something, or rather someone, weighing much heavier on my heart - Max. He lay exactly as I left him: his head tilted at an awkward angle, his eyes locked on the area where Grant last stood. I heard someone say once that they believed a person's soul stayed with his or her body a while after dying. Did Max see what happened to Grant? Could that have been the last horrifying sight he saw in this life before traveling to the other side? Was there even another side?

I dropped to my knees beside Max, ready to lift his head into my lap when he suddenly jerked into convulsions, choking violently. Elation ignited inside me like a Fourth of July sparkler. Max was alive! I didn't know how, but I didn't care. Maybe all my efforts really did make a difference; or maybe there really was someone upstairs looking out for us. Either way, I was eternally grateful.

When his choking turned into gasping ejections from his stomach and lungs, I turned him onto his side to help him expel the putrid mucus that lined his insides. I patted his back while renewed tears streamed down my face and soft giggles bubbled up.

"What are you laughing at?" Max asked when his vomiting finally ceased. He closed his eyes and drew in ragged breaths, laying his head on my knees.

"I don't know. The mysteries of life I guess." It felt completely alien to be laughing in a place like this. We had just been attacked by the worst demons ever encountered, Grant was killed and for a while there, Max *was* dead. What could there possibly be to laugh about? Maybe I was becoming delirious.

"What happened?" He tried to sit up, so I helped prop him against the wall.

"He's alive?" Charlie asked with surprise as he and Remie trotted up. I looked over and noticed that they consciously avoided stepping on... Grant's remains.

"What do you mean, I'm alive?" Max asked sounding suddenly alarmed.

"Um..." I hesitated for a moment. How do you tell someone they were clinically dead for at least five minutes or so? Maybe it was longer than that, maybe it was less; I had no clue. I decided there was no right way to tell him, so I just came out with it. "You were dead Max."

His first reaction was the complete opposite of what I expected. He started laughing. "Yeah, right. The demon just knocked me out." He started rubbing his head where a goose egg was starting to form. "You guys are kidding me, right?" When he looked up at our somber expressions, he knew it was true.

"Son of a bitch!" Max swore irately. He began a vigorous inspection of his body to confirm he was, indeed, alive. Satisfied with his assessment, he raised his hand for Remie to pull him up.

On his feet, Max swayed like a drunken sailor. "I got you." I inserted my body under his arm, and allowed him to bear his weight on me.

"We need to get out of here," Remie commanded looking around the hallways nervously.

"Lead the way," I said. Charlie took Max's other side and we hobbled down the hallway.

When we got to the end a thought struck me. "Wait!" I shouted louder than necessary. "Hold, Max," I said to Charlie, as I glanced around. I wanted to ensure my voice hadn't drawn the attention of any more hidden smoker demons that might be lying in wait.

He nodded. "Where ya goin', kid?"

"I got to do something really quick," I said trying to whisper through gritted teeth aiming my eyes back down the hallway. Charlie nodded in understanding.

"Don't go Abby," Max whined groggily. His alertness was wearing thin. Dying and returning to life must take a lot out of a person.

"I'll be right back," I whispered softly to him pecking his check. That seemed to settle him, and I took off down the hallway at a quick jog. I didn't want to spend any more time in this hospital than was absolutely necessary.

I spied a deserted army helmet lying on the ground along the way, and scooped it up. It might not have been the best choice, but it was the only option I readily saw available. There wasn't time to go hunting around for something better. Besides, Grant died honorably, and he deserved any sign or symbol of respect that we could give him. At least, I thought so.

Being careful not to gather up any of the demon's ashes - I'd send those back to hell, if I could - I used my hands to grab as much of Grant's remains as possible, placing them into the helmet. He deserved a proper funeral and burial, and should not be left in this den of demonic ruin. With Grant's ashes under my arm, I scurried softly back to the others.

"I'll take care of him," Remie offered. I was hesitant for a moment, not because I didn't want Remie to have him, but because I didn't want what was left of him out of my sight. I felt like it was my duty to ensure he was properly put to rest. I wanted to be certain he got the peace in death that he couldn't find in life; well not since the demons' arrival anyway.

"I'll take good care of him," Remie said reassuringly.

"Thank you."

I handed him the helmet, and a sense of grief washed over me. Seeing Grant's dark eyes lit up by a flickering blue flame inside him still haunted my mind, but I pushed it away. He was safe now, and nothing could ever hurt him again. I didn't want to remember him like that. I couldn't.

"Where's Grant?" Max asked when we reached the lobby. He had regained more than semi-consciousness.

"He's gone buddy," Charlie answered sounding fatherly. I could tell how much it hurt him to say the words. I was glad he answered, since I wasn't certain I'd be able to.

Max shook his head in disbelief, but didn't say anything. I watched him squeeze his eyes shut and wondered what he was thinking.

****

If it weren't for the unyielding summer heat, I might have believed we were walking through the gates of heaven. The double doors to the hospital were still propped open by the benches we placed there, and we took turns climbing over. I wasn't sure how long we'd been gone, but the sun had moved high enough in the sky for the skeletal trees to shade the pathway in an eerie pattern of shadows. It was just shy of a mile back to the compound, but the shade was too inviting and I knew Max would appreciate a short rest before our trek in the heat. The route out of the hospital seemed to have already exhausted what infinitesimal amount of "oomph" he had remaining.

Charlie lowered Max down beside me before he left to help Remie flip over what looked to be a golf cart, only fancier. It reminded me of what the university security cops drove around campus, which I saw when I went on a school field trip to check out college. If I'd known then that a demon apocalypse would soon prevent me from ever attending college, I would have never wasted my time that day. I would have ditched school and gone to the mall with the rest of my friends. Merely a few months later, the world, as we knew it, came to an end.

"What happened Abs?" Max asked his eyes pleading as he rested his head on my shoulder.

I tilted my head to lie atop his. "Shh... I'll tell you later. You need to rest now." And so did I. My mind bubbled with worry; how would I tell everyone what happened to Grant? Would they be angry with me? Would Taya ever speak to me again? Would Drew?

He weaved his fingers through mine then started stroking me gently with his thumb. Within seconds, his breathing grew deep and rhythmic. The sound of him snoring brought a slight smile to my face. I swore I'd never complain about his snoring ever again. It sounded like music to my ears now.

Charlie and Remie made quick work righting up the golf cart, and less than twenty minutes later they managed to get it running. Not that I expected them to fail. Those things probably ran on the same engine as a lawn mower, and even I knew how to get a lawn mower going. They drove up and we loaded Max into the back. He was sleeping so soundly, he didn't even notice. With only enough room in the front for two people, both Charlie and Remie demanded that I take the cart and drive Max ahead. They said they'd rather walk and catch up.

"No, Charlie you need to go and take Max. Eleanor needs you too," I insisted. I shoved him into the driver's seat, he plopped down heavily. "You too Remie." After everything we'd been through, I wasn't about to make Eleanor wait any longer. Who knew how much her condition might have progressed while we were gone?

"I don't know anything about medicine. You go," he said shaking his head.

"I need you to make sure Grant gets back safely. At least until I get there."

"Where are you going?" Remie and Charlie asked in unison their worry suddenly audible in their voices.

I put my hands up. "Nowhere. I just want some time alone to think. Ya know... about what I'm going to say..." I looked to the helmet that Remie held protectively against his chest.

"Think on the way kid. I ain't leavin' you behind," Charlie argued as he got out of the driver's seat. He winced with the movement, making it obvious the day's events had taken a toll on his body.

"Fine," I said with resignation. I didn't really have the strength, much less the desire to argue with them. Taking the time to think about how to break the news to Drew and everyone else would probably not make much difference. Never mind the fact that I definitely didn't have a way with words; there weren't any words in the world that would ease *that* pain. If Max had not come back to life, there wouldn't have been anything anyone could have said or done to comfort that wound in my heart.

The golf cart chugged along the empty roadways of the Air Force base like the little engine that could. We'd probably have made better time if we walked, but Max was in no condition for that, and the small umbra of shade we got from the cart's canopy offered a slight relief.

Charlie rested beside me, hugging the backpack to his chest and leaning his head against the support beam on the canopy. His eyes were squeezed shut, but the wrinkles on his brow made me doubt he was sleeping. Maybe he was trying to forget what he'd seen? His hands were shaking slightly, so I rested my right hand on his and gave it a small pat. He responded with a return squeeze, but he didn't open his eyes. Despite my awkwardness with words, I hoped I could give him a little bit of comfort. In all honesty, it comforted me too. That slightest touch of human contact kept my tears at bay. I had to focus on the good. We accomplished our mission, but at a great cost. We now knew the enemy we were facing when it came to the smoker demons. If we ever decided we were brave enough, or crazy enough, to go back to the hospital, next time our odds would be much better.

Rembrandt knocked on the roof of the cart, startling me out of my mental pep talk. I couldn't say I felt much better, but at least I wasn't a blubbering mess for the time being.

Remie jumped off the cart and strode up to the gap in the fence where we entered. I parked and walked to the back to help Max get out. His small catnap seemed to revive him, and he sat up looking more alert.

"We back?" he asked hopping out.

"Yeah. Can you walk?"

He nodded and started to make his way toward the fence.

Charlie came up behind me, laying a hand on my shoulder and causing me to flinch. "Hey, you okay?" He removed his hand looking at me concerned.

"Just an old wound that never healed all the way." I rubbed the sore spot on my shoulder.

"Want me to take a look at it?"

"Take care of him first," I said indicating Max as he squirmed through the fence. "And Eleanor."

"Okay, okay," he said before squeezing through the fence after Remie. I followed suit after one last glance behind us. There was nothing there but dirt and abandoned vehicles, yet somehow I knew this wouldn't be the last time I'd deal with a smoker demon.

"Ya know kid you don't always have to be the tough one. It's okay to let it fall apart sometimes," Charlie said as he wiped the sweat from his brow.

I sighed. He was right, but he obviously didn't know how stubborn I was. "I know Charlie. But if I'm not the tough one, who will be?"

"I will be. And Max will, and Rembrandt. I bet your brother and Taya would too. Hell, anybody on this base will. I know it hurts kid, but you gotta feel the pain. It's the only thing that will make you stronger."

What he was saying made sense. I had even tried the same argument with myself before, but my stubbornness won.

"You know why I came here?"

I shook my head, watching Remie and Max break into a jog as the first building of our compound came into view.

"I finally allowed myself to grieve for my loss. I accepted that my wife was gone, and never comin' back. I knew all along how crazy I was for stayin' in our house, prayin' that by some miracle she'd come home to me. I just didn't wanna face it." His voice began to tremble with emotion.

"But when you kids showed up, I realized there was still hope for those of us left behind. When I left that house, I promised Dorothy that I'd look after you kids."

My heart swelled with the emotion at his words. "Thanks, Charlie." A smile spread onto my face despite the grief that nagged at my heart.

"You ever need anythin', anythin' at all just let me know."

"I will." Without a second thought I wrapped my arms around him in a strong hug, and he hugged me back.

"You two coming, or what?" Max called out to us from under the open hangar door.

Charlie and I laughed for no reason at all, as we made our way back to the compound. It really helped to have him around. I missed my father terribly, and although no one could ever take *his* place, I was starting to think that maybe Charlie sometimes filled that hole. And maybe we were good for him too. We needed him, and something told me that he needed us.

****

Despite our fatigue, we headed straight for Eleanor. As we walked through the halls everyone cheered our return although they were totally oblivious of where we'd actually gone, and what we endured. Our appearances must have been somewhat alarming, and I saw morbid curiosity on more than a few people's faces. After Charlie fixed Eleanor we'd have some explaining to do. I didn't like keeping everyone in the dark about what was going on even though it was probably the safest option. Lying was lying, and I always preferred honesty.

"Hey, I'm going to go lay down," Max said as we turned down the hallway to the sick room.

"Yeah, go. Get some sleep."

He kissed my forehead before giving me a fierce hug. "I love you."

"Love you, too."

After he disappeared down the hallway, I followed Charlie into Eleanor's room. Wade and Taya were amusing themselves with a game of Go Fish, while Carter dozed with his feet up on the table. His journey book lay open atop his lap.

"You're back!" Taya squealed jumping out of her seat to give us all a hug. "Yuck! What happened to you guys?" she asked with a frown, wiping off the dirt and ash that transferred to her clothes while hugging us.

"Did you get what you needed?" Wade interrupted ignoring the fact that Taya had just asked a question.

"Yes." I looked at Charlie who was already headed for Eleanor's bedside. "Taya, get Lauren please."

"You got it." She marched out of the room seemingly pleased to have something to do.

"What shall I do?" Wade asked sounding antsy.

"I don't know." I walked toward Charlie as he began setting up a small operating table; laying out all the things we'd collected. "Charlie, what do you need for us to do?"

He looked up; setting his glasses atop his head. "I need clean towels, gauze, water, alcohol and..." He rummaged through the tools and cupboards for a moment before continuing. "And Lauren."

"Lauren is on her way. We'll get everything else you need." I pulled Wade toward the far end of the room, and directed her to a cupboard where we kept the towels, while I fetched everything else.

"How's she doing?" I asked Wade as we deposited our items on a side table for Charlie. He was busy in the sink washing his arms and face thoroughly.

"She's batshit crazy," she said sadly.

"Charlie will fix her up. She'll get better." We both stood at the end of Eleanor's bed, watching her sleep. She looked almost peaceful despite the fact that the black veins now covered her entire face. At least, she wasn't acting... well, like a demon!

"You don't know that." Wade turned away marching for the door. Her spikey hair bounced with the movement.

"Hey!" I yelled through clenched teeth tugging on her arm to make her stop. "You can't be like that."

"Like what? Realistic?" She tugged away from my grasp, and began adjusting the array of woven bracelets on her wrist, trying to avoid eye contact.

I sighed wearily, struggling for the right words but this time I remembered what Charlie told me just outside the compound. "I know it looks pretty bad now, but you can't lose hope."

She sneered in disbelief. "You haven't seen what she's been doing the last few hours! She's only sleeping because she probably wore herself out!" Wade whined sounding like a child trying to lay the blame on someone else.

I grabbed her by the shoulder and gave her a quick shake when she began to get hysterical. "Snap out of it, Wade! I know you're scared, but you need to be strong for her. What do you think Eleanor would do if it were you in that bed?"

She wiped at the tears on her face. "She'd never give up on me."

"Then don't give up on her. Okay?"

She nodded. "Eleanor is the closest thing I have to family Abby. If I lose her..." The sadness behind her unfinished words hung in the air like a raised guillotine.

Lauren walked in right then with Taya close at her heels. I took that as our cue to leave. I woke Carter up, and we all scurried out of the room to let Charlie and Lauren work a miracle. *Please God, if you're still up there, let them work a miracle.*

I led us all back to our room. I knew Max was sleeping, but we needed to discuss what happened. Plus, I wanted to know what went on during the short time we were away. Wade appeared to be ripping at the seams, and Carter peppered me with questions for the entire walk back to the room, but I refused to answer anything until we were all together.

To my surprise, Max wasn't sleeping. He was sitting on his cot with his head in his hands. "Hey, everything okay?" He looked up at the sound of my voice, and I could tell he'd been crying. His eyes were red and puffy. I now felt horrible for bringing everyone into the room. He needed some time alone, and I'd essentially put him and his pain on display for everyone. I was a terrible girlfriend.

"Yeah," he rubbed at his face trying to hide his emotions as we walked in. "I uh... I saw Drew on the way back to the room."

"Oh. Did you tell him?" I tried to keep my voice down, but tactics like that didn't work when Taya and Carter were in the vicinity.

"Tell who, what?" my brother asked his interest piqued.

Max expelled a breath, but I pushed my index finger against his lips concealing the pleasure I felt at the touch. Max had already assumed the difficult job of telling Drew about Grant; so I could at least take some of that responsibility and tell the rest of the group.

"You might want to sit down for this." I gestured to Taya and Wade. Maybe it was the tone of my voice or the expression on my face, but they immediately obliged.

"Abby? What happened?" Carter took on a timbre in his voice that I recognized very well. He knew I was the bearer of bad news. Like there was any other kind in a world like ours.

"We encountered the smoker demons at the hospital."

Taya gasped openly, while Carter and Wade looked completely dumbfounded. I might as well have been speaking in another language.

"W-w-what were they like?" Wade stuttered in visible fear. Taya grabbed her hand.

"Worse than anything we've ever seen," Max said coldly. He stood up and wrapped his arm around my waist. By the weight of his body, I could tell it wasn't just for comfort, but also to support him on his feet. The magnitude of everything that happened in the last few hours was altogether crippling.

"But everyone is okay, right? I mean you all look fine," Taya said in near panic.

"No," Max answered.

"We lost Grant," I said. The words tumbled out of my mouth in sobs.

I watched the faces of my friends and silent tears streamed down their cheeks. Taya dropped her head into her hands, and Carter walked over to her cot, wrapping her in his arms. He wiped the tears as they slid out from under his glasses.

"How did it happen?" Carter asked passing Taya off to Wade. She softly rubbed Taya's back, and it warmed my heart. I was glad they were becoming close, and if anything ever happened to me at least I knew Taya would have someone to lean on, and vice versa.

Max dropped back to his cot, unable to go on. He couldn't have told Carter anyway, 'cause he was dead at the time. Another bomb I still had to drop on everyone. Maybe I should hold off on telling that one... I wasn't sure how much more they'd want to know after hearing about the new nightmare that lived just a short distance away.

15

My brother dropped his pencil halfway through my story, and all the color drained from his face. Wade appeared to be on the verge of vomiting when I described what happened to Grant. All the while, Taya held her head in her hands. And at one point, she pressed her fingers into her ears not wanting to hear more. I didn't blame her. If there were a "delete" button inside my brain, I would have pressed it long ago.

"It turned him to ash?" Carter asked in complete disbelief. "How is that even possible?"

"How is any of this possible?" I raised my hands in the air as I dropped down onto the cot next to Max. I rubbed my hand on his back trying to comfort him. He hadn't said a word during the last thirty minutes while I recounted our ordeal.

"What do we do now?" Taya asked finally overcoming her emotions.

"Get the hell out of here, that's what!" Wade said matter-of-factly. "What if those things come back? How are we supposed to defend ourselves?"

"But they *can* be killed." Carter scratched his head with the eraser end of his pencil. "Right? You said you killed them?"

"Yeah, we killed at least four."

"How many of them are there?" Taya butted in.

"I don't know Taya, but at least, now we know there are four less of them." I did my best to sound optimistic.

"Four less? Seriously? What if there are four hundred?" Wade scolded us like we were out of our minds. Maybe we were, but if we abandoned our hope would we ever find it again?

"There aren't four hundred," Max's voice croaked angrily making us all clamp our mouths shut.

"How do..." Wade started but Max interrupted her.

"If there were four hundred we'd all be dead already. They got the upper hand this time because we didn't know what to expect, but now we do. They *can* be killed, and we *will* kill them. Simple as that."

"Max is right," Carter agreed directing his words toward Taya and Wade. "If those smoker demons were such a huge threat they would have attacked our compound long ago, but they haven't. Have they?" Without allowing them time to answer, he went on. "We've all endured and sacrificed too much to let some small band of demons stop us now. Who killed the hordes of spider demons at our door step? We did! Who killed demon hounds, demon birds, gremlins and smokers? We did!" The veins in his neck began to pulse as his face reddened. Feeling suddenly self-conscious, Carter retreated to his cot looking thoroughly surprised by his own outburst.

I couldn't hide the smile that cracked the cold shell of my body. My brother, the eternal introvert and mega-nerd just gave us the mother of all speeches.

"Thank you, William Wallace." I winked at him.

"Shut up!" his face reddened even more, but not from my teasing. I caught a fleeting glance from Wade as I turned around. I realized it was her expression that was getting him so worked up. He was trying to impress her, and it had obviously worked. Both she and Taya looked less vexed. I guess his animated discourse did the trick. Hey, whatever worked.

"Back to my original question," Taya said breaking the awkward silence of the room. "What do we do now? Go after the rest of the smokers in the hospital?"

"I think we should have a funeral for Grant," Max said sadly.

"I agree," I said.

"Yeah, he deserves that," Carter concurred.

"Okay, so let's get this started A.S.A.P. Taya, I need you to get everyone gathered together in the auditorium so we can inform them about what happened. Do you think you're up for that?" I looked at Max and he nodded, pulling himself up straighter. "After everyone gets filled in, we all need to gather for the service."

"I'll get everyone together in the courtyard with the airplanes," Taya said as she rose from her seat.

"Yes, that would be the perfect spot." I recalled the place she mentioned, drawing a visual picture in my mind. It was a small grassy area, circled by long retired military jets. Ragged flags still clung tenaciously to the poles that held them aloft for all to see. I couldn't have chosen a better place. "Remie and I will get the site ready while you guys do the rest."

"I'll go get started right now. Come on Wade, I could use your help," Taya said waving Wade toward the door. She gave Carter a brief glance, and after he offered her a small reassuring smile she left with Taya towing her out the door.

"I'm going to go see if I can track down Drew. He should be there for the service," Max said sounding less troubled even though his eyes said otherwise.

"You sure you're okay?" I whispered into his ear as he hugged me tighter, and with more fervor than I expected. "Hey, you're okay - we're okay." My lips brushed his earlobe as I spoke.

"I know. I'm just a little shook up. I'll be fine." He planted a firm kiss on my lips and one on my forehead before heading out of the room.

I turned around to find my brother standing alarmingly close to me. "Geez Carter don't sneak up on me like that. I almost swallowed my tongue!" I held my hand against my chest and caught my breath.

"Sorry, I didn't realize you were so jumpy. And I didn't sneak; you knew I was in the room," he said defensively.

"Whatever you say; smarty pants." I headed for the bathroom, ready to submerge my head in water. I didn't have time to do a thorough cleaning, but it would at least be nice to get all the muck off my face.

"Abby, I wanted to talk to you about something," he said trailing behind me.

"What's up?" I plugged the sink and emptied the contents of our water bucket into it. Splashing the water on my face, I began rubbing vigorously. It was surprisingly cold and felt heavenly.

"It's about Eleanor." I froze. Water dripped down my chin as a shiver ran up my spine. "I think there is some truth to what she is saying."

"What's she's saying?" I grabbed a towel and patted myself dry.

"I think no matter how we look at it, we should take what she keeps repeating under some serious consideration."

"You mean about something in the west?" I threw the towel in the sink, giving up on any further hygiene and chose to pull on a clean shirt from Taya's drawer.

"Yes." He pulled out a chair from our small desk and opened up his journal. It was newly filled with drawings and scribbles that looked nothing like anything I'd seen him do before.

"You didn't draw this, did you?" I asked him warily. I traced my finger along the eerie sketches. Tortured faces appeared to scream through the violent scribbles, their menacing eyes glaring from a dark corner of the page. It looked like a tidal wave of evil was splashed across the pages of the book.

Carter shook his head.

"What is it?" I shut the book not wanting to look at it any longer.

"Eleanor drew it during one of her fits."

"So, that's why Wade was so upset." Knowing what upset her made my heart ache for her even more. I don't think I'd have been able to handle that either.

"I think we need to go here Abby," Carter said tapping the journal with his finger.

"Go where?" My voice raised in pitch.

"This place that she is warning us about. This..." he pulled his glasses off and rubbed the bridge of his nose.

"You're not serious? That picture looks like evil ripped a hole into the world and let some of hell spill through."

"That's exactly what I think it is." Carter expelled a breath, replacing his glasses.

"You've lost your damn mind Carter! I just got done telling you how horrifying those smoker demons were, and that Grant died because of them, and you want to go knock on hell's gate?" I was fuming. My brother was beyond stupid. What in the world was he thinking? What happened to the Carter that stood against every decision regarding going after demons. There was no justification this could ever turn that into a good idea.

"Just listen to me for a second." He stood up and ushered me to toward the chair beside him. He was acting so incredibly calm and collected, which only made me more nervous. Something told me that he'd already made his decision about this, and now he was just letting me know it.

"Okay, I'm listening." I couldn't keep the agitation from my voice. I was ready to fight him on this with every fiber of my being. There was no way I would let my brother do this. We had a good thing going here, and as soon as we got the hospital pests... exterminated, we'd be golden.

"Have you ever wondered how the demons actually got here?"

"Well, yeah. Everyone has."

"So, keeping that in mind, wouldn't you expect that there must be some portal or place to enter through in order to get here?" He spoke slowly, hoping I'd catch on to what he was saying.

"What? Like a demon door?"

"Something of the sort. I'm thinking it's more like a tear between our world and hell."

"Carter." I expelled a heavy breath and felt the weight of the world drop back onto my shoulders again. "That sounds like something out of one of your video games."

"Maybe so Abby, but doesn't it kinda make sense? There are demons wreaking havoc all over the world. Why can't the notion that they have a way to get here be possible? Do you think they just materialized out of thin air?"

"Where are you going with this? Are you saying you want to find wherever this tear is?"

"I want to do more than just go there Abby. I want to close it."

"And how are you going to do that?" I couldn't keep the sarcastic tone of my voice controlled, and raised my eyebrows waiting for him to continue. He still hadn't convinced me of anything.

"I think we need to go to a place of power. Like where Norah mentioned. Maybe we can find our answer there."

I grasped his shoulder and squeezed. "You want to do this on a maybe?" My irritation now turned to concern. Maybe Carter wasn't as crazy as I thought. Maybe he was just desperate to make the world better; to do something to stop all the suffering. I couldn't be mad at him for that.

"You're always talking about not losing hope. I think we need to have more hope than just believing we'll live to fight another day. I can't live like that forever Abby. No one can. We need to have hope that this *will* end."

"That's why you have your journal. When the military, and government show up we can help fight to take back our world."

"Abby." my brother looked at me sadly. "That's not going to happen, and you know it." He sounded like he was confiding to me that he knew there wasn't any Santa Claus.

"You don't know that." That was the hope that I clung to most, and I wasn't willing to give it up. We would keep fighting until the cavalry arrived, and then everything would be okay.

"The demons are going to keep coming until they don't have a way to get here anymore. You always say how you want to kill them all, but wouldn't you rather stop them from entering?"

I opened my mouth to reply, but he had me there. Killing them, although satisfying, didn't seem to very effective other than to give us some time until the next horde rolled in. I'd never even fathomed that there might be a way to stop them.

"Makes sense, doesn't it?"

"I don't know. I've never thought of it that way, but going there," I pointed to his journal, "to that place Eleanor drew. That sounds like a suicide mission to me. Let's say we go there, how can we survive being in the proximity of a rip in the fabric of our world, while demons keep spilling out of it?"

"If you believe there's evil in this world, then don't you have to believe there is good, too? I can't believe that we weren't left with some way to defend ourselves."

All I could do was shake my head. My mind resisted his words, but my heart wanted desperately for them to be true. If there was a way to end all this pain, could I really turn up my nose at it? Could I live with myself, knowing I didn't at least try? Sure, maybe I'd die trying; no, I'd definitely die trying; but wasn't that how I wanted to go? Giving my life so others might continue to fight on?

"We can talk about this more later. I just wanted to let you know what I've been thinking," Carter said patting my back.

"Yeah, later." I felt a headache coming on, but I tried to ignore it. There were more important things I needed to deal with right now, and one of them was Grant's funeral.

Carter pulled me into an unexpected hug, and I stiffened at first until I realized how long it had been since we'd embraced each other. I suddenly missed my brother even though he was right beside me.

"I'm glad you're okay," he said pulling out of the hug.

"Me, too." I smiled weakly at him.

****

It didn't take long to find Remie and head out to the site we'd chosen. Beverly tagged along, carrying Grant's remains protectively against her chest. The sun had tilted in the sky, making its decent toward the mountains in the west. The west. Looking that direction caused a completely new feeling to bubble inside me. Fear? Doubt? Angst? None of which I wanted to experience, so I buried them away and ignored them like I always did.

The shadows of some of the jets stretched across the expanse of grass like beacons pointing the way. I thought choosing a spot would be difficult at first, but when I saw it, it just felt right. The largest, most impressive of all the aircraft was a huge, black stealth fighter. It was angular, and reminded me of an arrowhead. The very tips of its shadows touched the exact center of the grassy area, and I knew that was the place. Grant deserved a hero's sendoff in the shadow of the most formidable jet we could find.

I pointed to the place I'd chosen, ignoring the lone tear that tumbled down my cheek. Remie pulled out the shovel he brought along and went to work digging a plot for Grant. I joined Beverly under the shade of an aircraft wing while we silently watched Remie. It didn't take him long to dig a hole big enough to fit the helmet that held Grant's remains. I looked inside, and saw that someone had placed a tiny wildflower atop the ashes. I couldn't remember the last time I'd seen a flower.

"It's called Bird's Eye," Beverly said softly.

"It's pretty." The tiny flowers looked like purple daisies.

"You picked a good spot. It's peaceful here." Beverly sighed in a relaxing way. "Would you like to hold him?"

I nodded, and she handed me the helmet carefully. Just a few minutes later, the first people started trickling in for the service. I noticed that many of them carried small bunches of the same purple flower in their hands, Bird's Eye. A young girl carried a tiny bouquet in her fist, the soil still clinging to the roots of it. She smiled sheepishly at me. I'd never seen anything sweeter in my whole life.

I don't know what Max said to everyone about what happened, but there was something different about the people in our compound. They were grieving, there was no doubt of that, but there was something else. I just couldn't put my finger on it.

Max and Taya came to my side when everyone was gathered together. My nerves rattled through me, but not because I was nervous. This funeral meant we'd have to let Grant go, and I wasn't sure I was ready to do that. My body began to shake. I knew he was never coming back, but I just couldn't accept that he was gone even though I carried all that was left of him in my hands.

"You can do it," Taya whispered words of encouragement beside me. She took my hand, while I held the helmet in the other and squeezed. Max pressed his hand against the small of my back, lending me some comfort and I finally stepped forward. My legs were heavy, like they were filled with lead. Every step became more difficult, and I wasn't sure I'd make it to the plot that Remie dug. But with Max and Taya at my side, I managed to walk the small distance.

The silent crowd watched me as I eyed them hesitantly. Some nodded their encouragement, others offered sad smiles. I spied Carter at the forefront, straight across from me, with Wade wrapped under his arm. Her face was sorrowful. I searched the crowd further, looking for Drew, and panic jolted through me when I couldn't find him.

A hand rested gently on my shoulder, and I could feel its trembling through my whole body. I turned to find Drew standing beside me. His eyes were swollen with tears and his face was red, but he offered a closed lip smile.

Drew reached for the helmet, and I handed it gently to him. We both held onto it for a moment, both our hands trembling with emotion. When he nodded, I let go and retreated into Max's arms.

Drew stepped forward to the edge of the small plot, as though he were standing at the rim of a cliff. I suppose in some ways he was. Drew opened his mouth to speak, uttering a small gurgling sound, and then closed it again. He wanted to say something, but he didn't seem to have the strength to utter the words he was thinking. They were too painful.

Words were never my friend, but I felt the urge to say something. Like Charlie advised me, we needed to lend strength to each other. I might be weak with emotion right now, but I was going to give Drew everything I had left. I was going to give Grant, everything too.

I stepped forward beside Drew, placing my hand atop his arm. His shuddering slowly subsided. "We come together today to mourn the loss of one brave man. To share the grief we all have, and perhaps find the strength to bear that grief." I choked on the last few words, and swallowed hard. I had to keep it together.

"There are no words to express what we carry in our hearts. Words pale in the shadow of grief; they seem insufficient to even begin to measure Grant's brave actions; or how losing him will forever wound our hearts. We must honor him not just in the words we speak today, but in our actions from this day forward. We will live our lives with honor, valor and selflessness; just as Grant did."

I turned to fully face Drew and placed my fingertips along the edge of the helmet, bowing my head. "I will remember you, Grant."

Tears cascaded down my cheeks as I stepped away from Drew and Grant. Max pulled me into his strong arms, holding me close to him as my body shuddered. I felt Taya move beside me, and I looked up to see her copying my actions and placing her fingers delicately against the helmet. She held Drew's grief-stricken gaze before bowing her head and repeating my words.

"I'll always remember you, Grant." She pressed her fingers to her lips and then placed them on the edge of the helmet. "Please watch over us," she whispered softly.

Drew began sobbing openly, no longer able to conceal his utter despair. Max pulled away and stood beside his friend, placing a strong hand atop his shoulder while the other touched the rim of the helmet.

"I will remember you," Max said the words in a strong, firm tone because he meant every one. I watched his jaw clench as a tear rolled down his chin.

Everyone in attendance began to walk forward, placing their hands on the helmet and repeating my words. Simple words that held more power than anything I'd ever seen.

When everyone had finished saying goodbye to Grant, we all watched as Drew lowered him into ground with a tilt of the helmet. There was a long moment of silence until a gust of wind whipped the flags above our heads, snapping them in the air. We all looked up to watch the tattered American flag dancing in the breeze. I vowed, then and there, to keep fighting, to never give up and to do whatever needed to be done to win this war over evil. For Grant, for Norah, for Judy, and for Savannah, as well as my father, Max's parents, Remie's daughter and Charlie's wife. For everyone.

Carter was right. We needed to do more than just keep fighting the demons. We needed to stop them permanently.

The crowd slowly trickled away until it was just Drew, Max, Taya, Carter, Wade and me. We each took a handful of soil and sprinkled it into the grave with Grant, until he was fully interred. Drew planted the helmet securely above the mound as a marker.

"Thank you for what you said," Drew spoke for the first time, his voice cracking with the effort.

"I meant every word." I pulled him into a hug, which he returned with fierce sadness.

"I don't know what to do now. Grant was always with me since the beginning. He was like my brother," Drew said his voice hoarse.

"We keep fighting," Max answered his voice full of encouragement.

"Yeah," Taya agreed. "We keep fighting until we send every demon back to hell!" She took on an expression of defiance I'd never seen in her before.

"No." The sternness in my tone nearly startled me. I'd opened my mouth to speak without even realizing it. I was only thinking it, but for some reason my voice decided what I was thinking needed to be said.

Everyone turned to me with confusion plastered on their face.

"We need do more than just fight." I looked at Carter meeting his gaze without blinking. He nodded his support, acknowledging his thanks that I now believed him. I knew he was right. "We need to stop them."

"What do you mean?" Max asked sounding baffled.

"What I mean is; we are heading west."

It would take a lot of convincing to get everyone on board with our strategy, but I hoped that with Carter's logic, and any luck with Eleanor, we could do it. If Charlie could just heal her, perhaps she could give us the necessary insight we sought through what she'd experienced.

I knew it was a drastic and dangerous decision, but it was the right one. If we continued as we were, we'd just keep fighting demons until they eventually plucked us off, one-by-one, like petals on a dying flower. Carter was right; we needed to stop the demons from ever entering out world. I always said I planned to make the demons pay for what they'd done, and now was the right time to do it.

"What's in the west?" Drew asked.

"Vengeance," I answered.

Other Titles by Megan Duncan:

Agents of Evil Series
Released
Chaos
Vengeance (Coming Soon!)

Warm Delicacy Series
Savor
Indulge
Devour
Revenge (Coming Soon!)
Royal Blood (Warm Delicacy Series 1-3)

Falling From Eternity (A Paranormal Romance)

The Long Road Home (A Contemporary Romance)

Find out about giveaways, new releases and more on Megan's blog:
www.meganduncan.blogspot.com/

Made in the USA
Middletown, DE
10 December 2015